ALCHEMY
OF
SOULS

BOOK THREE
OF
THE HUNDRED HALLS
A HUNDRED HALLS NOVEL

THOMAS K. CARPENTER

Alchemy of Souls
Book Three of The Hundred Halls
A Hundred Halls Novel

Hardcover Version

by Thomas K. Carpenter

Published by Black Moon Books

Cover design by Ravven
www.ravven.com

Discover other titles by this author on:
www.thomaskcarpenter.com

ISBN-13: 978-1-958498-02-6

The Hundred Halls Universe

ALCHEMY OF SOULS

CITY OF INVICTUS

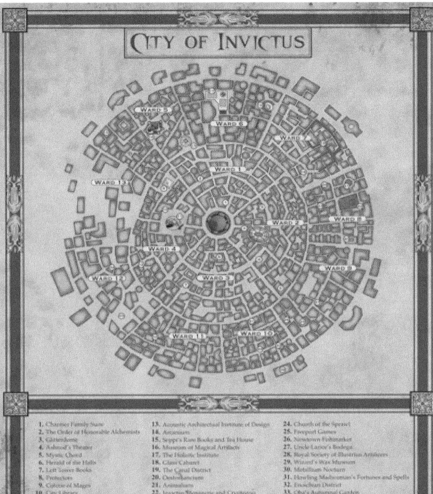

ONE

Aurie knew days like this weren't meant for her. Yet it hadn't been one solitary day, but a whole summer of them, one after another like train cars, all in a row. She'd kept expecting the hammer to drop, but every day the clinic had stayed open and the number of patients had increased. By mid-July, everyone in the district knew her name and greeted her with a wave and a smile as if she were family, even if the smile was a mouth full of jagged teeth, or the wave was attached to a set of glistening claws. Here she was, the last day of the summer before classes started, and nothing had happened. It was a miracle.

As the end had approached, she'd decided to hold a Farewell to Summer party, giving everyone a last chance for treatment before she was buried in class work. During school year, the clinic would be open on Sundays, but it just wouldn't seem the same.

Much to her embarrassment and surprise, the district used the occasion as a little festival. Colorful tents filled the square, around which Hannah was being chased by a throng of laughing children with enchanted wands that changed her hair color every time one of them touched her with one. Hannah's hair was currently bubble gum pink with flame-orange tips.

Annabelle, Nezumi's daughter, her thick tail sticking out from her little overalls, jumped out of a stall to tag Hannah with her wand.

"Rocket ships!" yelled Annabelle with a slight, but thoroughly adorable lisp. Her teeth were still coming in.

It wasn't technically a color, but the spell interpreted it anyway, changing Hannah's hair white with black bands.

After a few rounds of the game, Annabelle came to see Aurie and threw herself into her arms. She smelled like clover and cotton candy.

"Hey, Ladybug," said Aurie, laughing. "Don't wear yourself out too much."

"No wear out," said Annabelle.

"I got you something," said Aurie, pulling a bracelet from her pocket. She showed it to the little girl, who bounced on her heels, clapping her hands. "It has your name on it."

"Magic?" asked Annabelle.

"Yes," said Aurie, slipping it on the girl's wrist. "Special magic to protect you."

"Th...th...thank you," said Annabelle, getting the *th* sound right on the third try. "I love you, Auriebella."

Annabelle threw herself into Aurie's arms for another hug. She loved the way Annabelle didn't hold anything back. Aurie squeezed her tight and kissed her on the forehead. Annabelle rejoined the game, squealing with delight.

The parade of laughter disappeared into the tents, leaving Aurie ready to attend to her last patient.

"She's a treasure," said Ms. Cartagena, smiling from beneath her cowl.

"I'm sorry," said Aurie, turning her attention back to the old woman. "Before I got distracted, you were saying that your elbow is hurting? My spell showed it checked out as pretty healthy, like twenty-year-old kind of health."

The woman beneath the cowl smiled. She wore a full-length black dress with a veil as if she were the wife of the deceased at a funeral. Only a pale arm was sticking out.

She chuckled knowingly. "I must confess, I only got in line because I wanted to say thank you for what you've done for the district."

"You didn't have to do that," said Aurie.

"But I have," she said. "Besides, it was an excuse to get out on this wonderful day. Nothing but blue skies and the kind of clouds you can spend an afternoon daydreaming by."

Aurie looked back over the city. The warm sun on her face made her wish Pi hadn't left, but she was getting together with Ashley, her old friend from Coterie, and Aurie didn't want to get in the way of that.

"The summer has been too perfect," said Aurie. "Almost like it can't be real. It makes me worry that doom is around the corner."

The old woman tapped a bony finger on Aurie's hand. "Doom is always around the corner. No one escapes it forever, but when the good days come, enjoy them and don't look back. You never know when the next one will come."

An ache formed between her breasts, as if something was pressing against her. She tried to sigh and make it go away, but it had caught fast.

Annabelle came running up, pigtails bouncing, a giggle at the edge of her lips ready to burst forth like bubbles.

"Ms. Aurelia. Ms. Aurelia," said Annabelle, tugging on Aurie's sleeve. "Can you come play with us?"

"Maybe after a little while," said Aurie, forcing a smile. "I'm chatting with Ms. Cartagena. But don't go too far. Your dad said to stay near the clinic."

Nezumi, Annabelle's father, had gone in search of undercity mushrooms to bring to his wife, who was a fine chef. He'd been Aurie's biggest cheerleader since the clinic had reopened at the beginning of summer and had her and Pi over for dinner weekly, though Aurie wasn't sure he really liked Pi. Aurie had seen him sniffing the silverware after meals to see if she'd cursed them.

After Annabelle left, Ms. Cartagena said, "She's a sweet kid."

"She's been through a lot, though you can't tell. Nezumi tells me that she has nightmares about what happened last year and wakes up screaming a couple times a week," said Aurie, the ache in her chest squeezing tighter. While it'd been Patron Frank Orpheum who'd hypnotized the district and turned them into zombie-like thralls, she'd been the one to get Nezumi and his family mixed up in it. Aurie watched Annabelle for them when they worked. She liked to think she did it because she was a good kid, but Aurie knew there was a locomotive full of guilt driving it.

Ms. Cartagena clucked her tongue. "Good riddance to that jack-ass Orpheum. I never did like his Orpheum Vaudeville Traveling Show. Pompous ass probably hypnotized people into thinking they'd had a good time."

"Vaudeville show? He hasn't done that for—"

Ms. Cartagena hushed Aurie. "No math, young lady. You're not supposed to know how old I really am."

Aurie was well aware that Ms. Cartagena was the type of supernatural creature that lived a long time, but she wasn't rude enough to ask which one.

Before Aurie could say anything, Ms. Cartagena tensed, her eyes glowering. She clucked her tongue again.

"You have a visitor," said Ms. Cartagena loudly, then in whisper, "Careful with this one."

To Aurie's unfortunate surprise, Camille Cardwell was standing outside the booth wearing a fuzzy turquoise jacket and a big chunky necklace around her neck. The woman was the owner of the *Herald of the Halls*, and the mother of Aurie's rival, Violet Cardwell, a pretentious blonde twit she had the unfortunate experience of sharing a Hall with.

"I'll be taking my leave," said Ms. Cartagena, sliding away spryly.

"I'm only taking charity cases, though I have heard the *Herald*'s sales are down," said Aurie, right as she noticed a young man with Camille wielding a tiny and expensive camera. Aurie muttered a curse word under her breath.

"Such is life," said Camille, sighing, "but my misfortunes shouldn't keep me from being generous with my wealth."

Aurie felt like an ass for the comment, especially when she knew that Camille gave extensively to Golden Willow and other charities. It was Violet she had a feud with, not the mother.

"My apologies," said Aurie, glancing at the camera, silently wishing that neither it nor Camille was there. "That was rude of me. How can I help?"

"It's not how you can help me, but how I can help you," said Camille. "I got word of the good works you've been performing here in the Enochian District, and came to offer a helping hand. Financial of course—actual work is hell on my nails."

She was a charming old socialite, and Aurie found herself liking Camille a smidge, even if she'd gotten her kicked out of Golden Willow and had birthed a blonde monster. Aurie just wished the mother didn't wear the same musky plum perfume as her daughter. It always made Aurie want to gag.

"I appreciate the offer, but..." said Aurie, eyeing the guy with the camera.

Camille noticed her staring. "Oh, silly me, I forgot about him. Dave's just taking footage for the article in the *Herald*. As you said, paper sales are down, but online is up, up, up. We're going to do a few posts on the district with the highlight being your clinic. After all, you're quite the hero after winning the contest last year, and not even with a full team. Fighting those giant bugs must have been awful, just awful. And now this work with the clinic will make you a hit with my readers. I know it feels a little exploitive, but it's good for the district."

Aurie's face warmed with embarrassment. Despite her feud with Violet, the *Herald of the Halls* had written glowing articles about the Harpers winning the contest. A beat reporter had interviewed both Pi and her earlier in the summer. Aurie had never expected Camille herself to stop by. She'd been preparing to decline the help, but realized pettiness was driving it and changed her mind.

"The district would be happy to take any help you can provide," said Aurie, realizing that Camille was making a lot of sense. "And thank you for your support of Golden Willow. Your generosity has helped a lot of people."

Aurie took a deep breath. The musky plum perfume wasn't as bad now that she was used to it. In fact, it was becoming more lovely by the second.

"There, there. You see, you're coming around," said Camille with a wink. "The district is thriving now because of you. You're *protecting* them, *defending* them. Keeping them safe."

Aurie was feeling lightheaded, and a part of her was aware that this was unnatural, but the part of her in control didn't care. Whatever Camille was saying seemed to make a lot of sense—it wasn't like she hadn't spent last year fighting off a patron. Why shouldn't the district benefit?

"Dave, darling," said Camille, gesturing at the tents. "Get a few wide shots of the area. I want to make sure we have good scene setting."

"I really must be going," said Aurie, feeling drowsy. It had to be something in the perfume that was doing this. She needed to get away.

Camille reached out and grabbed Aurie's bare arm. A tingling sensation traveled through her limbs, until Aurie felt like she could jump over a three-story building in a single bound.

"Yes, darling. You're a great hero, who does heroic things," she said, then pulled her hand away, peeled a layer of fake skin from her palm, torched it to ash with magic, and winked. "Good luck."

Despite the feeling of invincibility coursing through her veins, doom started rotting in her gut. She could taste it like bile.

As Camille and Dave the camera man walked away, a shout went up from the street. Screams erupted as tents fell like leaves. Desperate to see what was going on, Aurie leapt onto the dragon fountain.

What she saw brought denials to her lips. It couldn't be. They'd left them in the contest last year. A half-dozen deadly bugs marched through the festival, slicing through tents, advancing on the fountain. At first she thought they were an illusion, until she remembered she couldn't be fooled by that kind of magic because of her skill with mendancy. Once she knew they were real, rage filled her. Why had these bugs entered her world, threatened her friends? Aurie summoned a piece of the sun to her fist, ready to unleash it.

Racing between the tents, barely ahead of the bugs, was Annabelle. She'd dropped the wand. Her face was etched with fear, a high-pitched scream issuing from her lips in one long siren.

"Get behind me!" Aurie screamed, mentally urging Annabelle to run faster. The nearly eight-foot-tall bugs were right on her tail, so close she didn't dare use destructive magic, so she threw a bolt of force with her other hand to knock the bugs back and give Annabelle room.

The little girl scrambled past the fountain. With Annabelle safe, Aurie tapped into her well of magic, going deeper than she'd ever gone. As the faez flowed out, like water priming a pump, it connected with a second well—the dragon fountain. Power raged through her.

The bugs had stopped advancing, but the power kept flowing. Like a double helix, the twin wells of faez flowed up and out of her, spilling out around her in golden destruction. To Aurie it felt like she had a sun bursting from her chest. Nearby tents charred to ash in moments. The giant bugs teetered backwards, and she realized they were costumes. Frightened human faces stuck out of the bodies of the olive-green bugs. The limbs were held by wire and only appeared to move.

But the power kept flowing, filling the fountain with faez. She felt like she was holding a nuclear bomb inside her chest. She couldn't stop it, like a river rushing over its banks: faez, sweet golden faez, power without measure came out of her. A part of her realized that if she could harness it she could become a god.

It was like drowning and ecstasy all at once. She'd never felt so alive. Straight up into the sky, Aurie threw a beam of fire. Like a pillar of god, the fire went through the clouds, a signal to the world of her existence.

She was ready to claim her place in a new pantheon centered around her, Aurelia Maximus Silverthorne, when she heard a terrible cry of pain from directly behind her.

Annabelle hadn't kept running. She'd hidden by the fountain, and now she stood a few feet away, her overalls crisped black, flame dancing around her like a thousand bright devils, screaming. Other figures were lying in crumpled heaps, clothing smoldering.

The magic ceased, a cornea of unspent power rippling into the sky. Before she could call upon a spell to repair the destruction she'd unleashed, someone tackled her from the fountain.

Crushed beneath a heavy body, Aurie could only see Annabelle's motionless form ten feet away. The bracelet she'd given the little girl had fallen off. People were yelling, putting out fires, trying to fix the damage.

Aurie pushed the man off her, crawled to Annabelle's still form, and took her in her arms. Tears fell from her cheeks. She held the girl as men tried to pull her away.

"What have I done? What have I done?" she muttered, unbelieving. "What have I done?"

TWO

The statue of Invictus stood over one hundred feet tall, looking out upon the city in what Pi always thought of as annoyed resignment, like a parent who loved their children but was so sick of watching and caring for them. She knew this was a bit of projection, since that's really what she thought of the role of head patron. While she'd been waiting for Ashley, Pi had overheard tourists speaking in enraptured tones about how wise he appeared. She knew this was a load of crap. Power didn't imbue wisdom, only made people more intense versions of whatever they already were, which always brought about a settling disquiet as she recognized her own flaws in constantly seeking power.

The lower half of the statue was covered in scaffolding and tarps, beneath which jackhammers thundered their concrete-busting tune. The theater and gift shop at the base of the iconic statue were getting upgraded, a generous gift from a wealthy donor.

"Ms. Pythia Silverthorne," said Ashley Bellamy in her aristocratic Southern accent as she stepped out of a black limousine, "you look like you should be on the cover of *Trends* magazine."

The two girls embraced. Ashley had been her only true friend the year she spent in the Coterie of Mages. They'd kept in touch, but the rigors of class work had interfered with mutual plans.

Ashley held her chin and raised an eyebrow. "That leather jacket is divine. Did you have that tailored?"

Pi was wearing tight jeans and a white tank top, off-the-shelf clothing, but the leather jacket made everything look designer—a trick of its power. The dark leather was the color of the deepest sky on a moonless night. When you looked directly at it, it appeared matte black, but if she was distracted and paying attention to something else, she thought she saw galaxies spinning across the surface. A few weeks ago, half asleep in her bedroom, she thought she saw a meteor shoot across the back.

Pi smiled coyly. "The winnings from the contest have afforded me certain luxuries."

As much as she trusted Ashley, Pi knew it was prudent to keep the details about the jacket secret. It'd been a reward from the contest, and even after a summer, she still didn't understand the extent of its magic.

"Thank you for the letters this summer," said Pi. "I'm sorry I didn't write back as much. Aurie kept me busy at the clinic, which speaking of, thank you for the generous gift! That money went a long way towards helping people from the district out."

Ashley blushed. "You weren't supposed to know."

"How did you get your grandfather to give money to the clinic? I didn't think he'd be the kind of guy who supported our kind of work," said Pi.

Ashley gave a sly smile. "My esteemed grandfather gives a lot of unregistered money to political causes. I was able to divert a goodly sum to a variety of other affairs, including the clinic. The fact that the money is normally quite hush-hush means he cannot try and claw it back without attracting attention."

"Merlin's balls, was he pissed?"

Ashley gave a wide-eyed sigh. "Pissed might be the understatement of the year. He called me a traitor to the family name. He was ready to disown me, might still. Only my status in Coterie, and that he's already 'lost' his daughter, stayed his hand."

"Are you going to lay low for a while with him?" asked Pi.

Ashley's eyes lit with an inner fire. "Hell, no. That wrinkled old prick, pardon my tongue, has got it coming to him. I don't care that he's family. How can I do nothing while you and your sister risk yourselves? I've lived a very privileged life. I need to start using that to help others, rather than hiding behind it."

Pi threw her arms around Ashley and gave her a kiss on the cheek. "You're amazing, Ashley. What do you need my help on?"

Ashley pulled them to the building side of the sidewalk as tourists streamed past. The noises of the city—cars, voices, honking, sirens—were ever-present, until Ashley snapped her fingers to give them a bubble of privacy.

"I'm on a scavenger hunt," said Ashley, visibly annoyed. "Whoever collects the most items on the list gets their choice of third-year rooms. I *have* to win so I can get the Griffon Lodge. It has the best wards and a spectral butler. But mostly it's about the wards. Brock DuPont and Bree Bishop started being a couple last year, and they've been knocking off the rest of the class one by one. We're down to sixteen. If I don't get the Griffon Lodge, I'm not sure I can fend them off. Especially since my grandfather has made his displeasure known to the rest of the alumni. The last attempt was right before finals. They'd enchanted my blankets to strangle me in my sleep. The only reason I survived was because I'd been sleeping in my closet and woke when the blankets were trying to slither in."

Pi remembered Brock DuPont. His parents owned the Smoke & Amber bar. "I'm all yours. What's on the list?"

The parchment was yellowed with age and the lettering was in exquisite calligraphy. There were twenty-five items, and eight of them were crossed out.

Pi pointed to one of the items. "Pin from fifth year at a different Hall? Which one?"

"Oculus," said Ashley with a grin.

"You sly dog, Ash. How'd you steal from a seer? Shouldn't they have foreseen what you were going to do?"

"Knowing the future and stopping it are two different things," said Ashley.

Pi kept reading. "A selkie's pubic hair? Gross."

Ashley rolled her eyes. "Don't even ask how I got that."

The easier items on the list had already been acquired, though easier was quite relative. Any one of them could have gotten Ashley killed.

"What do you need help with? Though to be honest, I'm not sure how anyone can do better than this. Hellhound lice? Ewww...really?" asked Pi.

"Since Brock and Bree are sleeping together, they only need one room, so they're working in tandem. It leaves me at a disadvantage," said Ashley.

The desperation in Ashley's eyes was enough. It wasn't hard to imagine how difficult it was in Coterie. Pi had been almost murdered a half-dozen times during her first year. She also felt guilty because if she'd stayed, the two of them could have banded together against the others.

"Gotcha."

Ashley leaned in and pointed at an item halfway down the list.

"Feather from a cherubim," read Pi. "If you would have told me earlier I could have done some research on where to find one."

"It's okay. I traded some favors for a name and location," said Ashley, giving a little shudder at the word favors.

"If you have a name and a location, what do you need me for?" asked

Pi.

"You know what a cherubim is?" asked Ashley.

"Roughly, but give me the details," said Pi.

"The realm they come from is a bit of a higher plane of existence. Even when we see them here, we don't really see all of them. They have four faces, which, to our human eyes, look like a lion, owl, human, and eagle. They also have more wings than necessary," said Ashley.

"Aren't they sometimes called a sphinx?" asked Pi.

Ashley nodded soberly. "That's the one."

"Crap," said Pi, "you don't need my help. You just have to answer its question."

"If I'm wrong it'll try to eat me," said Ashley. "Which is why I need you."

"Got it," said Pi. "I'm your backup plan."

"I've done some research. If you can get away, they won't pursue, but that's the hard part, getting away," she said.

In certain ways, a sphinx was stronger than a demon lord. The cherubim channeled faez differently than most supernatural creatures. If a demon was the typical high school jock who threw you in the trashcan and gave you swirlies, then a sphinx was the bright-eyed hacker kid who changed all your grades to D's for not going to Homecoming with him.

"You look like you want to back out," said Ashley.

"No way. I said I'd help. I'm thinking about what protections we need," she said, though Pi was also wondering if this encounter could benefit her. There was a question she really wanted answered, and the sphinx would be able to provide said answer.

Ashley gave a nervous smile. "He lives a few blocks from here."

While they walked, they talked about the mundane details of their lives in the Hundred Halls, including favorite professors and living conditions. Pi was sharing a suite with her sister, and unlike Ashley, their room had been awarded by vote. The suite had a massive bathroom, including a tub that filled itself with a large variety of liquids upon demand. Pi had taken a warm sand-infused mud bath earlier in the week, and her skin was still glowing from the exfoliation.

They arrived at the address. The sphinx lived above a convenience store that had bars across the window.

"Not exactly living in the lap of luxury," said Ashley, looking despondent.

"Maybe he wants quick and easy access to Twinkies at all hours of the night," said Pi.

"I'm worried this isn't the right spot. Or my source was lying. I can't imagine a proud creature like a sphinx would choose to live here," said Ashley.

"Could be a good thing, Ash. He might not be as strict on the ol' sphinx code. Instead of a riddle, it might be a question you can answer using the intertubes," said Pi, patting Ashley's shoulder. "Phone a friend or something like that."

The stairs were narrow, and graffiti had been carved into the wood paneling with an ink pen. It wasn't even the good graffiti, the kind that made you feel like you were in an outdoor art shop. It was the nasty, racist graffiti that normally lived on truck stop bathroom walls.

Ashley knocked on the door. It sounded like it was made of balsa wood. A TV set was playing, one of those million magical police procedural shows that the networks loved, and Pi hated. After Ashley knocked a third time, a muffled voice shouted something that sounded like "come in."

The door opened without them touching it. Revulsion set in when the stench hit them. Old pizza boxes were stacked as high as the ceiling, with a narrow row between. Even without seeing them, Pi could sense the thousands of cockroaches crawling through the cheese-crusted cardboard skyscrapers. The sphinx was a hoarder, full-fledged intervention-level hoarding.

They followed the sound of the TV until they came upon what could be called a living room if one were being extremely generous. A hairy guy in his underwear was ensconced on a crappy folding lawn chair from the previous century. The aluminum tubes looked ready to collapse from his weight.

Thinking they were in the wrong place, Pi grabbed Ashley's arm to pull her out before the guy noticed them, but she shook it off. Ashley made an exaggerated eye rolling motion, then nodded towards the guy.

Pi didn't understand, until she realized what Ashley was doing. She looked around the room, trying to keep the hairy guy on the lawn chair at the edge of her vision. When she saw it, she nearly exclaimed. It was the sphinx, though not in the Egyptian lion with a human head kind of way. There were lots of dirty, beaten gray feathers, multiple faces and eyes, and a lumpy body. The creature looked like it'd been sleeping in an ashtray for about a decade. The human form was just a projection of its otherworldly self.

"Leland Smiley?" asked Ashley.

The hairy guy in his tighty-whities finally noticed them. "You're not the Albert's Pizza guy."

"We're here to trade," said Ashley, who was standing as still as possible as if any movement might result in the filth from the room permanently adhering to her.

Leland squinted at them. "Whoever told you how to find me is going to have to answer some hard fucking questions."

"I want a feather," said Ashley.

"I don't have time," he said, gesturing towards the TV. "My show's on."

"I'll pay the price," said Ashley, crossing her arms.

"Not interested," he said.

"We're mages from the Halls," she replied.

This got his attention. He licked his lips in anticipation. "I haven't had mage flesh in a long time. You know how this works, right?"

"I am aware of the conventions," said Ashley.

"What about you, girlie?" asked Leland, patting his hairy legs. "You here to sit on my lap, or just killin' time?"

"I need an answer," said Pi, catching a what-the-hell glance from Ashley, and shrugging in response.

"A ménage à trios," said Leland with a disgusting smirk on his lips. "Who's first?"

"I am," said Ashley, bracing herself.

Leland cracked his neck by pulling on the side of his head. Then he stretched his fingers like a pianist about to perform at Carnegie Hall.

"I'm a little rusty," he said. "As you might notice, I've been trying to avoid this line of work."

"Ask the question," said Ashley.

"Remember, no helping each other. You got that?" he asked.

They both nodded, then Leland Smiley tapped on his chin for a bit before he realized the TV was still on. He snapped his fingers, and it switched off. After a couple of minutes a slow smile rose to his lips, and just witnessing it made Pi want to scrub herself with sandpaper.

"A rich man and a poor man are in a bar in New Jersey with Springsteen on in the background. The poor man turns to the rich man and says, 'I have an amazing talent; I know almost every song that has ever existed. I'm willing to bet all the money you have in your wallet that I can sing a genuine song with your choice of a lady's name in it.' The rich man laughs and says, 'Okay. How about my daughter's name. Gertrude Simon-Sloan.' The rich man goes home poor. The poor man goes home rich. What song did he sing?"

Ashley repeated the riddle quietly. Pi started working through it, though she didn't want to get too wound up on it since she'd have to answer her own.

Leland watched Ashley much like a lion would an antelope. Somehow, Pi could imagine his jaw unhinging and swallowing her whole.

"I'm waiting," he said after a couple of minutes.

Ashley closed her eyes, cupping her hands over her mouth almost in a praying position. She mumbled to herself.

While Ashley was thinking, the answer appeared in Pi's head. Probably because, unlike Ashley, she wasn't trying too hard, which made solving problems easier. The song was "Happy Birthday," but it didn't do a damn bit of good if Ashley couldn't figure it out.

"One more minute," said Leland, stirring on his lawn chair.

Ashley gritted her teeth and clenched her hands. Pi was trying to will the answer across the space. She wasn't allowed to say anything, or violate the rules. She thought about texting the answer, but decided that was the same thing.

"Twenty seconds," said Leland.

He started mouthing his countdown, which didn't help Ashley at all. It was down to the last seconds, when Pi hummed the first two notes of the song: one long, one short.

As Leland's eyes widened, Ashley shouted, "'Happy Birthday!'"

He jabbed a finger in Pi's direction. "You cheated."

"Nope," she said, crossing her arms defiantly. "Just clearing my throat."

He looked ready to murder her, but narrowed his eyes and in a cool voice said, "Fine. One feather."

He plucked it from his back and handed the greasy, limp thing to Ashley. She held it with two fingers and quickly dropped it into a baggie as if it were contagious.

"Your turn. What is your request?" he asked, menace in his eyes.

A stone formed in her gut. She had no doubt that he was going to ask an insanely difficult question. But she needed an answer, one that would help her understand who she was, and why she always sought power. She didn't think that it only came from her parents' death. It had to be more than that. Had to be something deeper, more ingrained into her being. And for that she was willing to risk a lot.

"What is my heritage?" she asked.

The question seemed to surprise him. He raised an eyebrow as if he were accessing the answer and chuckled softly. The bastard was taunting her with his knowledge.

When he didn't have to think about his question, Pi knew it was one he'd been saving for a particularly troublesome client, one that would likely result in an incorrect answer.

"What is your heritage?" he asked.

At first Pi thought he was repeating her question for posterity's sake, but when he slid back into his lawn chair and placed his hands behind his head, she realized what he was doing.

"You can't do that," said Pi. "That's not fair. It has to be a question I can answer."

"Now you're worried about being fair? You cheated me out of my due," he said. "Suck it up, Princess Buttercup, and answer the question."

Pi thought about making a run for it, but as soon as it crossed her mind, the door to the apartment slammed shut.

"I'll give you the same amount of time I gave her. Two minutes," he said.

"That was more than two minutes!" said Pi.

"Felt like two minutes to me. Time's a wastin'," he said.

Pi paced between the pizza boxes. Leland was smirking.

"Let's get out of here," she said, and pulled Ashley towards the door.

Leland yelled after her, "You're not leaving."

As he'd said, the door was locked. Pi stepped back and put her boot into it. The impact jarred her to the hip.

"It's the nature of a sphinx's power," said Ashley. "We can't get out while you owe him an answer."

"The hell with that," said Pi. "There's always a way out. He's only more prepared than we are."

Pi flexed her fingers, then tried a few unlocking spells. Nothing worked.

"They teach that in Arcanium?" asked Ashley.

Pi shook her head.

"Twenty seconds!" yelled Leland. "Then I'm coming to eat you!"

"Merlin's tits," said Pi, glancing around the room. "I have an idea, but I need more time."

Ashley moved towards the living room, pulling a trio of perfectly round stones out of her pockets. She started rotating them in her palm, the motion quickly building speed until they were a blur, turning them into a disc. She added faez into the spinning stones until the room stunk of ozone.

"Dinnertime!" yelled Leland.

What came limping into the room made Pi think of a cross between a lion and an eagle that had been dragged behind a speeding car for about fifty miles.

Ashley hit the dirty sphinx with a spell from her stones, exploding cardboard boxes around him like confetti. The sphinx was momentarily deterred, but marched forward.

While Ashley was keeping the sphinx off her back, Pi began a complex spell in Egyptian. It was something she'd learned in preparing to retrieve the Rod of Dominion meant to break down barriers. She assumed that the ancient wizard that had written the spell down had reason for it.

Pi pulled a blue paint pen from her back pocket and scrawled hiero-glyphics on the door while the battle raged behind her. There were fifteen glyphs to create, and if she got one wrong, the backlash from the spell would probably enslave her to the sphinx rather than break its barrier.

With the glyphs complete, Pi said a few words in ancient Egyptian, and the spell activated. She was hoping for the door to be blown open, or some other sign that it'd worked, but nothing. She checked the handle to find it locked.

"How's it coming back there?" asked Ashley. "I'm running out of tricks."

Using the materials at hand was the mark of a great mage. Ashley's latest spell had formed a giant cardboard box around Leland. Hunks of old cheese were stuck to the outside. But based on the bulges, the sphinx was due to break out soon.

"I'm working on it. You don't happen to have a piece of amber, do you?" she asked.

"Sorry, fresh out," said Ashley.

With a piece of amber, she could try another ancient spell that she'd learned. Something that dated to Mesopotamian times that had come up in her research.

As she rubbed her temples, her arm bumped against a lump in her jacket. Pi reached inside and found a pocket she hadn't noticed before. She pulled out a golden lump about the size of a marble.

Using the amber, Pi worked the new spell. As she said the words, ancient phrases that she'd memorized but had no idea what they meant, golden cracks formed in the door. Encouraged by the sign, Pi kept repeat-ing the incantation.

"Hurry, Pi!"

Right before Leland escaped, Pi's spell broke down the barrier. The two girls sprinted down the stairs with Leland hot on their heels.

They burst into the street and turned to do battle with the sphinx. To their surprise, rather than the mythical form, the version of Leland Smiley in his tighty-whities stumbled into the street.

Drawn by the sudden motion, pedestrians stopped to point at him and pulled their cell phones out for pictures.

Pi grabbed Ashley's hand and kept walking. After a dozen steps, Leland shouted, "Fucking witches!" and flipped them off.

Yelling over her shoulder, Ashley replied, "Bless your heart!"

"Sick burn, Ash. Sick burn," she said.

"That was too close," said Ashley. "Sorry about your answer. What was that about anyway?"

"Don't worry about it," said Pi, trying to hide her disappointment.

A flash of light from the other side of the city drew their notice. Everyone on the street had stopped and was staring in that direction. Despite the taller buildings, they could see that the sky was lit up with something bright.

Ashley pointed into the clouds. A billowing ball of energy was rolling upwards as if a volcano had erupted and shot its lava charge into the atmosphere.

"What the hell is that?" asked Ashley.

"Looks like an explosion of some kind. Seems like the direction of the twelfth district. Lots of old magics left there, waiting to cause havoc," said Pi.

"Really? I didn't know that," said Ashley.

Pi squeezed her friend's shoulder. "Be glad whatever that is, it isn't our problem, because that's sure to cause a truckload of trouble."

THREE

The waterfall beneath Arcanium thundered into its pool, sending flecks of water against Aurie's ankles. She stood right at the edge of the path, reluctant to enter Semyon Gray's quarters. She'd heard he'd been in Tokyo and had to catch a flight back to deal with the repercussions of the incident.

Aurie was sick with grief over what had happened. Since she was a mage of the Hundred Halls, no charges would be brought by the outside authorities. She wasn't out of the woods with her fellow mages, but that eventuality was nothing compared to the guilt that had etched into her bones like acid. She hadn't slept in three days.

The other students had been mostly supportive, though she saw the looks in their eyes when they thought she wasn't paying attention. They were wondering if she was going to lose control again.

The final toll had been three dead, fourteen injured, and one still in critical condition. Aurie had tried to visit Annabelle, who still hadn't woken up, but Golden Willow wouldn't allow her in the building due to the risk she presented. A call to Dr. Fairlight hadn't gotten her anywhere either, as the doctor refused to talk about Annabelle's condition. Aurie worried the damage was greater than the Rod could heal. If Annabelle died, Aurie would be devastated.

She'd tried to call Nezumi, which had been the hardest call she'd ever made in her life, but no one had answered. Either Nezumi and his wife were too grieved to answer, or they refused to speak with her because of what she'd done. Either way, she didn't blame them.

Aurie walked through the waterfall. On the other side, she found the tiny silver dragon Menolly catching minnows by dunking her head into the water when one would swim past. To her surprise, Menolly scampered over and bumped her face against Aurie's leg, so she knelt down and scratched the creature's scaly snout. Menolly made rumbling noises in her belly similar to a cat. When the little dragon had gotten her fill of attention, she gave Aurie a little squawk of "thank you" and resumed her fishing.

Feeling a little less frayed at the edges, Aurie steeled herself and went into Semyon's office. Her patron was seated on the other side of the desk in his formal robes. His hair was even grayer than it'd been last year. She was expecting him to be wearing a fearsome expression, but his face was filled with such sympathy that it nearly brought her to tears.

"I know this is going to be hard to hear, but it's not as bad as you think," he said.

"Not as bad as I think? Three people died. More were hurt. There's a little girl who I hold dear to my heart that hasn't recovered yet. How can it not be as bad as I think?" she asked, her voice cracking.

"Professor Mali told me what you told her. I have a few suspicions about what Camille gave you. Honestly, that it wasn't much worse is quite surprising," he said, though his gaze indicated there were repercussions he was unwilling to speak about.

"You believe me?" she asked.

"Of course I believe you. Now, don't mistake my message. This event has caused terrible complications that will take considerable time and energy to unravel"—he glanced away as if this burden had come at a bad time—"but that guilt that you are currently torturing yourself with has to stop right now. You are not at fault. I'm not sure Camille Cardwell knew exactly the extent of what was going to happen, though if she did the implications are troubling, but I know for sure that she wanted to destroy you."

It was as if she'd been pulled out of the rubble after an earthquake. Aurie took a deep and quivering breath. Hearing those words from him was relief beyond measure. It hadn't erased her sadness or grief, but she didn't feel like she was being pulled apart by pliers any longer.

"Are you steady enough to tell me what happened?" he asked.

"I am," she said.

"Good. You're going to need to be strong. I think this is the first time a student has caused an international incident. When you released that built-up energy into the sky, it entered the atmosphere and burned up a Chinese military satellite," he said.

"I haven't started World War III or anything, have I?" she asked.

He made dismissive motions with his hand. "Not at all. The Chinese government, like every government in the world, relies on us for their mages. They can no more boycott the Hundred Halls than they could oxygen, or water. For better or worse, we are the only place they can come to for mage power."

She felt a little wobbly thinking about it.

"Please sit," he said, motioning towards the chair. "I don't need you passing out on my floor. And explain what happened. Every last detail. We'll get to the hard part after I hear how Camille did this."

With her voice shaking more than she would have liked—she hated the idea of being weak in front of her patron—Aurie went through the details of the day. Semyon asked numerous questions, which reminded her of the first time she'd met him.

Afterwards, he stared at his bookcase, rubbing his chin in thought.

"I assume you've seen this," he said, picking up a copy of the *Herald of the Halls* that had been on his side of the desk and tossing it to her. The paper landed in her lap.

"Special Issue: WILD MAGE THREATENS CITY

It could have been much worse. That's what the authorities say about the release of wild magic during a festival in the Enochian District.

The local Protector's guild explains that Aurelia Silverthorne, third-year student of Arcanium, mistook some costumes as a threat and unleashed a significant amount of magic on the festival, killing three, injuring twenty-seven, including a young girl who still hasn't recovered.

This paper's owner, Camille Cardwell, was nearly immolated when she had the misfortune of attending the festival to bestow a large gift to the community. She said: 'the heroics of the bystanders risking their lives to tackle Aurelia Silverthorne when the magic grew too much for her to handle was nothing short of a miracle. I was frightened for my very life.'"

Aurie dropped the paper in her lap. She knew the talk online was getting outrageous, but she hadn't known they'd devoted a whole edition to the event.

"There's a dozen articles about what happened. A piece on the man who tackled you. Another on that girl still recovering in Golden Willow. More about those that died. There's also a few pieces about the monster attacks that have been happening in the city and speculation on how they can be related to this event," he said gravely.

"Monster attacks? Isn't what happened at the festival bad enough? Am I to be blamed for everything that happens in the city from now on? I can't even fathom how they would pin that on me," she said, exasperated.

"Seismic detectors as far as West Virginia noticed the event. They're saying the release of magic weakened barriers in the city, or wakened creatures long dormant in the undercity," he said.

"You actually believe that to be true, don't you?" she asked.

He sighed like a doctor about to explain his patient had cancer. "You remember where you were standing that day?"

"Yeah, I was on the dragon fountain," she said.

"Notice anything strange about it?" he asked.

She didn't know what he was getting at, but went along. "Not really."

"How did it survive the release of magic? You took out a Chinese satellite ten miles above you and broke windows as far as the fourth ward. Shouldn't an ordinary brass fountain have been annihilated in the release?" he asked.

Aurie remembered something she'd heard last year when the Harpers had gone against what they thought was a simple demon. Echo had told them that the four fountains around the city were important.

"It's a well of power," she said.

Semyon's nose wrinkled. "How did you know that?" He shook his head. "Never mind. I shouldn't be surprised about anything when it comes to you. Yes, it's a well of power, but that's not exactly an apt description. I'd call it an anchor, or a pillar. Think about the foundation of a house. If you want to keep it strong, you build it on bedrock."

"A house of magic?" asked Aurie.

"It's called the City of Sorcery for more than the Hundred Halls. When you released your magic, you tapped into the conduit for the city. It's like accidentally plugging your vacuum into a power line. You're lucky you weren't annihilated by the outflow. Only your strength as a mage kept you safe, though I would be careful around the wells, because you might not be able to control it next time."

"What does that have to do with the monsters?" she asked.

"When you shook the pillars of the city, it knocked a few things loose. The use of magic leaves residue, unspent faez, that settles in dark places. There's a lot of leftover magic beneath the Hundred Halls, as well as forgotten experiments, or mistakes that people wanted to hide," he said.

"So I *am* a danger," she said.

"Aurelia," he said softly, "we're mages. We're *all* a danger. Invictus included. Keep in mind that even he was not immune to the hubris associated with mages. He came from a time before the halls, when chaos reigned. He did terrible things in service to power. Through this he realized that humanity would destroy ourselves with war. It's the reason he created the Hundred Halls. By binding us together, he kept us from killing each other. It's why the patron system has worked so well. A little bit of each of us is bound to the other halls. Invictus himself still exists within us all. Which reminds me. This might be a little early in your career to bring this up, but given the recent events, you might be wondering this already. You have the level of power capable of being a patron—at a later date, of course, but it's within you. You also have the vision and the ambition, which is important."

"Me? A patron?" she asked, incredulous. "What about that Invictus is dead?"

The reminder put Semyon back into his chair. "Eventually someone will find a way to take the position of head patron."

It was clear to Aurie in that moment that Semyon's constant exhaustion the last few years was from his attempts to find out how to achieve that position. If he didn't, one of the Cabal patrons would. She hoped it was Semyon.

"Earlier," she said. "Earlier, you mentioned that there are complications from...from, well, you know."

He rubbed his hand across the edge of his desk. "The general public has always tolerated magic, either because of jealousy or fear. We are the 'haves' and they are the 'have-nots.' This agreement, especially the immunity from prosecution, frays during difficult times. It's bad enough that we're fighting amongst ourselves, but if the public turns on us, then the Halls themselves could be at risk and then by proxy, the world."

Aurie could see where this was going. Semyon was working his way to saying it, but hadn't gotten there yet because he was afraid of what she would think. For years, she'd always thought of patrons as near-mythical beings full of godlike wisdom and experience. The gray hair, deep lines around his mouth, the hesitations—these reminded her that he was mortal, just like she was.

"They want to offer me up as a sacrifice to people's concerns," she said.

He blinked twice. "Yes...yes, that's it. They cite your lack of control as the reason. That you're a risk to the mage community as well as the population at large."

Aurie sat up, looking her patron in the eyes. "I've been reading the bylaws. What do you think they'll do?"

"The only course of action is a trial of your peers," he said.

"They'll stack the jury against me. I'm sure that's been Camille's intention all along. It'd be easy for them to fill it with Cabal members, or others sympathetic to the Cabal. And there'd be no way to keep them from intimidating those that weren't. It wouldn't matter what I said. They'd kick me out and take my magic," said Aurie.

"I'm afraid there's no other way," he said, clasping his hands. "We'll just have to find a way to convince them."

"There is another way," said Aurie. "It's in the bylaws, an obscure rule from the early years. I had to go back to a previous edition to find it."

Semyon raised an eyebrow. "I see someone has learned the importance of good research."

It wasn't so much that she'd learned, but that she'd been awake for three days, wracked with guilt. Doing the research had taken her mind off what had happened, though fleetingly.

"When they bring the charges, I want a trial by magic," she said. "It's my right to ask for it."

"I've been a patron of the Halls since the beginning. I don't recall this rule," he said.

She pulled a yellowed and tattered book from her carryall. He took it and read through the marked sections.

"It's only been used twice, both of them in the first decade of the school," she said.

He was busy reading, but remarked, "I was a bit more bookish then. I suppose a cataclysm could have happened and I wouldn't have noticed."

"The trial would be judged by three patrons, chosen randomly from the available halls. Exactly what will be required will depend on those patrons. They will decide what I must do to prove myself," she said.

"Aurelia. Do you understand what you're asking? It could be anything. They could give you an impossible task," he said.

"I'd rather have a slim chance of winning than no chance. If it's a trial by peers, I'll lose for sure. But a trial by magic will give me a chance. They set the conditions, I have to prove it. Probably something that shows my control over Arcanium magic. I would assume it would have to do with verumancy or mendancy. The only thing I ask is that you delay it as long as possible to give me more time to prepare," she said.

"Are you sure about this? It seems risky," he said.

"Less risky than the other way," she said.

He considered it for a while before nodding.

"I will present your request to the other patrons and do my best to delay it as long as possible, giving you more time for learning, and the public a chance to forget," he said. "So do your best to stay out of trouble until then. If something else happens, they could easily argue for the immediate removal of your magic."

FOUR

Third-year students lived in the Tower of Letters, which was on the back-side of Arcanium, facing towards the city center. The suite that Pi and her sister shared was much larger than their apartment in the thirteenth ward. While they had separate bedrooms, a study area lay between them.

Pi was standing at the window watching a parade of Oesteomancium students march through the street. The bone-bending mages had recon-figured their limbs into outlandish shapes that made them look like stilt-walkers, or denizens of a freak show. The month of October was practi-cally their official holiday, and everyone called their hall the Weird Circus.

"What's the bloody point?" asked Pi, tapping on the window.

Aurie and Xi Chu were preparing for an exam in Obscure Languages. They'd been mumbling in worm-tongue for the last few hours, driving Pi to distraction.

"Bloody?" asked Aurie. "Are we English now?"

Pi lifted one shoulder in a weak shrug. "Trying it out. You know, for Rigel."

"Sometimes magic is exploring what is possible," said Xi thoughtfully as he looked up from his tomes.

Pi knew she shouldn't make a face, but she couldn't help it. Almost everyone in Arcanium was focused on knowledge for knowledge's sake without seeing the bigger picture. "Magic, like everything, is a means to an end. If you're not trying to accomplish something with it, why bother?"

Aurie frowned, that disappointed older sister expression on her face. "Which is why you're failing Mysteries and Existentialism. Sometimes we have to prepare for challenges we don't expect."

Pi rolled her eyes—away from Aurie's gaze so she didn't get a lecture—and went back to the window. Despite the constant danger, and the elitist attitudes, she missed the Coterie of Mages. They knew how to get things done. It was no wonder the Cabal seemed to be in control of the Halls these days. They weren't sitting on their laurels worrying about how to ask a praying mantis what a moth tasted like.

She wasn't paying attention until she heard Aurie exclaim. A message wisp hovered in the middle of the room.

"What?" asked Pi.

Aurie had a strange expression. It made Pi a little worried.

"We have to go down to the police station," said her sister.

A thousand things went through Pi's head. None of them favorable. She blurted out, "Did the zombie squirrel bite someone?"

It was Aurie's turn to be surprised. "What?"

"Never mind," said Pi. "Why do we have to go to the station?"

"It's our uncle," she said.

"Mom doesn't have a brother," said Pi.

"No, the one that disappeared all those years ago in Siberia. Dad's older brother. Uncle Liam. He's at the station. They picked him up for loitering near the Bank of Invictus," said Aurie.

After the stunned silence, the sisters headed to the station by way of the Red Line. On the train, they talked about what they knew of Uncle

Liam. Pi couldn't help but get excited. Of her family, she'd only known her parents. Maybe Liam could fill in the blanks for her, help her figure out who she really was.

"I don't believe that Uncle Liam ever met us," said Aurie. "Dad didn't talk about him much. I think Liam's about ten years older, so he was probably gone by the time Dad was grown up."

"He was an adventurer," said Pi breathlessly. "That's probably the side of the family that I'm more like."

A punch in the arm brought Pi around. "If by adventurer, you mean reckless idiot, then yes, you're probably a lot like this Liam."

Pi ignored her sister. "I wonder why he came back? Maybe he's supposed to tell us our secret past—like we're related to royalty, or maybe fairy queens. It would explain a lot of things."

"Don't get your hopes up," said Aurie. "He's probably here because he heard about our winnings from last year."

The police headquarters had huge angular pillars crossing in the front as if they thought it was the Fortress of Solitude. Pi had never met anyone from Protector's Hall that she'd liked, and her experience with its patron, Bannon Creed, hadn't helped.

But most of the officers at the station weren't mages. Not all crimes were magic related, or required magical abilities. The check-in officer led them to an open-plan office. It looked like every station she'd seen on TV, except there were fewer officers in robes.

When Pi saw a handsome older man with ginger hair and a jaw line that reminded her of her father, she knew it was Uncle Liam. He had a sleeve of tattoos that formed a blanket of leaves on his left arm and a scar that intersected his right eyebrow. While she knew he was in his early to mid-fifties, he didn't look it. He whistled a little tune that made her think of ancient cities with wooden bridges.

An overweight Protector with a wad of chewing tobacco in his cheek spit in the trashcan right when they strolled up. He had a messy sandwich in one hand and a clipboard in the other.

"You tellin' me you're related to these two? I read about her in the *Herald*," said the Protector, gesturing with his sandwich as parts of it fell onto the floor. "Damn near killed a whole district. If it were up to me, I'd put her in a cage like she belongs."

Aurie looked ready to put a fist into his mouth. Pi wasn't happy about what he said either, but she wasn't about to start a fight in the middle of police HQ.

"Excuse me, Protector Cox," said Pi, keeping her voice calm. "We didn't come down here to be insulted."

Protector Cox turned his girth towards her as if that would somehow intimidate her. She could see in his gaze he was used to getting his way, and that talking back usually earned a nasty spell from him. While she wasn't going to start a fight, she certainly wasn't going to back down.

"Listen, missy," he said, wiping his mouth with the back of his hand. "I'll damn well insult you if I want, and you'll take it, unless you want to join your uncle in chains for threatening an officer."

It bothered her that the other officers within hearing range hadn't made a move to help or refute his challenge. She opened her mouth to say something, but a gesture from Uncle Liam made her reconsider. Despite the magic-inhibiting manacles on his wrists, his fingers were working through a spell. He winked and mouthed the words, "Keep talking."

"We're just here to get our uncle," she said, speaking slowly to keep the Protector's attention. "We're not here to start any trouble."

"Damn right," said Protector Cox, bits of food and chew coming out of his chubby mouth. "Learn your fucking place or I will put you in it."

He took another bite of his sandwich, then stopped cold. He had a look of inward concern. His stomach made a gurgle that was loud enough to draw the attention of officers at the other desks.

Protector Cox straightened, appeared to want to put his hand to his rear, but decided instead to make a run for the bathroom. He dropped his sandwich and clipboard, and not even five steps away, everyone heard his bowels unload. The stench of a sewer was immediate and overpowering, drawing the notice of everyone in the open office. He tried to quietly waddle out of the room, but a round of flatulence made his exit anything but private.

When he was gone, the office burst into laughter. He wasn't well loved, that much was clear.

"How did you do that?" asked Pi, impressed.

"I couldn't let that bastard bully my nieces. I've met his kind, and it's even worse on the inside."

"Thank you," said Pi.

Uncle Liam cocked a grin full of adventure and held the manacles up. "Can you get me out?"

His accent was clearly Irish, but the rough edges had been smoothed away by time.

"In the middle of a police station?" asked Aurie incredulously.

"Would you rather Protector Cox return after he realizes that someone might have put a spell on him? I am wearing spell-dampening manacles after all," he said.

"Which means he'll think it was us," said Aurie. "You jerk!"

"Aurie, hush," said Pi, gesturing at the other officers. "We don't want to draw any more attention to us."

"Sorry about that. I didn't think of that when I did it. Sometimes I act before I think, especially in times that like. Like I said, I don't like bullies. Girls?"

"Fine," said Aurie, "but make it quick."

Pi dropped to one knee and started working on the manacles. She was about halfway through figuring out what spell would unlatch them when she heard her sister.

"Pi...hurry up."

She noticed a group of officers moving through the office in their direction. Uncle Liam regarded her with a smirk on his face. Despite the danger, he seemed to be enjoying himself. Pi couldn't help but feel the same way.

When the manacles came off, Liam stood, brazenly opened the drawer on the desk, and pulled out some personal effects that Protector Cox had confiscated.

As the officers neared, Liam tipped an invisible cap, whistled a ditty, and said, "Officers."

To Pi's surprise, they went right past without so much as a word. Uncle Liam moved towards the exit. Pi couldn't believe that no one was stopping them. They walked out the front and onto the street, making it a few blocks before Aurie turned on their uncle.

"What the hell do you think you're doing? We've never met you before and now you have us breaking you out of the police HQ? Are you insane?" asked Aurie.

The outburst drew the notice of people on the street. Pi put a hand on her sister's arm. "Maybe we should find a quieter spot for this discussion."

"No," said Aurie. "I want answers before I go anywhere with him. We don't know him at all. We don't even know that he's really our uncle."

Liam's expression turned to a wounded puppy pushed into the wintery night. "Girls?"

"My sister is right," said Pi. "We don't know you, and you put us at risk back there. She can't afford any problems right now. Why did they have you anyway?"

He held his hands wide. "My introduction wasn't supposed to go like this. I'll explain, but can we get something to eat while we talk? I'm savagely hungry."

They found a chain restaurant nearby called Soups & Spells. The soups came in little cauldrons with runes on them. The runes were pure fakery. Liam ordered a stew, while Pi and her sister ordered coffee.

After he ate his stew, Liam dropped his spoon in the bowl, quietly passed off a belch, and put his hands on the booth table.

"I didn't even know either of you existed until a couple of months ago. I was passing through London when I saw the article about winning that contest last year. I wouldn't have realized we were related except for the mention that you were the kids of Kieran and Nahid. Honestly, the news that hit me in the knickers the hardest was that they'd passed. I had no idea. I feel like a gimp for not being there at the funeral," he said, despondent.

"Where have you been all these years?" asked Aurie. "Why didn't you ever contact your brother?"

Uncle Liam rubbed the edge of the table absently, searching for the words. He looked like the kind of guy with a complicated past.

"Let's just say, your uncle Liam made a lot of mistakes when he was younger, and it took a long time to fix those mistakes," he said in his Irish brogue. "As for Kieran, we never really got to know each other. He took off to join the Halls while I was away. Maybe the last time I saw him was when he was seventeen. A good lad he was, and a damn fine scrumhalf for the Whitestone RFC, just like I'd been. I followed the articles about his rugby exploits while I was away. Made me feel like I knew him."

In him, Pi saw the same wanderlust, desire to know family, and need to search for power that she felt. Aurie, however, was frowning deeply. She didn't trust him, that much Pi could see, and it was probably a fair evaluation.

"Why are you in Invictus?" asked Aurie.

"A bit of business," he said. "Don't worry, it's all on the up and up.

I'd planned on stopping by to meet you two, but Protector Cox was shaking me down for cash, threatening to have me sent back to Ireland, and I wasn't going to have any of that nonsense."

His brow furrowed as he checked the clock on the wall.

"I'm sorry to do this, but I have to get going. Got an appointment with some people that don't like when a fella is late. Don't want to end up in tatters, if you know what I mean," he said, and as he got up, he bit his lower lip. "And you wouldn't mind picking up the tab? Haven't had a chance to pick up the local scratch. Good. Thanks."

He started to leave, when Pi said, "Can we meet up again? I'd love to hear more about your adventures. Maybe you have some stories about the family."

He nodded as he walked backwards. "Yeah, yeah. After my business is wrapped up, I'll look you both up. Next time is on me, and we'll do it right, have a real meal."

The bill arrived a moment afterwards.

"I can see why Dad never talked about him," said Aurie.

"I don't know," said Pi. "I kinda liked him. Not sure I'd trust him with two pennies, but it's nice to know we have family again."

"Is it really family if you've never met them in your life and they just show up, right after you've come into money, and nearly get you into trouble with the local authorities?" asked Aurie.

"Not the most ideal of circumstances," said Pi. "But..."

"Face it, Pi. You are who you are. Learning where our families came from isn't going to change anything. I don't think you could trust a word he says anyway," said Aurie, throwing a couple of tens down on the check. "If we don't see him again, I think we'll be better off."

Pi didn't refute her. There wasn't any point. She'd known her sister wouldn't like Liam the moment she'd laid eyes on him. Yeah, he wasn't trustworthy, but he was family, and he might know a thing or two about their history. As they slid away from the table, Pi discreetly took the spoon from the bowl and shoved it in a spare baggie that she had in her pocket. Even if he didn't look her up again, she would find him.

FIVE

Freeport Games was filled with kids playing board games. Aurie saw Hannah, Brian Travers, and a few others playing Settlers of Catan in back. She kept her hood up and ducked into the back, heading through the maze-like hallways until she came upon the elevator room. A steel platform suspended by a heavy-duty winch on the ceiling hung above a hole that went hundreds of feet into the undercity.

Hemistad was hunched over an open crate on the platform, grumbling to himself. He wore a wrinkled tan jacket that looked like it'd been donated. He was the owner of Freeport Games. Aurie and her sister had worked for him in various capacities over the years.

He was normally a little grouchy, but she sensed a deeper agitation, as if he were a dog with his hackles up. The exact nature of Hemistad's supernatural origins had never been made clear, but Aurie didn't have to be a mage to know he was dangerous to the wrong people.

He closed the crate and frowned. "I thought Pythia was helping me. Don't you have that clinic to look after?"

A pit opened in her gut.

"She was busy, and I wanted to help," she said.

It shouldn't have surprised her that he didn't know about what had happened. He'd been abroad the past few months searching for something.

When he frowned again, his bushy eyebrows covered his eyes. "I'm not sure this is the kind of magic you'd like to get involved with."

Pi had warned her that Hemistad operated in gray areas, which was why it was usually her sister helping him. But Aurie needed information that he probably wouldn't want to give, and helping him was the best way to get it.

"I'm expanding my horizons," she said.

"I'll assume you brought what I asked for."

Aurie joined him on the platform. He grabbed the pendant, but didn't hit the button right away. He stared at it for a while before handing it to Aurie, and walked back to the crate.

She stabbed the button with a thumb. The platform lurched downward, the steady whine fading as they descended. Hemistad leaned against the crate as if he were a doomed prisoner.

"Can you at least tell me what we're doing?" she asked as they neared the bottom.

"Nothing you need to worry about," he said gruffly.

The platform hit the rock floor with a thud, jarring Aurie's teeth together.

Without turning to her, he banged on the crate. "Bring this and hurry up, I want to get this over with."

He marched into the darkness without another word. Aurie conjured a wisp into existence and told it to follow Hemistad, before turning her attention to the crate. It was about four feet to a side. She pulled a purple paint marker out of her pocket and wrote "light" on five sides, imbuing it with verumancy. Trying to put her arms around it revealed the flaw in her plan. The crate was too unwieldy to pick up and carry.

Aurie dug into her carryall, which had a portal back to her room. The desk had been set up with reagents and magical supplies, but she needed something mundane. She pulled the plastic bag of rubber party balloons out, took four balloons, convinced the bag to close itself, and put it back on her desk.

Convincing the air she blew into each balloon that it was helium wasn't hard. Gases were the easiest materials to lie to, since they were rather fluid by nature. Aurie had found the more solid the item, the harder it was to convince. Once the balloon was full, she tied a string around the bottom and hooked it to a corner of the crate. With all four corners connected, the crate lifted off the steel grating of the platform. Aurie gave it a gentle push, and the crate floated across the rocky floor. After attaching a fifth string to the box, Aurie tugged it along behind her.

The wisp on Hemistad bobbed ahead faintly, sometimes disappearing behind pillars that went up into the darkness, other times reflecting on puddles, or shimmering along cave walls.

Aurie was content not to catch up to him, as he seemed rather maudlin. She doubted he would be a good traveling companion.

The darkness of the undercity was less imposing than it'd been on her first trip two years ago. She felt more confident about her abilities, but not so much that hubris would leave her unguarded. She kept a spell at the tip of her tongue should it be necessary.

As they passed through tunnels and smaller caverns, Aurie recognized the path. They were headed to the place that they'd encountered the Hunger. When they reached it, Hemistad circled the room twice before settling on a flat rise near the center.

"Set it up here," he said.

"What am I setting up? You haven't told me anything," she said.

Hemistad pulled a yellowed scroll tied with a piece of string from his pocket and threw it at her. It wasn't a scroll, but a collection of pages ripped out of a tome, and the string was dental floss. She pieced together the spell from a few glances.

"We're building a cage?" she asked.

"*We're* not building anything," he said. "You are. That's what I need you for."

"What are you going to do?" she asked.

"I need to find the Hunger," he said.

"Is that what we're catching?"

He marched away. "If I would have wanted you to know, I would have told you."

The rough nature of his answer made Aurie wonder if she'd made the right choice to help him. Too late to back out now.

The crate opened at a touch, revealing a pile of aluminum frames and a brass urn about three feet tall. Aurie pulled everything out, placing the frame pieces along the edge of the level area, and the urn to the side.

A series of runes circled the rim of the urn. The style indicated it came from the Slavic regions, but the ancientness of the script suggested it was at least a thousand years old. Aurie tapped on the brass lid with a fingernail only to have something tap right back. The spell didn't mention the urn, so Aurie decided to leave it alone.

Assembling the aluminum cage took about twenty minutes. It was a rectangular shark cage with hooks for placing buoys to keep it floating in the water. There were no buoys, which suggested Hemistad only wanted it as a scaffold for the spell.

Wielding a purple paint pen—which was the most ubiquitous tool for the resourceful mage—Aurie neatly drew runes along the edge pieces of the cage. These were not related to the Slavic runes on the urn, but standard enchantments used for warding possessions.

Aurie had always thought of them like a programming language. The order of the runes was important along with the syntax. God forbid you wrote the wrong rune, so after each one, she checked it against the spell. She repeated the rune phrase four times for each side, which meant twenty-four times total. The work was tedious, and by the end she was writing them from memory. The exact meaning of the enchantment wasn't entirely clear. It came from a realm of spellcraft that she was unfamiliar with, but as long as she copied it precisely, she had nothing to worry about.

Hemistad appeared the moment she clicked the cap back on the paint pen.

"Is it finished?"

"Did you find your Hunger?" she asked.

His mouth bunched up. "Is it finished?"

"Runed and ready to catch sharks," she said, disappointed by his lack of response.

He stared at the cage as if it were a jail cell that he was being put into for life.

"You may go," he said, never once taking his eyes from the cage.

"What about the virgin's blood?" she asked, pulling the vial from an inside pocket.

He held his hand out. She gave it to him.

Getting the blood hadn't been as hard as she'd thought. An enterprising mage had set up a website for sharing or trading hard to find reagents. There was a Filipino mage who was apparently making a killing by staying a virgin and selling vials of blood. The kind of spells that needed virgin blood tended to be icky, since they were usually associated with sacrifices and other ancient rituals.

"Good luck, Hemistad, with whatever you're doing," she said, backing away.

He didn't say anything, so she hurried her pace. She really didn't like the idea of hanging around when the Hunger showed up. She also wanted to get away before anything happened so that she wouldn't feel guilty if whatever he was doing was a little sketchy.

Around the time she was leaving the cavern through an old sewer tunnel, a young woman's voice back at the cage stopped Aurie in her tracks.

"Don't look back, don't look back, don't look back," she mumbled.

The last time she and Pi had gone to the undercity, the Hunger had tricked them by appearing as a young girl who'd gotten lost. This had to be something similar.

"Just keep going," Aurie whispered to herself.

An anguished young woman's voice reached her across the room. "Don't do this, Hemistad. You'll regret it."

Aurie looked over her shoulder. A faint glow illuminated the center of the cave. She couldn't see details, but it appeared Hemistad was standing outside the cage, while another person, the young woman presumably, was inside the cage.

"Sacrifices have to be made," he said. "Even if they are unpalatable."

"But you've done so well all these years. Why go back to what you were before?" she asked.

"We can't avoid who we are, even if we don't like that person," he said. "Let's get this over with, there's killing to be done."

A steady roar like a fierce wind rising rumbled into the room like a storm moving through an old forest. Aurie sensed the presence in the darkness, the Hunger. In her mind it was a great hungry maw, never satisfied, a bottomless pit of need. She took a step into the room, but a primal fear forced her from the chamber, almost as if she were being pushed away by invisible hands.

Once Aurie turned away, the need to flee took over and she raced back to the platform that would take her back up to Freeport Games, feeling like whatever Hemistad had become was chasing her. *There's killing to be done.* The words chilled her heart. What had she unleashed upon the world?

SIX

One hundred one-foot-tall gnomes holding bats and wearing bright red painted hats filled the Astroturf square. An attendant from the Transmuters' Hall was standing in front of a wall full of stuffed unicorns. He had long stringy hair and a red striped shirt.

"Three balls for five dollars," he called out. "If it has a rainbow ticket inside, you win a fluffy unicorn!"

Pi leaned into Ashley, who was clinging to her arm. They were both a little tipsy. They'd spent the last few hours at a bar in the seventh ward before coming to the carnival, which was run by the smaller Halls as a fundraiser since they didn't have rich alumni.

Behind them a Ferris wheel rotated while benign geists scared the people on the ride. The sounds of bells, chattering children, and popping spells was a blanket of sound that turned each part near indistinguishable. The carnival took up at least three blocks in the street.

Ashley poked her in the arm. "Win me a unicorn."

"You can buy a unicorn," said Pi.

"But it's not the same as having my friend, the great Pythia Silverthorne, win me one," said Ashley with a slight slur to her words. "Come on, Pi, don't you love me?"

Laughing, Pi pushed her away and reached for her clip of money. She found it in an inside pocket, but not the one she'd put it in earlier when they were buying shots. The leather jacket worked like that.

The attendant handed her three balls after she gave him a fiver. "Good luck."

"I get to use magic, right?" she asked.

He looked insulted by her question, so she took that as her answer.

"The ball has to break the gnome," he said. "No blasting them with fireballs or anything."

Pi pulled her hand back out of the pocket that had a few explosive seeds in it.

"Which one do you think has a golden ticket in it?" she asked.

Ashley squinted at the gnomes. "I'm not big on divination. It feels like cheating."

"They'll revoke your pin at Coterie if they hear that kind of talk. Cheating is a Coterie special," said Pi as she hefted a ball. "Or has living in the Griffon Lodge with your protections made you complacent?"

Ashley's eyes went wide with thought. "Ohhhh...did I tell you? Brock tried to use a passwall spell to get into the Lodge, but he didn't know about the specter that lives in the walls. By the time they found him, the specter had aged him ninety years. They don't think he'll be back this year, if ever. Without Brock to watch her back, I don't think Bree will last the semester the way the other third years have been talking."

A pang of regret tugged on her heart as she eyed the gnomes. Pi cupped the ball and whispered to it for a few seconds. When she was finished, she wound up and launched the ball at the gnomes in front. The ball flew from her hand like a major league pitch, right at a little ceramic gnome. But as quick as she'd thrown it, the gnome swung the bat, knocking the ball away from the field.

"Stupid gnome!"

Quick as a flash, the gnome raised its little fist and flipped her off before resuming its previous form.

Ashley dropped to her knees in laughter. "Oh my god, Pi. I wasn't expecting that. You just got shut down by a gnome!"

"I guess you don't want a unicorn stuffy?" asked Pi with her hands on her hips.

Ashley crawled over, tears in her eyes, laughing hysterically as if she'd been drugged. "Please, Pi. Try again. I do want one."

Nearby carnival-goers were eyeing the pair of them uneasily. With cheeks warm from the attention, and the beginnings of a grin tugging the corners of her lips upward, Pi poked Ashley with the toe of her boot.

"Get up, you're embarrassing your hall," said Pi.

Once Ashley had calmed herself, Pi turned her attention to the ball. At this point, she didn't care as much about the stuffed unicorn as not being made a fool of by a ceramic gnome. Whoever had enchanted them had done their job well.

For her second attempt, Pi tried a different tactic. Instead of going for speed, she went for weight. By the time she was done with the spell, she could barely hold the ball. It took a couple of more spells on her arm before she could prepare the throw.

After the windup, she launched the ball at a cluster of gnomes in the middle. Two gnomes tried to swing at the ball, but it blew their bats to dust, before demolishing a third gnome behind them. Unfortunately, the gnome was empty.

None of the gnomes dared to give her the finger. In fact, they looked a little scared now that they could see what she could do.

"Alright, my little garden tyrants," she said, pulling out a handful of fives. "Which one of you has a golden ticket in your belly? Fess up or I'll make sure and destroy every last one of you."

The gnomes didn't move, but a couple of them made eye motions towards a gnome on the left side that looked like it was doing its damndest not to be noticed. Before they could get wise to her, she sent the final ball at the gnome at great speed. It cracked it in half, revealing a golden ticket.

The attendant grabbed a stuffed unicorn from the wall and shoved it in Pi's gut. "Here's your unicorn."

Then he went into the back of his booth and took out a few replacement gnomes for the pair that she'd broken. Pi handed the unicorn over to an excited Ashley, who bowed upon receiving it.

"You are a true and excellent friend, Pythia Silverthorne," said Ashley.

"And you are a girl with serious family issues," said Pi.

"Only that I wish you were my sister," said Ashley.

"Not with your creepy grandfather," said Pi. "Let's get out of here. I have a test in bibliomancy on Monday. I have to turn a book into a homunculus. The spell work might as well be quantum physics for all that I understand it."

The train station was five blocks away from the carnival. They decided to walk to sober up before they got back to their respective Halls.

While they walked, Ashley told awful unicorn jokes. She was halfway through her third, a groaner about what unicorns call their fathers, when she glanced at her wrist and turned back up the sidewalk.

"Someone's following us," she said in a hushed voice.

Pi resisted the urge to turn and look. "Did you see who it is?"

"It was a dark shape slipping into the shadows," she said, then her face turned hard. "I bet it's Bree, trying to get me while I'm out of the Griffon Lodge. Great...and I'm all liquored up. I know a spell, but oh god, it's worse than the hangover."

"Do it quickly, before she does anything," said Pi as they kept walking.

Ashley made a few discreet gestures that looked like she was signing her name, and then pinched the middle of her forehead, squeezing and tugging until a brown slug slipped from her knotted muscles. Once it was out, she flicked it towards the sewer like a snotty booger.

"That was unpleasant to watch," said Pi.

"We're still being followed," said Ashley, pointing to her watch. The face of the timepiece showed the surrounding streets covered in mists with a dark shape moving through them.

"Handy," said Pi.

"I don't think she knows we know," said Ashley as she faked a drunken stumble. "Let's turn the tables on her with an ambush."

In a loud voice, Pi said, "I know a shortcut," and dragged Ashley into the alleyway.

Once they were out of sight, they ran through the narrow passage, hopping over discarded beer bottles and broken sacks of garbage with their guts hanging out.

"She's following," said Ashley, glancing at her watch. "Let's hide behind here."

They huddled behind a blue dumpster with a rust-rotted bottom. It smelled like old diapers. A distant siren faded in and out of hearing.

"Where is she?" asked Pi, after a minute of waiting.

Ashley tapped on the face of the watch as if the hands were stuck. "It's not showing her anymore, which is weird. Heck, it's not even moving, and it doesn't need to be wound. This is a gift from my grandfather. A scrying watch. It kept him alive during his time in Coterie. It should show anyone that intends to harm me."

"Does that mean she ran off?" asked Pi.

Ashley tapped on the edge of the watch. It throbbed red. "We're still in danger. But the face is blank."

The hairs on the back of Pi's neck went up. The smells of the alleyway disappeared, replaced by damp forest, autumn leaves crushed and decaying. Pi sensed a presence moving towards them, an aching emptiness.

"It's not Bree, whatever it is," said Pi, pulling a bag of salt from a pocket. She quickly made a circle around them. As she chanted to complete the barrier, a zephyr whipped down the alleyway, blowing the salt away.

"Do you have any more salt?" asked Ashley.

"Nope," said Pi. "I guess we're going to have to do this the hard way."

The shadows deepened around them. Pi felt oppressed, as if the shadows were solid things, pushing against them.

"This feels awful," said Ashley with a grimace. "What is it?"

The crushing presence wanted her to give up, to lie down and not resist. "It's vaguely familiar."

Pi summoned a trio of wisps to burn away the shadows, but they persisted.

"Let's get out of here," said Ashley, tugging on Pi's jacket.

"It wants us to run," said Pi. "It'll only make it stronger. I think."

They put their backs to each other. The shadows crept towards them like ink spilling.

"What the hell is that?" asked Ashley.

At the other end of the alleyway, low shapes moved towards them. Pi was going to suggest they head the other way when she noticed the same shapes coming from the other side.

"We're trapped," said Pi.

The shapes were small like dogs, but upright rather than four-legged. When they hit the circle of light, Pi gasped. The gnomes from the carnival booth marched with bats raised.

Pi launched explosive seeds at her side, while Ashley buckled the pavement, sending it rippling at the gnomes, knocking them away like bowling pins. The pair dished out destruction, but there were hundreds more gnomes than they could deal with. The whole alleyway was filled with them.

A scream echoed behind Pi. Ashley had been knocked down and was being carried away by them, but Pi couldn't help because she was nearly overrun on her side.

A gnome hit her in the leg with a bat. She kicked it way, cracking it in half. The two halves cackled, while more gnomes came on.

Pi fought them off, throwing magic wildly. She lifted the dumpster and threw it at a squad of gnomes, crushing them to dust. She ran after Ashley, who had disappeared down a side alley.

Her wisps were put out, plunging her in darkness. Shapes moved at her. She fought like a cornered bobcat, striking out with magic in all directions, forgetting about everything but getting to Ashley. Nothing was going to stop her.

Then, as suddenly as she was without sight, the alleyway returned, illuminated by the nearby streetlights. It was completely empty, except for the destruction she'd rained down on the dumpster. Trash had been spilled in all directions, scorch marks littered the walls, and not a single gnome was in sight.

At the far end, where they'd entered the alleyway, a young couple had stopped and were staring at her. Even from a distance, she could sense the look of horror on their faces.

"Ash," she muttered, and went running in the direction that she'd been dragged away.

It worried her that there'd never been any gnomes. Something had been playing tricks with her mind.

She turned the corner to find Ashley staring at the brick wall, arms limp at her sides. As soon as Pi saw her, she knew something was wrong.

Pi touched her hand to find it cold and the skin hard like marble. Ashley's gaze was blank, her mouth slightly agape. Her chest was neither rising nor falling, and she had no pulse.

A few spells revealed that Ashley wasn't technically dead; it was as if her soul had been ripped from her body so suddenly that it'd forgotten to collapse. Like a tablecloth yanked from a dinner setting, so the dishes and glasses remained exactly as they were before.

SEVEN

The other Arcanium students filtered into the Athenaeum, chatting amongst themselves, while Aurie and Pi spoke quietly in the back. It'd been a couple of weeks since Aurie had gone into the undercity with Hemistad.

"I'm telling you, Aurie, the feeling I had that night was pretty damn similar to the time we fought the Hunger. It put illusions in my mind, just like the Hunger did to us, making us think we were helping some girl who'd gotten lost in the undercity. What happened to Ashley was probably what would have happened to us if we hadn't fought it off long enough for Hemistad to return," said Pi.

"I'm not disagreeing," said Aurie. "I'm just not sure it's that simple. Sure, Hemistad was messing with the Hunger again, and I know what he said about killing, but it seems like too big of a coincidence that he would attack you and Ashley later that night."

"It's what I felt," said Pi, despondent. "It was something old and hungry in that alleyway. And it made me see things just like the Hunger."

Her sister looked either on the verge of tears or about to punch someone in the face. A couple of mornings, Aurie had found Pi asleep on the couch in their common area with an open book on her chest. She'd been trying to find a spell to restore her friend. They'd moved Ashley's body to an old warehouse in the twelfth ward until they could figure out what to do. Pi didn't trust the authorities, and they both knew that even Golden Willow couldn't help Ashley, since her soul had been ripped from her body.

The class began when Professor Mali rolled in. Her gray hair had been braided tighter than usual, giving her a severe look, but there was also an underlying sadness, much like Patron Semyon. If Aurie had to guess, the pair of them were working against the Cabal, while trying to run a Hall at the same time. They'd been keeping it up for years, and it was wearing on them.

"What is power?" asked Professor Mali, her strong voice cutting through the chatter, reminding the students to settle down. She rolled back and forth a few times until she was sure she had the class' attention.

"Anyone? What is power?" she asked again.

Hands went up around the classroom. She called on Deshawn.

"Having the freedom to do what you want, even when others disapprove," he said.

Her lips wrinkled in consideration. "Possibly."

She pointed at Xi.

"A potential of energy that can be used when activated by a specific and controllable means."

"Quite exact," she said, giving Xi a nod. "We're getting there. Pi?"

"The currency of control."

Professor Mali showed a wry smile. "How Machiavellian. All good answers. Though they do not show the whole picture. How do you use power? What is the mechanism? Yell out your answers."

"Use faez."

"...trigger something."

"Press a button!"

Aurie thought about it and said, "You decide to use it."

Other answers flew around the room. The professor nodded along, but did not make any signs that they'd hit the answer she was looking for.

When the answers stopped coming, she wheeled in front of Violet's desk and stared at the blonde girl with unnerving intensity. At first Violet stared back, a nervous smile on her lips, but as the professor kept at it, Violet grew more uneasy. This went on for minutes. The tension in the room increased, not only for Violet, but for the rest of the room, who started sharing glances, wondering what was going on.

The effect on Violet grew more severe over time. After the ten-minute mark, she looked ready to run out of the room. Even Aurie felt a little sorry for her, if only because she was a fellow human being. Right before Violet looked like she was going to break into tears, Professor Mali rolled away.

"What did I do to Violet? Did I use faez, or trigger something? What happened?" asked the professor.

"You intimidated her," said Deshawn, who looked angry about what had happened.

Professor Mali shrugged. "I simply sat unmoving in my chair. Why is it my fault that she interpreted it that way?"

"Because you have power over her," said Pi.

"But I didn't use that power," said the professor, and she paused to let it sink in. "So how again did I use it?"

The class muttered with partial understanding. Aurie didn't quite know what the professor was getting at.

The professor snapped her fingers, and a fifth-year student in robes rolled a cart into the room. A cube of marbled granite rested on the cart. After the fifth year left, the professor positioned herself across from the cart, staring intently at the cube.

Aurie thought there was going to be a repeat of the staring contest with Violet. But after about thirty seconds, the professor lifted her hand towards the stone and said in a loud voice, "Mali!" It wasn't a normal shout, but a focused word that sounded more like a martial arts yell. It came from the professor's gut and reverberated through Aurie's head.

The stone split, the two halves falling away from each other to crash onto the metal cart. There was a stunned silence afterwards, then a few students started clapping.

"That was the coolest thing ever," said Deshawn, who appeared to have forgiven the professor.

"Thank you, Deshawn," she said, the corner of one lip tugging upward. "But I think 'cool' is an understatement. Does anyone know what kind of magic that was?"

To Aurie's surprise, Pi yelled out, "You used your true name."

Aurie gave her sister a questioning eyebrow, which was returned by the shrug of one shoulder.

"Thank you, Ms. Pythia. Yes, I used my true name. Dispel any thoughts about a true name being some secret moniker that can be used to control you. That's the stuff of fiction. A true name is an acknowledgement of your whole self, an understanding of your power, and the actualization of it. During your first year, you spent time in the Verum Locus, to get in touch with yourself, who you really are. It was a painful but necessary lesson on your way to becoming a great mage. Our next lesson will take another step towards that goal. We won't meet again for a month, but when we do I want you to join me in the Essence Foundry. Bring with you some items from your childhood that mean something to you. And there's some reading to do." She snapped her fingers, and a list of twenty-eight books wrote itself on the chalkboard, receiving a collective groan from the class. "All of them need to be read by the start of class or you will not be allowed in the foundry. The next assignment could have disastrous consequences if you get it wrong. I will not tolerate students who aren't willing to properly prepare. Any questions?"

Deshawn raised his hand, and she called on him.

"Aren't we going to learn how to use our true name? Because that'd be super handy in the kitchen. Need to slice that bread? Deshawn! Dice some onions? Deshawn!" he said, making action poses each time he said his name.

Professor Mali's eyes lit with mirth. "Yes, it would be 'super handy,' but no, you're not going to learn how to use your true name. This year, anyway. What you'll learn in the Essence Foundry will put you on that path, but there are no guarantees. Not everyone is capable of learning their true name. Maybe ten percent of fifth years can use it by graduation, and at best, one in three alumni eventually learn it. Sorry. Class dismissed. And get to reading! I will test you before you are allowed into the foundry!"

Aurie gathered her books, and was prepared to leave when Professor Mali rolled up. She waited until after the other students had left before speaking.

"Yes, Professor?"

"Semyon was hoping to speak to you today, but unfortunately, he's currently out of the country. But he wanted to pass along that the other patrons have agreed to the trial by magic. The first hearing will be in December," said Professor Mali.

"Do we know who my judges will be?" asked Aurie, and as soon as she did, she knew the news was bad.

"I'm sorry, Aurelia. It couldn't have been any worse. The choosing is supposed to be random, but Semyon believes they may have tampered with it," said the professor.

"Who?" asked Aurie.

"The three patrons who will be assigning your task and judging will be from the Coterie of Mages, the Order of Honorable Alchemists, and the

Protectors," said the professor.

"All Cabal. They stacked it against me," said Aurie. "Do I even stand a chance?"

"Technically, their job is only to assign a task and judge whether or not you completed it," said the professor, then added when Aurie made a face, "Remember, you asked for the trial."

"I am well aware. At least this way I have a chance," she said.

The way the professor looked at her didn't inspire confidence.

"When is Patron Semyon coming back? I was hoping to talk strategy with him," said Aurie.

"His schedule is currently unknown to me. I'm sorry, Aurelia," said the professor as she wheeled out of the room. "I'll leave him a message, but I don't know when he's coming back."

EIGHT

The Goblin's Romp was a seedy bar full of shady characters. A row of Harleys sat out front. The guys in black jackets with Bad Moon Rising on the patch looked wolfish as the full moon neared. Pi stayed on the other side of the bar and rattled the ice in her whiskey. Technically, she wasn't old enough, but bars like this didn't care about serving to minors, as long as they could prove they could wield magic. Power mattered.

She hadn't touched the whiskey, as she had no intention of getting drunk. She'd only ordered it to keep the bartender from hassling her. Drinking was out of the question. Not when she was planning on going into the undercity as soon as her escort arrived. Though it would be news to him of his role.

She checked the watch on her arm, the one that Ashley had been wearing when she'd been husked. The scrying part didn't work for her, since the magic was bound to their family, but it still told time. Pi'd kept it as a memento of her friend, a promise that she'd fix whatever had been done to Ashley. She glanced to the door, and someone stepped next to her. Hot breath washed over the back of her head. It smelled like whoever it was had been eating garlic pizza.

"Can I buy you a drink?" asked a husky voice.

Pi bit her lip while she contemplated what to do. She knew what he saw. Her magical leather jacket had taken a rougher look inside the Goblin's Romp. The edges looked weathered and torn. With her hair shaved on the one side and the nose rings, she looked like she belonged.

With a snap of her fingers, she let blue flame engulf her hand. Eyes from around the bar fell upon her.

"I'm not here to drink," she said.

The guy backed away. "Right."

Right about the time she thought about taking a sip of her whiskey, Uncle Liam ducked through the door and headed towards the back. She caught him halfway, grabbing him by the arm.

"Liam."

As he turned his head, a smile formed on his lips, then quenched itself as soon as he realized who it was.

"Pythia? What are you doing here?" he asked. "How did you find me?"

"I'm a mage," she said, matter-of-fact.

He seemed quite perturbed. "I'm sort of busy right now. Can we meet later?"

"You've been in the city for nearly two months and you haven't visited. Look, I don't know anything about our family, and when you showed up, I hoped that I could learn more," she said.

He glanced at the back of the bar. "I'm really busy. Can we meet another time and I'll be happy to tell you all the tales you want."

"Let me go with you into the undercity," she said, hoping it hadn't come out too desperate. She'd been waiting forever for Liam to contact her, but when he hadn't, she'd taken matters into her own hands.

"I'm not even going to ask how you know that's where I go, but that's where the ride ends, lass. You can't go through this way. They only let certain folks pass, and for sure, no Hall mage is gettin' through," he said, starting to move towards the back.

She set in behind him. When he approached a brick archway, a broad-shouldered bouncer stepped out of the shadows. Liam showed him something in his palm, and the bouncer nodded his head to let him pass.

He looked back. "Sorry. Not my rules."

When he went into the darkness beyond the archway, Pi showed the bouncer the rune Radoslav had given her years ago to show that she worked for him. The bouncer frowned as if he'd been looking forward to telling her "no," and then reluctantly let her pass. Being linked to an infamous maetrie had its advantages, even if it'd nearly gotten her killed last year.

Pi caught up to Liam at the spiral staircase. It was about ten feet wide and it made big loops downward. Peering over the edge revealed a darkness that went beyond sight. Liam was already on the second layer.

"Wait up!" she called.

"You're a tricky one, aren't you? I see the Devlin blood runs strong in ya. Fine. You can come, but you can't get in my way, nor can you speak a word of this to anyone. If you cause problems, you have to promise to leave; otherwise strike it from your mind," he said.

"I promise," she said, drawing an "X" on her chest.

She tried to contain her excitement. He seemed to sense it and sighed.

"Ask away, Pythia. I can see you're going to explode otherwise," he said.

"Call me Pi. Only teachers call me Pythia," she said.

"You're a cocky one. Couldn't I teach you anything?" he asked, laughing.

"Back in the police station," she said, "you used magic on that Protector. I know you didn't learn magic in the Halls. Is that why you went to

Siberia? So you could find a dragon as your patron?"

He held his hand out in a shushing motion. "Not so loud, my little clever niece. Not that I'm worried about someone down here turning me in, but I don't like givin' away my secrets."

Warmth exploded in her chest at the thought of a dragon as a patron. "What's it like? Are they as big as the reports?" she asked.

"Bigger. She's as big as a mountain and as old as history. Claimed she knew Alexander the Great back in the day," he said with a wink.

That she was jealous of Liam didn't surprise her. The Hundred Halls had always felt too small for her. Pi wondered if her sister hadn't been around if she might have pledged herself to something as powerful as a dragon. Of course, doing so was majorly illegal, but it would have been tempting.

"Is that why you disappeared for so long? Did you have to gain the dragon's trust?" she asked.

"So many questions," he said. "We don't have time for the full sto-ry—maybe someday later I can regale you with the details—but I can say that having a dragon for a patron isn't always what you think it's going to be. They're a vain and capricious race with little regard for the wants of humans. As long as I served a purpose, she was willing to put up with me. And that's all I'm willing to say about that right now."

"Do you know where our family comes from? I know you knew my grandfather and grandmother before they died. I guess your mom and dad...sorry, this isn't coming out quite right. But Dad never said much about it, just that they died when he was young and you were mostly gone by then," she said.

Liam slowed and put a hand on her shoulder. His green eyes were tinged with sadness. "I do know a thing or two about them, and I'll tell you the story, but not right now. This isn't the place for things like that."

The darkness in his gaze worried her.

"Uncle Liam. You can't just say that and expect me not to wonder," she said. "I have certain urges. Desires. Is it because of them? Do I have some otherworldly heritage that's driving me in this way? I need to know. Please."

"Not now, lass. Not now," he said. "We're almost to the bottom and I need you to understand some things before we get there. You can be a mouse for me, right? Good. I'm picking something up, let's call it a package. Once I have it, we can talk, but until then, I need you to keep your mouth shut. It's going to be wobbly enough with you there."

Any questions she had were silenced as she noticed the warm glow from beneath them. The spiral staircase had burrowed through the rock for hundreds of steps. It'd felt like she was walking around the inside of a grain silo. But then it opened up into a massive lighted cavern filled with a small town.

"It's called Big Dave's Town," he said, his long strides picking up steam as they neared the bottom. She had to skip steps to keep up.

Pi knew there were places to live in the undercity, but she hadn't had any idea how big they were. There were enough houses that at least a thousand people were living in this cave alone. For the most part, the style was something out of a post-apocalyptic movie, but some of the houses were almost cover of *Home & Garden* magazine quaint.

The shady cast of characters she'd encountered in the Goblin's Romp continued in Big Dave's Town. Men and women openly carried weapons, magical and mundane. A guy in a trench coat had a semiautomatic hanging over his shoulder. A pale woman with a crimson birthmark that halfway covered her right eye carried a runed katana on her back.

Non-humans were present in Big Dave's Town as well. A trio of folks with thick tails like Nezumi's pushed a cart of junk across the cobblestone road.

The scent of low-level faez stayed in the background like a metallic taste that wouldn't go away. She thought something touched her mind, but it slipped away before she could tell what it was. Telepathy magic was practiced by a few non-human races, but she didn't see any present.

Uncle Liam led her to a tunnel on the far side that was lit with lanterns at regular intervals. It didn't escape her notice that on the way through the town, everyone had given them a wide berth despite the cheerful song on her uncle's lips. A few people gave her questioning stares, but most preferred not to let their gaze linger long. What that meant about her uncle Liam, she wasn't quite sure.

They traveled for another ten minutes, taking a few turns at crossroads. The way was marked with signs, a far cry different from the areas of the undercity she'd been to with Hemistad. Uncle Liam kept checking over his shoulder to make sure no one was following, though the passage was populated enough that it seemed a ridiculous gesture.

After a small detour off the main tunnel, he stopped at a side passage that went into an unlit cavern. A crisp chill haunted the opening, as if it were the open door of an icebox.

"You might want to wait here until I'm finished," he said. "This part of the journey is a little unpleasant, in more ways than one."

"Do I look like I'm a delicate flower?"

He put his hands on his hips and looked at her, clearly deciding whether or not to let her come along.

"You had me join you this whole way. What's a little further? I'm family after all," she said.

His face changed as if an idea had come into his head.

"Fine," he said with a mixture of amusement and concern. "But if you know any enchantments against cold, you might want to use them now. And when we get to Lilith's house, keep your mouth shut, and don't say a word about anything you see there, especially about her looks. They call her Lilith the Ghoul, if that gives you any indication."

Something about the way he said it made her think she might regret her decision to come along.

"Lilith is the trader?"

He nodded.

Before they went in, Pi cast a few spells. Protecting oneself against the cold was simple magic, though the severity of the cold seemed like something beyond a wintery breeze. Pi applied a second layer just in case.

Even with the spells, Pi gasped before she'd even taken a third step inside. It felt like she was being dipped in liquid nitrogen.

A hundred feet into the cavern, they came upon a cinderblock building with icicles hanging off the roof. Liam banged on the door, warming his hands between hits.

After a minute, the door opened, revealing a woman who looked like she'd once been beautiful before half her jaw had fallen off.

"Who is she?" asked Lilith through a voice box on her throat. It came out female, but computerized.

"This is my niece, Pythia," said Liam as he tried to go in, but Lilith didn't open the door any further.

"You did not say anything about her," said Lilith, pointing a ravaged finger at Pi.

"Darling Lilith, she's fine. She's a Hall mage if that's any consolation to you," he said.

"You are just saying that to be mean," said Lilith.

Without a jaw and normal voice inflections, it was hard to tell if she was truly mad or being sarcastic.

Liam cocked a grin in Pi's direction. "Lilith was once in the Hundred Halls until her accident."

"Which Hall?" asked Pi.

"Coterie," said Lilith, and this time the anger came through the voice box as static. Pi nixed her earlier assessment, deciding against revealing that she'd once been in Coterie. Lilith clearly had some lingering resentment.

The inside of the house was like any other, except every surface had a patina of frost on it. Even without casting the usual detection spells, Pi surmised the whole place was covered in spells. Whatever had happened to Lilith in Coterie had been bad, and she'd come to the undercity to survive. As tolerant as normal folk were about magic, it only counted when the practitioners looked like them.

Lilith lead them to a barn behind her house. It looked like one of those buildings you ordered by mail.

"It's in there?" asked Liam.

"I did not bring you here for the view," said Lilith.

Liam took a step towards the building.

"Forgetting something?" asked Lilith, holding out her hand.

Liam reached into his jacket and pulled out a small book. Pi only got a brief glimpse but it had red and black lettering with bits of bone along the spine. It wasn't much of a guess to assume it was a spell book. Pi never understood why some people bound the books with crazy-ass bling that only made you look like a psychopath when you were carrying them. On the other hand, it could have been bound by someone with a scrapbooking fetish.

"I will leave you to it," said Lilith, throwing him a key. "You know how this works, right?"

"Don't insult me," said Liam.

His sudden rudeness surprised Pi. Liam licked his lips and cracked his knuckles. Inside the barn was a crate the size of a small car. Before he stepped inside the barn, he glanced at Pi, that earlier darkness coming to the forefront as if he were about to reach some long sought after goal.

The key rattled the lock. Pi tensed.

"Stay back. All the way back to the house," he said, waving her away.

"The first impression is the most important. She has to bond to me."

Pi backed up across the yard. In the moment before Liam unhooked the lock from the front of the crate, Pi felt a presence touch her mind. It was curious, and unmistakably wild.

Before he could completely remove the lock, the crate burst open, knocking Liam onto his back. A creature covered in reddish fur along its back with a white star of fur on the front came bounding out and hit Pi in the chest with two paws. Pi was convinced that she was about to be eaten and summoned faez to defend herself when the creature licked her across the face.

Intelligent, green-gold eyes stared at her as if Pi was supposed to understand why she'd been knocked down.

"Um, hi," said Pi tentatively.

Pi climbed out from under the creature. At first she thought it was a wolf, but it was much too large to be a wolf and had more sharpened features. The creature pushed her hand with her muzzle in hopes of being petted, which Pi obliged.

"What is she?" asked Pi, knowing without a doubt that the creature was female.

Uncle Liam was furious. He cursed for a good minute in what she could only assume was Gaelic by its many throaty consonants. With his hands jammed in his ruddy hair, he looked back and forth between the crate and her as if he couldn't believe what had happened.

When a tickle of mischievousness touched her mind, Pi understood that the creature had bonded to her rather than Liam.

"Oh no," said Pi. "I'm so sorry."

"I told you to move back to the house!"

She pointed behind her. The door was only a few feet away. "I did."

Liam paced, glancing at her every time he turned back around.

"I'm sorry, Uncle Liam. I didn't mean to do it," she said. "I know you're pissed, but can you tell me what happened? What she is? Maybe I can make it up to you somehow?"

He took a step towards her, and Pi didn't see a carefree uncle, but a man who was not above killing. Pi took a step back against the house, and the creature beside her started growling.

He seemed to recognize what was happening and held his palm out. "My deepest apologies, Pi. I'm not a nice person when I get angry. Aye, I know you didn't mean to do this. It's my fault, after all, for letting you even come near." He shook his head, and his next words were spoken more to himself than her. "I should have known better. I did know better. I was going to have her wait in the bloody tunnels. I don't bloody know why I didn't have you stay outside."

He sighed and looked up, realizing that he'd been thinking out loud. "She's a kitsune."

Pi was scratching around its neck and found a runed collar. The markings were heavy with magic.

"Don't take that off," he said. "If you do, she'll rip your throat out. While it's on, she thinks you're family."

"What's her name?" she asked.

He nodded towards the kitsune. "Ask her."

Before she could say the words, a name appeared in her mind, and Pi spoke it aloud. "Inari."

"What do we do now?" asked Pi, staring at the kitsune. It appeared that life had just gotten more complicated in ways she didn't understand.

Uncle Liam had one hand on his head and tugged on his hair. It was going in all directions and gave him almost a fae look. The sleeve of tattoos on his left arm glowed like embers.

She looked at Inari, who seemed totally disinterested in the conversation and was pawing at the frozen ground.

"I have some things I have to check on," he said, looking distracted.

"I don't understand, Uncle Liam," said Pi. "Why did we come down here to pick up this kitsune?"

He opened his mouth twice before finally speaking. "It's complicated. But you're going to have to take care of her for a while until I can adjust plans."

"Complicated? That's an understatement. Where am I going to put her? What does she eat? I don't know anything about kitsunes, and we're not allowed pets in Arcanium, especially magical ones."

Uncle Liam shrugged and headed towards the exit. "You'll figure it out, lass. You'll figure it out."

NINE

A Cauldron of Coffee was a shop across from Freeport Games. Aurie had frequented it to grab a tray of drinks for an all-night gaming session, but had never bothered to actually sit at a table. She was waiting for her sister, who had told her to meet her here, rather than the shop, which seemed rather strange.

But then again, things had been rather odd lately in the suite the last few weeks. There was a lot of banging around in Pi's room, and Aurie swore she heard growling. It had gotten noisy enough that the other third years that liked to study with Aurie had asked to meet elsewhere. She'd been meaning to see what was going on, but whenever she got around to it, the idea slipped her mind.

When Pi arrived, she threw herself into the chair across the table and grabbed the steaming cup of coffee that Aurie had bought for her. She flipped her hood back over her leather jacket. Car lights flashed by the window.

"Black with a shot of honey?" asked Pi, eyebrow raised. "I swear if you give me that pumpkin spice crap again I'm going to enchant your headbands to strangle you."

"I thought you might like to try something new," said Aurie. "Or aren't you as adventurous as you like to say you are?"

"Drinking spiced barf is hardly what I'd call adventurous," said Pi.

"You're safe anyway, because they only have it in October," said Aurie. "So what's going on, sis? Why are we hanging out here instead of where our friends are?"

Pi pulled a stack of papers from the inside of her leather jacket—way more papers than should reasonably fit—and threw them on the table.

"Um, *Herald of the Halls*? What gives?" asked Aurie.

"Yeah, I get it. I hate the Cardwells too, but we need to be reading this more regularly. A lot going on in the City of Sorcery that we need to be aware of. Read on, I'll drink my coffee."

While Pi curled up on her seat and sipped at her steaming mug, Aurie paged through the dozens of newspapers. It wasn't hard to see the central theme, though Aurie didn't understand what Pi was trying to imply.

"I get it," said Aurie. "Monsters are coming up from the undercity and attacking people. I'm well aware of the not-so-subtle references to the reason why they're occurring. I'm preparing for my trial, after all."

Pi shifted forward and grabbed one of the papers, opened it to the center page, and pointed at an article with her dark blue fingernail. "Read that one."

Aurie scanned it, mumbling the words as she read. "...the body, bereft of soul, could have been a mannequin for all intents and purposes...is this what it sounds like?"

"I found six other instances that describe what happened to Ashley," said Pi.

"So whatever's doing that is still out there," said Aurie.

"The weird part is they're all Hall students. Not a single one from the same Hall." As she listed them off, she counted with her fingers. "Coterie of Mages, Senders, Oculus, The Daring Maids, Eros, Metallum Nocturne, and Sanctums."

"That can't be a coincidence," said Aurie.

"In a few cases, the paper confirms that the souls have been ripped from the body, but no one has made any connections between the cases, not even the police," said Pi.

"How do you know—" Aurie cut herself off when she saw her sister's expression. "Never mind."

"These are just the bodies that have been found and reported in the paper. There could be more," said Pi.

"It's the Cabal," said Aurie.

Pi shook her head. "I thought that too, but why kill one of their own? No, that's too easy. We can't assume everything bad in the city is coming from them. Not when there's a more logical answer."

Her sister's gaze drifted across the street.

"I don't know, Pi..."

Pi leaned in and spoke in a forced whisper, desperation coming through her tone. "Why not? We've both seen the Hunger, something messed with my mind the night Ashley was taken, and even Semyon warned us he was extremely powerful. We don't know what he is, but we know he's dangerous."

"It seems like a coincidence," said Aurie. "Why would he attack Ashley while she was with you, knowing full well that you've seen the Hunger?"

"I've thought of that, but here's the thing. I've been watching him the last couple of weeks. He's been going out each night, and I've tried to follow him with varying success. Three nights ago I tracked him to Metallum Nocturne. The next day they found the husked body in the Hall," said Pi, jamming her finger at the article in the paper. "It's Hemistad. Period."

A feeling of sinking made Aurie a little dizzy. Could they be working for a soul-eating monster? She'd always assumed he was an old werewolf, or something around that level of power, but sucking souls out of bodies so quickly that the body hardened right after was something quite terrifying.

"You might be right," said Aurie.

"Might be right?" asked Pi, a little too loudly, drawing a few stares. She lowered her voice. "How can you not see it?"

"I'm not disagreeing," said Aurie. "I can't imagine that..."

"That we've been working for a monster," said Pi. "Look, I don't want to believe it either, but I want to find out what happened to Ashley, to see if there's any chance I can restore her. If I can catch him in the act, I might be able to learn what he did."

"I'll help. Tell me what you want me to do," said Aurie.

She pointed across the street. "It's getting near closing time. We wait here until he leaves and follow him."

"What if he doesn't go out?" asked Aurie.

"He's been going out almost every night," said Pi, frowning, "but most nights I lose him."

While they waited, Aurie drank coffee and read the *Herald of the Halls*. Her sister was right, she should have been reading the paper more regularly. There was a lot going on in the city, and Aurie sensed the Cabal's fingerprints all over it.

Two hours and four cups of coffee later, Pi tapped on the table and nodded towards Freeport Games. Hemistad had left the shop, heading east. Pi tucked the many papers into her jacket, and the pair walked out of A Cauldron of Coffee with their hoods up.

Before they'd left, Pi had given Aurie the seashell trinket they'd won in the Grand Contest last year. It allowed two-way sub vocal communication across short distances, but not any further than a block. It was as close to telepathy as one could get with magic.

When Hemistad got on the Blue Line, Aurie and her sister joined the train a few cars back. A storm hovered over the ocean to the east, brightening the sky with brief flashes, but it didn't appear that it would move over the city.

After a half-hour, Hemistad exited the train in the fifth district. They were worried that he was headed to Arcanium, which wasn't far from the station, but he headed towards the Stone Singer Hall instead.

At no time did Hemistad check for followers, which gave Aurie ample opportunity to study his hunched form. He marched down the sidewalk without deviation. Anyone coming the other direction had to step out of his way. One poor guy in a suit lost in his smartphone got a shoulder from Hemistad that threw him into the wall. The cry of accusation died on the man's lips as if he sensed Hemistad was not a man to be messed with.

Aurie worried what his demeanor indicated to her. He was a man on an unpleasant mission.

The only time he hesitated was when he neared Stone Singer Hall. The massive building in the shape of a flower took up an entire city block. Colored lights played against the petals. Hemistad's head lifted, and he scanned back and forth as if he were a radar dish. He sniffed once, twice, then as if he'd locked on target, moved away in a hurry.

Before, he'd been sturdy and relentless in his forward progress. Now, he moved so much like a predator that Aurie expected him to drop down on all fours. They had to break into a run to keep up.

The hairy old man cut down a side street that led to the Hall, gaining speed as he went. Aurie thought he was going to ram the door, but he hit the wall and went straight up, climbing it hand over hand as if it were a minor slope. He went up and over, slipping between the valley of two petals.

"Holy crap, did you see that?" asked Pi, mouth agape. "I haven't seen that before."

"How could I miss it?" said Aurie.

"What the hell is he?" asked Pi, shaking her head.

They stood at a pair of stone double doors with runes around the edges. Aurie didn't know much about this Hall, except that these same doors existed on every side.

"This is why I keep losing him," said Pi. "He keeps going in the Halls while I'm stuck outside."

"Then we have to go in," said Aurie.

"Are you crazy?" she asked. "You know how dangerous our Hall wards are, and we're supposed to be the bookish nerds of the university. If I knew he was coming here and had time to prepare, it might be different."

"But we don't," said Aurie. "Don't you want to stop him?"

"I was hoping we could wait outside and get him when he came out," said Pi. "And I guess you believe me now?"

"Not completely, but it's hard not to see the connection," said Aurie. "The way I see it, if we don't get in, someone's dying tonight."

"How do we get in?" asked Pi, looking up.

"We need Hall pins," said Aurie. "Most Hall wards are built around them."

At that moment, the doors opened and two male students marched out. Pi raised a mischievous eyebrow towards them.

"Gentlemen!" said her sister, startling the two students. "Have you been embraced yet?"

They halted, sharing confused glances mixed with cautious smiles.

"No?" said the first, with a tone of hopefulness.

Pi clapped her hands together, shaking them in a prayerful way as she stepped close. "Then let me tell you about our Great Tentacled Master. Our Lord Cthulhu. He wishes to have you in his bosom!"

Talk of Cthulhu turned their hopefulness into dread. They backed away from Pi. "Um, sorry, no thank you."

As they half-walked, half-ran up the street, Pi called after them, "But he gives great hugs! No slime, I swear! Or maybe only a little slime!"

Pi turned back to Aurie, flashing her palm open, revealing a Hall pin in the shape of a musical note.

"Have you in his bosom? Gives great hugs?" asked Aurie.

"I was improvising, give me a break," said Pi.

"You only got one," said Aurie.

Pi shrugged. "I went creepy too early, didn't get a chance at the second pin. But I got a strand of hair from each of them."

"That's okay. We'll make it work," said Aurie, examining the pin.

Using a bit of transference magic combined with mendancy, Aurie was able to spread the enchantments from the pin between them.

After preparing the pin, the sisters set to work on defeating the outer wards. There were two layers of symbols around the outside of the door. By drawing over them with a new set of symbols, they rerouted the electricity the wards would release back into the spell, rendering them inert.

"It's not going to last long, maybe twenty minutes if we're lucky," said Aurie.

When they approached the door, it opened. They moved inside. Aurie expected an alarm to sound. The outer door closed behind them.

"Maybe they don't have major protections," suggested Pi. "I mean, who wants to steal from a bunch of math-obsessed civil engineers who have a serious fetish for glee clubs?"

Somehow Aurie didn't think that was true, and she was proved right about five steps later. The entryway looked like something out of the Renaissance, with marble statues lining a sweeping staircase leading upward. Passages went beneath the staircase, either left or right.

The statue of a bearded king with a trident turned his head and said, "Password."

Rather than answer, Pi grabbed Aurie's sleeve and ran into the left passage. Aurie looked back to see the statue moving after them.

When Pi reached for her explosive seeds, Aurie stayed her arm. "Nothing loud. So far it hasn't alerted anyone else."

"That we know of," said Pi.

The statue was about thirty feet behind them. It appeared to be increasing speed. Aurie didn't like the look of the trident.

The halls were maze-like. They took turns at random. When they realized they weren't going to be able to lose the statue, Pi pulled a round, flat piece of metal from an inside pocket. She rubbed the surface and whispered, "Expand," until it filled the hallway. She anchored it on the walls with a few spells.

A stone fist dented the barrier, startling them, but did not break through.

"Maybe we can lose it," said Pi.

The twisting hallways left them frustrated. The statue hadn't caught up to them, but they were now very lost, and hadn't seen any signs of the students that lived in the Hall.

"I think this maze is part of the defenses," said Aurie, after a few minutes of wandering. "We need a way to find Hemistad soon, or get the hell out of here. If we can."

"I almost forgot," said Pi, pulling a piece of amber from her pocket. "I linked this to him when I was in the shop a few weeks ago."

Pi blew on it, waking the amber. A glow formed on the right edge. The glow led them out of the maze and into the apartments. Right away, they saw a group of three students heading across a study area. It was late in the night, and the living quarters had a subdued feeling, as if most were already asleep. Faint singing could be heard from a different direction.

They followed as the glow deepened into the living areas. While Arcanium had all the trappings of an expensive library, the Stone Singer Hall would make a museum look shabby. A few times, they had to backtrack to avoid Stone Singers.

When the glow on the amber went out, Pi tapped on the stone. Chills went down Aurie's spine. They stood at a four-way.

"He's hunting," said Aurie.

"I feel it too," said Pi.

A shadow moved across a hallway down from them. The hairs on her neck were at attention. When Pi grabbed her arm, a little noise came out.

"I saw it," said Pi, pointing the other direction. "Or something any-way."

"It went this way," said Aurie, nodding the way she'd seen the shadow, which was the opposite direction Pi had pointed.

"Damn it's fast," said Pi.

"Check down that hall. I'll go this way," said Aurie. "I'll keep in contact with the necklace."

As Aurie crept down the hall, she felt a pressure on her skin as if the air was condensing around her, which made the nearby singing a counterpoint. Whoever was practicing had a lovely voice. Soprano, if she had to guess.

Looking back, she didn't see Pi. "Where are you?"

A voice came back through the seashells. "It went this way. Tracking it."

Aurie hurried back the other way. Almost as soon as she did, she sensed something behind her. She spun around, nearly tripping over herself in the process. Nothing was there.

"Pi?"

The singing was rising to a crescendo. Aurie felt probing against her mind. When no answer came from her sister, she took off at a run.

A thumping reverberated through the floor as if a battle was taking place.

"What's going on? Pi? Answer me," said Aurie.

Something was wrong. Something was very, very wrong. Then it hit

Aurie. The singing had stopped.

She moved back in the other direction, where she thought the singing had been coming from. A form was crumpled on the floor. It was Pi.

Fearing the worst, she knelt down, expecting to find her sister's soul removed. To Aurie's relief, Pi groaned and climbed to her feet.

The sounds of students rousing reached them. They had to get out.

"We're too late," said Pi, pointing into the room.

Aurie had been so focused on her sister, she hadn't noticed the door was open. A reed-thin girl with thick glasses stood before a podium with a music book open. Her hand was frozen in a raised position, her eyes blank.

Aurie walked in and touched her skin. Hard as a rock. She was nothing but a husk.

"I'm sorry," she said.

"We have to go," said Pi.

They took off back the way they came. A few times they almost ran into students, but managed to avoid them. Pi led them to the maze.

"The enchantments are about to wear off," said Aurie. "We have to get through here quickly or we're going to be trapped."

Pi pulled out the amber stone. "We have to hope he's outside again."

They ran through the maze, following the glow on the stone. At times, the glow flipped sides, which they realized was a trick of the maze. When they found the entryway, Aurie breathed a sigh of relief.

"Let's get out—"

The words died in her throat as the bearded statue stepped in front of the door and raised its trident to throw. Aurie was going to be too slow. Before she could summon her magic, Pi threw an explosive seed, blowing the statue in half. Dust rained down upon them as they ran through the shards of statue, escaping into the cool November night.

TEN

The bed was a cozy refuge against the cold November day. Wind blew leaves against the window, muting the car honking and sirens that permeated the city.

Pi had her naked back against Inari, the fox-like creature that she'd bonded with in the undercity. The first few weeks, Pi had made Inari sleep on the floor, but each morning, she awoke with the kitsune in her bed. She gave up when she realized that Inari wasn't going to listen and that sleeping against her soft fur was magical.

Wind buffeted the window, startling Pi enough that she opened her eyes and realized she was going to be late for her class on lexology.

"Oh crap," she said, stumbling out of bed, knocking a book on the floor. "I swear I set the alarm."

Pi picked the book up. *Sumerian Secrets of the Ancient Soul*. It was one of the many books she'd gotten from the Arcanium library in her research to figure out how her fellow Hall students were being turned to soulless husks. She put it back onto the "To Be Read" pile near the bed, which was as tall as she was.

She gave the alarm a quick examination. It appeared to be in working order, and she hadn't set it on PM instead of AM.

A whine came from the covers on the bed. Inari's pointy snout was sticking out of the pile.

"Yeah, I know. You're hungry," said Pi as she was hurrying around the room trying to find her books for class. "So am I. But there's no time for food. I'll get us breakfast when I get back. I have a little time before my next class."

Pi almost walked out before she remembered she needed the enchanted vellum she'd prepared the night before. It was in her warded armoire, where she kept her reagents and other materials under protection. After she unlocked and disabled the wards, she removed the vellum from the front drawer.

A cold nose poked her in the elbow, followed by a pathetic whine. She looked into Inari's golden eyes. "I'm sorry, Inari. I told you. There's no time. Maybe next time you'll make sure I wake up when I'm supposed to."

The look the kitsune gave her almost made her feel bad about scolding her.

Aurie was studying in the common area between their rooms. She looked up from her tome. "Oversleep?"

"Yeah." Pi sniffed her armpits. "I could use a shower."

"Did I hear barking in your room last night?" asked Aurie as Pi left the suite.

She and Inari had been playing around, jumping from the bed to the floor and back like giggling schoolchildren. She recalled a little barking, but hadn't been worried because she'd enchanted the room to be soundproof.

"Wasn't me," said Pi, closing the door behind her.

It was painfully awkward that she hadn't told her sister about the kitsune yet. She would soon. It was only right, plus it would be nice to have help taking care of the massive creature. Sneaking Inari up to the domed garden on the roof for bathroom breaks was becoming a major hassle.

Professor Longakers gave her a raised eyebrow when Pi skidded into class twenty seconds late. The rest of class, a mix of third and fourth years—thankfully no Violet Cardwell—snickered with anticipation.

"Ms. Pythia. You know my rule," said Professor Longakers.

"What's the penalty?" she asked, cringing. She wasn't in the mood.

Professor Longakers was the squarest, tweed-jacketest professor in Arcanium—practically the living embodiment of the Hall. His classes focused on the use of words within spells, and how understanding the proper linguistics of language—difficulty compounded by the hundreds of languages used—could allow a mage to modify a spell to fit the needs of the moment. But he was also an aficionado of hip-hop and slam poetry, and he put that love on display in his classes.

He pulled out his smartphone and started tapping on the screen.

"You have to do Reginald's Handy Mug Repair spell, but the item is a pair of glasses." He pulled his wire-rimmed glasses off his face and bent them into pieces, snapping them at least three times before tossing them onto the carpet.

Seconds later, an old school '80's rap beat came over the speakers in the room.

The whole point of the exercise was that most of the words actually didn't matter in a spell. Many times, the effect was hung on a few key phrases that could be manipulated if you understood how the magic worked, but changing the wrong word could be deadly. Thankfully, this wasn't Coterie, and the professor had given her a relatively mundane spell. But she still didn't want to be embarrassed in front of her classmates.

Pi bobbed her head to get into the beat, then let the words of the spell flow, adding lines for fun and adjusting the spell words as she went:

"The professor's spectacles, broken and wrecked

need to be straightened, whole and without affect

returned to a good line, giving eyesight to the blind

so I divine, at two-four time

the correct rhyme, sweet sublime

to ill this magic, or let my grade be tragic."

The final finger gestures solidified the spell as it flowed into the glasses, and like a slow-motion movie in reverse they reverted to their original form.

Professor Longakers retrieved them and placed them on his face. After a brief inspection, he clapped his hands together.

"Well done, Miss Pythia," he said. "Better than new."

Xi Chu gave her a fist bump as she took her seat.

The rest of the class went as normal. They were working through some Slavic spells that the professor claimed had come from Baba Yaga, though Tristen Loren had to go to the infirmary when he used the word "bra" instead of "flaw" and got himself tangled in a webbing of connected bras that kept reattaching themselves as they tried to cut them away.

Pi paid attention enough to take notes, but her mind kept going back to Ashley and the experience in the Stone Singer Hall. She'd been trying to convince her sister they needed to confront Hemistad, but Aurie didn't think they had enough proof. The only argument that had swayed Pi was that letting him know that they knew might spook him, and if he left the country, they'd never figure out how to fix Ashley or the others.

When class was over, Pi went by the Arcanium student store and picked up a package of red licorice for Inari as an offering for yelling at her earlier.

Inari tackled her at the door, digging her snout into the package as soon as Pi pulled them out of the grocery bag. While Inari ate, Pi went to her reagents armoire. In her haste to leave earlier, she'd left it unlocked.

"I need to make a run to the apothecary, it seems," said Pi with a sigh.

She made a list which included moonglove, cloverdust, obsidian chips, imp fingernails, and electric lichen. As she closed the cabinet, Inari was back at her elbow whining.

"Bathroom, huh? Let's go. Aurie's at class," she said.

Inari followed her into the empty hallway. The stairs to the domed garden went straight to the roof. The kitsune squatted behind the massive blood orchid, which was currently closed. When it was open, it liked to bite people.

Once Inari was back in the room, and after promises of taking her to the dog park later (for whatever reason, everyone assumed Inari was a giant husky with red fur), Pi headed for the kitchens, but realized on the way she was going to be late for her alchemy of ink class. Pi's stomach grumbled in protest.

Halfway to The Inkwell, the ink lab in the north wing, Pi ran into Deshawn.

"Hey Pi, do you have any obsidian chips? I'm all out for some reason, and so is the apothecary," he said.

"Me too," she replied, checking Ashley's watch on her wrist. "Sorry. Late for class."

She made it on time and took her seat next to Aurie at the table nearest the front. Professor Gill came in moments later. She was a blonde-haired and blue-eyed elegant woman, impeccably dressed in a pencil skirt and white blouse.

The task for the class was to mix a batch of acidic ink for demon summonings. It required a number of dangerous materials, including arsenic and concentrated brown recluse venom. Accidental poisonings happened at least every other week in Professor Gill's class.

Pi leaned over to her sister.

"Got any food? I'm starving," said Pi.

"Why didn't you eat after lexology?" asked Aurie.

"Got busy."

Aurie arched her eyebrow in that mom-way that annoyed Pi. "Do you or do you not have food?"

"I don't, but I have the carryall," said Aurie, handing it over.

The miniature portal in the bag went back to a table in the suite. They kept various emergency supplies within reach, including food bars. Pi pulled one out and immediately tore into it.

"You shouldn't eat that now," said Aurie. "You might accidentally poison yourself."

"I know what I'm doing," said Pi between bites.

She ate three food bars between mixing and didn't spill one drop of ink—a success by any measure.

After class, she returned to her room with the intent to study, but ended up roughhousing with Inari. They played a game where Pi had to touch Inari's collar before she could get her teeth on Pi's arm. Pi wasn't sure where the idea had come from, but it was a game they played regularly.

Hanging out with Inari, despite the inconveniences, was becoming one of her favorite things to do. Her parents had never let her have a pet when she was a kid, and since then she'd been too poor to afford one. Not that Pi thought of Inari as a pet, but it was the closest analogy. At times, when Inari was asleep on the bed, Pi had terrible thoughts about why her uncle Liam had paid Lilith the Ghoul for the kitsune. Something seemed wrong, but she couldn't quite place her finger on it, and besides, Pi was giving the kitsune a wonderful place to live. Better than that old cramped crate, anyway.

Before she left for class, Pi promised Inari another bag of red licorice. The kitsune watched her leave with surprising focus.

Everyone had their own table in Runic Calligraphy, so she couldn't chat with Deshawn while Professor Chopra droned on about the importance of flourishes on the anchor runes when warding against extraplanar creatures.

Pi spent the time thinking about soul magic. It was a little-understood area of magic due to the difficulty of acquiring working material. Mostly, it was used as a unique signature, like a fingerprint, when designing certain spells or items. One could key a door to only allow certain souls through. But that's not what Hemistad, or whoever was stealing the souls, seemed to be after.

Aurie didn't seem to be convinced that it was Hemistad. Pi wasn't completely on board either, but she didn't have any other ideas. Which meant they needed to either confirm that he was the one or eliminate him from the investigation.

Violet Cardwell was drawing a rune on the blackboard, the chalk screeching annoyingly until Pi's fingernails hurt. She was about to throw something at the board to make her stop, when something about the rune sparked a memory and set her mind tumbling with thoughts.

"What rune is that?" asked Pi, the words coming out before she remembered she was in class.

Violet spun around and gave her a dirty look.

"Welcome back, Miss Pythia. I see we're having a little daydream," said Professor Chopra to the laughter of the class. "Just a minute ago, I asked everyone to copy this rune on their paper."

"But what rune is it?" asked Pi, trying to hide her impatience.

Professor Chopra made an one-shoulder shrug. "I have no idea. It was something I found in a book once."

"Do you remember what book?" She realized the rest of the class was looking at her oddly, so she added, "It's for an extra credit project that Professor Mali asked me to do."

She picked Mali, since she knew no one would actually ask the professor since everyone was terrified of her, even the other professors.

Professor Chopra frowned. "I think it was something about the faerie horticulture. I believe it was the *Leaves of Fae.*"

"Thank you!" said Pi, moving towards the exit until the professor said, "Miss Pythia, where do you think you're going?"

"I have to do something," she said, cringing at the vagueness.

"If you don't want to fail my class, you will return to your seat," said Professor Chopra.

"But I'm practically getting a hundred percent," said Pi, inching towards the door. She searched for something to say that would get her freed from class. Her mind was teetering on understanding something, and she didn't want to miss it. "I could take the final today and ace it."

By the look on the professor's face, and the reaction of the class, she knew she'd gone too far.

"Let's see about that," said the professor, marching to the middle of the room and unrolling a sheet of paper onto the floor that was about three feet wide and five feet long. He slid a piece of sheet metal under the paper. Then he grabbed the long brush, which was nearly as tall as she was, and a bucket of ink.

"Caustic rune, using the whole sheet of paper, without lifting the brush, and has to be strong enough to eat through the steel," said the professor, holding out the brush. "If you complete it, you can leave class. If you fail, then you fail the semester."

Not only was a failing grade bad for her career, but she'd lose her spot in the suite, which meant she wouldn't be able to keep Inari in the Hall.

Pi considered the difficulty of the task. She'd never used the long brush before, and creating the rune required a delicate touch and a judicious use of faez. She was going to return to her seat and wait for the end of class until she heard Violet snicker.

Pi grabbed the long brush out of the professor's hands. The handle was strong and well balanced. She took a deep breath, dipped the bristles into the ink, carefully wiped off the excess on the lip of the pot—one drop would ruin the rune—and began. The rune required seven strokes and two twist-flourishes. Pi moved through them like a ballet dancer at Carnegie Hall. By the time she was finished, she knew it was perfect.

As she set the long brush back in the ink pot, the rune activated and sizzling filled the air as if a rasher of bacon were on the stove. The rune burned through the steel plate in half a second and kept going. Before Professor Chopra could put it out with a fire extinguisher, it'd eaten through the floor. The marble flooring, supporting beams, and ceiling material for the next floor down disappeared in a cloud. The students in the classroom below theirs barely got out of the way before the floor collapsed.

The whole class stared at the hole in stunned silence. Pi was worried she'd gone too far, but Professor Chopra whistled appreciatively.

"Enjoy your day, Miss Pythia."

Pi didn't waste any time and raced back to her room on the other side of Arcanium. She needed to look at the sketches of runes that Aurie had made from the night she went with Hemistad into the undercity, the ones on the strange urn in the crate.

She burst into her room, expecting to be tackled for the bag of red licorice she'd promised, only to find an empty room. Thoughts of the rune went out of her head as she worried about what kind of mischief Inari might be causing.

"Not good," she said, and checked Aurie's room next. No sign of the kitsune.

Pi grabbed a hunk of reddish hair that Inari had shed, and cast a tracking spell on it. She raced back through the hallways, wondering where the kitsune could be.

When the trail led to the waterfall beneath the school, her stomach sank into a pit. The spell led her to Patron Semyon's quarters. She knew he was out of the country.

All sorts of bad theories went careening through her head. If this whole thing with her uncle Liam was to get the kitsune into Arcanium, then she'd majorly screwed up. The stolen Hall pin and enchantments to bypass the wards alone would probably get her expelled.

Pi put the toe of her boot onto the invisible path through the waterfall. She had no idea if it worked while Semyon was gone. When her foot found something solid, she breathed a sigh of relief.

"Hello, down there in the water," she said. "I'm not here to cause trouble. I just need to find out what my kitsune is doing. Please let me pass. I'd prefer not to drown. I really wouldn't look good as a bloated corpse. It's a complexion thing."

Pi didn't get any response, so she took steps forward until she was almost to the waterfall. Undulating shapes moved through the water directly beneath her. The presence of something large and terrifying nearly made her run back to the safe side. She forged ahead, hoping that whatever it was, it understood her intentions.

When she reached the other side, she was so surprised she nearly fell into the water.

Inari was lying on her stomach, paws dipped into the water. Next to her was Semyon's dragonling, Menolly, who was fishing for minnows.

"Inari! You nearly gave me a heart attack when I found you missing," said Pi.

The kitsune's expression turned to remorse. She stood up, and her tail slipped between her legs.

The dragonling momentarily looked up, before scooping a minnow out of the water and shoving it in her mouth. The tail was wriggling as she swallowed it down.

Pi pointed towards the exit. "Back to the room. Before anyone sees you."

Inari slipped past her. Menolly squeaked at the kitsune, a tiny goodbye, before a belch slipped the silver dragonling's lips.

Before Pi left, she checked the wards around her patron's inner door. They looked intact. What she'd thought had been subterfuge had only been loneliness.

When she caught up to Inari back in her room, Pi promised the kitsune she'd take her back to play with Menolly again. This seemed to cheer up the kitsune, who'd been sulking since she'd come back.

The events of the day caught up to Pi. It'd been a surprisingly stressful day. She lay on the bed, telling herself that she'd only close her eyes for a few seconds, to fall deeply asleep, dreaming of runes whirling around her head.

ELEVEN

The first thing Aurie noticed when she walked into the Essence Foundry was the heat. Beads of sweat burst onto her forehead as the bright-orange light of the blast furnace washed over her. A quick spell brought a measure of relief from the suffocating fires.

The students inside the foundry milled around the room waiting for Professor Mali to finish quizzing the students outside. Aurie caught a whiff of musky plum from behind her.

"You should put your head in there," said Violet. "It might improve your situation."

No one was standing near, so Aurie spoke her mind. "I know what your mom did. She's got the blood of those people on her hands and that little girl, whose parents sorely wish she'd get better."

Violet reacted as if she'd been shocked. "I don't know what you're talking about. I saw the videos. You're a dangerous mage who has way too much power and not enough sense. How dare you blame my mother for your failings."

It was Aurie's turn to be shocked. Either Violet was an excellent liar, or she knew nothing about what her mother had done.

Before Aurie could say more, Professor Mali rolled into the room. Aurie wandered back to the table with her name on it. Pi's table was on the other side of the room, which had probably been the professor's intention. At least she'd put Violet Cardwell as far away as possible, directly in front.

"Knowledge is power," said the professor. "It's the motto of Arcanium. It's true to a point. Power is the ability to influence your surroundings. Through learning, we increase our power, and our ability to leverage our desires. But power without wisdom is dangerous. Does anyone know the difference between knowledge and wisdom?"

She called on Deshawn. "Knowledge is having a supermodel's phone number. Wisdom is knowing that there's no point in calling it."

The class had a good laugh, even Professor Mali, who chuckled despite herself.

"Thank you, Deshawn, for your excellent example," she said. "Wisdom is knowing how and when to use your power. Mages are the most powerful beings on the planet. You can do things that others cannot even conceive. It's a wonder that the world, out of fear, does not wipe us out. And maybe that's the wisdom of the normals, to know that there would be a terrible price to pay, and that they would lose an opportunity for greater things. It's why we have the Hundred Halls, and put such a heavy price on being able to control our magic. Magic without control is like carrying an unstable bomb in your pocket. You never know when it might go off."

Though the professor didn't single Aurie out, she felt it just the same. A few classmates stole glances in her direction.

"In the early years of Arcanium, when classes were less formal and more self-driven, we lost hundreds of mages because they were experimenting with magics they didn't understand, nor could they control. Even our patron has deep scars from the damage he inflicted in his early years before Invictus found him and offered him a place in the school. After you graduate, and if you've earned his trust, he might tell you a few stories that would chill your heart. It's why we spend a lot of time on activities that on the surface seem unrelated to magic. Why spend so much time in the Verum Locus your first year? Why attempt to use your true name when most of you will never achieve it? Today we embark on another journey for wisdom: a soul golem."

Violet raised her hand immediately. "My mother told me I should never use my soul for any magic."

A wry smile ghosted the professor's lips. "She is very correct, and very wrong. Yes, you should never use your soul for magic. It's a finite resource that disappears quickly, changing you along the way. But you can imprint your soul on objects that allow you a modicum of control over inanimate objects, or in this case, a golem. But the control will only work if you have built your golem to accept your imprint, which means you must understand yourself to build it properly. The difficulty of this task will not be the technical magical aspect, but acquiring the knowledge of yourself."

From across the room, Aurie caught Pi's expression before she hid it behind a mask of indifference. Her sister's mind was in flux about who their family had been, and who she was. This exercise would be difficult for her.

Aurie wasn't naive enough to think it wouldn't pose challenges for herself. Despite her confidence, she was aware that she had problems with control.

The professor indicated the back wall with a sweep of her hand. Swivel chairs squeaked as everyone turned to look. Covering a long table were dozens of silvery golems. They had big bellies and blank faces. Each was about two feet tall.

"Today, you will take control of your golem. You know how to accomplish this task, or you wouldn't have been let into the foundry. You must master this task, because the difficulty only increases. By the end of the semester, the soul golem must be capable of defending you against danger without your involvement. If it cannot, then you will not be asked to return for your fourth year, because the challenges and dangers in Arcanium only get harder."

While the rest of the class moved to collect their golems, Aurie went to her sister's table.

"You okay?" asked Aurie.

"What? Yeah, no problem. I got this," said Pi.

"Then why haven't you moved?" asked Aurie.

A hint of darkness passed across her sister's eyes. "Like the professor said, we have to know who we are. I'm figuring that out. What are you going to use in the heart binding?"

"I can't tell you that," said Aurie, putting her hand on her sister's arm. "You have to figure that out for yourself. *Dooset daram.*"

The smile Pi hung on her lips was only meant to keep Aurie from asking more questions. "*Dooset daram.* You'd better get back to your table. All the good supplies are being taken."

It wasn't like Aurie knew much better how she wanted to make the golem. But she was willing to try, even if she didn't know how, which gave her a moment of insight about her sister. For all Pi's perceived recklessness, she was actually quite disciplined when it came to the magical arts. She liked to give the impression that she was winging it, but Aurie knew better. Pi usually spent every waking moment working on her craft.

Which made her wonder what Pi was working on in her room. She had the room warded for sound and magical scrying. Did she have a secret project she didn't want Aurie to know about? She'd thought about breaking into the room on more than one occasion, but every time she approached the door, the idea slipped from her mind. Away from the suite, she could sense that something or someone was keeping her from doing so, which worried her about what Pi was mixed up with.

Only a few golems remained when Aurie collected hers. It was lighter than she expected, and the metal was cool, despite the heat of the foundry.

Back at her table, she examined the golem. Half-lidded eyes stared back as if it were just waking up from a long nap.

"Who are you, little golem?" she asked. "Or I guess I should ask, who am I?"

The other students moved with deliberation as they worked on their golems. Even Violet, her blonde hair bouncing as she listened to headphones as she worked.

There were three parts to linking a golem: the heart, the mind, and the soul. The first part was the heart. Aurie unlocked the chest of the golem. Metal scaffolding hung from the inside, where she would place her chosen items to act as its heart.

Aurie dug into her bag. She pulled out a picture of her parents from the day they'd graduated the Hundred Halls. It wasn't even a real photograph, since everything had been destroyed in the fire. Aurie had printed it off the internet. The edges of mother's floral scarf peeked out from her graduation robes. If there'd been any object she could have picked to have survived the fire, it would have been the scarf, just to be able to smell it and feel like she was home again.

The paper crinkled beneath her fingertips as she squeezed tightly. Aurie ran her thumb across her father's picture. He was flexing his arm, showing off the Whitestone RFC rugby jersey beneath his robes. Staring at the picture reminded Aurie of how similar her father, Kieran, and his older brother, Liam, looked. After she'd stared at it for a few minutes, she folded it up and tucked it into the golem's scaffolding.

A quick tug on a strand of hair produced a sharp sting on her scalp. Aurie pulled a second strand of hair, shorter and colored purple on the end, from her carryall, and twisted the two together, before tying them into the golem.

Next, she scoured the supply cabinets for the proper reagents. Aurie gathered bark shavings from an ancient aspen tree network for flexibility and family, the dog tags of fallen soldiers for duty and structure, and a few micrograms of plutonium to represent her power and instability. The last item was kept in a special warded locker.

She approached Professor Mali for permission.

The professor seemed to weigh Aurie with her gaze. "Are you sure about this, Miss Aurelia?"

"Positive," she said.

"You realize that if you make a mistake, it could kill you and your fellow students, not to mention make this foundry unusable for the foreseeable future," she said.

"I am aware," said Aurie. "I promise you I will take the proper precautions. I know the spells, and you know I can cast them."

The professor appeared reluctant. "Very well. I give you my permission. Do not disappoint."

She would have to work some spells to keep it inert; otherwise her golem would become radioactive, making it unusable.

After placing the other items into the golem, Aurie prepared to remove the wards from the plutonium. Immediately, the radioactive material tried to escape her spell, forcing her to improvise, but after a tense minute, she successfully transferred it into her golem.

The second part, the mind, was created using speaking paper. Aurie collected a stack of the crisp vellum and brought it back to her table.

She was a little self-conscious about starting until she realized the rest of her class was busy talking to themselves. Aurie looked to her sister's table, only to find it empty. This exercise was hard for the both of them, but even more so for Pi. She hoped Pi had only stepped out for a moment of fresh air, though the single remaining golem on the back table said otherwise.

Her younger sister was convinced that their uncle held the key to understanding their family, but Aurie thought that he was here in town after their winnings. Though Aurie had few memories of her parents talking about Liam, she remembered that they thought little of him. Aurie just hoped that Pi wouldn't be hurt too badly when she learned her uncle wasn't the guy she'd hoped he'd be.

Aurie set a fresh, completely blank piece of speaking paper in front of her, activated it with a touch of faez, and began. "Hello, I guess..."

As she spoke, the words appeared on the page in flowing script.

"My name is Aurelia Maximus Silverthorne. I am twenty-two years old. This exercise is much harder than I thought it would be, because I'm not sure what to say. How do I tell an inanimate object who I am?" She paused, concentrated. "I guess I can be a bit of a perfectionist, and I like things that I know will work."

The words had filled up the page, so Aurie stopped speaking. She folded it in half, then folded it again so it was one long strip of paper, and fed it into a slot in the back of the golem's head.

Realizing that it would be easier to talk if no one could hear her, she placed an enchantment on her table that muffled her voice beyond a few feet.

After the first couple of sheets, she got used to the exercise. Aurie would let the speaking paper transcribe a story, filling up multiple sheets, and then she would fold them and place them into the golem. The act of putting them in the golem was more cathartic than she expected, so Aurie delved deeper into her feelings as if she were talking to a therapist.

Aurie talked about growing up, feeling jealous of her younger sister, who had been more naturally gifted at everything. Even though they were separated by two years, Pi had often equaled her in school or the fledgling magic they covertly practiced.

Once their parents had died, the tables had turned. Pi had to rely on

Aurie, which came with a certain amount of guilt, as Aurie enjoyed being better than her sister at coping, but hated the reason why it had come about.

The story that was most difficult to tell was the one about her pet gerbil, Pepper.

"You'd think we named him Pepper because he had spots or something. He was nearly pure white except for a brown blotch on the side. We named him Pepper because Mom and Dad only agreed to one pet, but Pi and I wanted two, so we thought if we named it Pepper, they'd eventually buy us Salt. Anyway, that's not the point.

"One day I was making everything in my room levitate, using a spell I found on the internet. We'd just seen the movie about Jedis, and I wanted to be one. I was wearing my tan fluffy bathrobe, marching around the room, giving ridiculous speeches before levitating random objects to prove my power. After I ran out of things to lift, I decided to see if I could do it with Pepper. He was on my bed, sniffing around, nose twitching. He smelled like cedar from his habitat, which I kind of liked. He had big black eyes, and I liked to think that he loved me, since he would curl up on my lap when I was watching movies on the laptop.

"Pepper was standing on his back legs, looking up at me. He trusted me. I thought the spell was safe. I'd used it on everything in the room already. I knew the words, the finger manipulations. What I didn't know was that the levitation spell worked by pulling the object up from the top using a small distortion field. When I was grabbing a book, it was solid enough to move as one. I would have known that it wouldn't work if I'd performed the spell on anything flimsy.

"I didn't realize what I'd done right away. I mean it worked. I lifted Pepper a foot off the bed. I didn't do it very long because he seemed distressed by the whole thing. It wasn't until he landed on the bed and he made a soft, wet cough, and a drop of blood appeared on my bedsheets, that I realized what I had done. Pepper didn't make a noise. He just lay on his side and after a few labored breaths, died."

Aurie cupped a hand over her mouth, trying not to sob. Tears blotted her vision, turning the foundry into a watery-orange blob.

She knew she was crying, not for Pepper, though she'd cried for weeks after that day, but for Annabelle. Nezumi's daughter was still in the hospital, unresponsive to medical or magical attention. Dr. Fairlight had told her that Annabelle had been caught in a backlash of faez, which had stopped her heart and put her in a semi-stasis. Faez was the raw stuff of creation, and the faez had changed her. It was why the Rod of Dominion wouldn't work—she wasn't sick, or injured, but changed in a way they couldn't understand enough to fix.

Dr. Fairlight had let Aurie sneak into the hospital to see Annabelle late at night on a rare occasion when her parents weren't waiting for her to wake up. It had almost appeared as if Annabelle were only sleeping, except her vital signs were so low they were almost nonexistent.

"I'm sorry, Annabelle," said Aurie, the words tumbling out of her mouth and onto the speaking paper. "I wish I could take it all back, go back to that day and make sure it didn't happen. Even though it was Camille Cardwell who triggered it, by spraying me with some potion, making me believe that we were being attacked by those awful bugs from the Grand Contest, it was still my magic that hurt you.

"That's the thing that worries me. Had it been anyone else, that wouldn't have happened. Semyon once told me that I have more access to faez than anyone he's ever encountered. What if it's too much? What if I'm a danger to this world? I took out a Chinese satellite with the blow off, but that's nothing compared to what I did to you and your parents.

"When I first met Nezumi, he told me that mages were bad. Too dangerous. I'm beginning to worry that he's right. That I'm too dangerous. There was a time I thought I could do enough good things to make up for the bad things I might do by accident, but I worry that won't be enough. I'm sorry, Annabelle. I'm sorry for not being good enough for you, just like I haven't been good enough for my sister, or my parents."

The words she'd spoken had not only been etched into the paper, but etched into her heart. Between schoolwork, the huskings, and everything else going on, she'd barely had a chance to understand what had happened that day. Sure, there'd been grief. Every day that Annabelle was in the hospital, unresponsive to treatment, she grieved. But voicing that grief had opened those wounds bare.

Aurie folded the sheets and slipped them into the back of the skull of her golem. By the last sheet, she was numb. As she turned her head to wipe her eyes on her sleeve, something moved at the corner of her eye. It was quick, sliding across the floor so rapidly, Aurie almost missed it. But she knew what it was as soon as she saw it. It was a small stack of speaking paper that had been covertly placed near her, recording her confessions.

Aurie flew at Violet, who tucked the stack of papers into an inside pocket of her designer jacket before she reached her.

"Give those back!" said Aurie, the eruption drawing the notice of everyone in the room.

"What are you talking about?" asked Violet

The look of surprised innocence proved to Aurie that the earlier interaction had been full of lies. Professor Mali rolled up.

"What's going on?"

"She recorded my conversation using speaking paper. She has it in her pocket," said Aurie.

"I really don't know what she's talking about," said Violet, shrugging one padded shoulder. "I was putting the finishing touches on my golem when she came screaming up to me. Look, Professor Mali, she's got a long history of unstableness going all the way back to when she attacked me for no good reason at Golden Willow. I really think she shouldn't be allowed to be in the same classes with the rest of us. It's too big of a risk."

Professor Mali didn't seem to be buying any of it. "Then let's dispel this accusation by opening up your jacket."

Violet huffed. "I really can't believe I'm being asked to do this. I'm not the one going to trial for lack of control."

The steel gaze of the professor was enough to get Violet moving. She opened up the designer jacket, revealing nothing, not even a pocket.

"Why are we surprised?" asked Violet. "When she's the criminal."

"A moment," said the professor, who cast a few spells. When she was finished, she frowned and glanced at Aurie in a way that made her question herself.

"I'm sorry," said the professor. "I can detect no extra-dimensional pockets where she might have hid them away. As far as I can tell, there are no papers."

Aurie had to fight back the urge to bring down a pillar of flame upon Violet's head, burning that smug expression off her perfect face.

"I'm sorry," said the professor, rolling away. She looked like she was questioning her own spells, which at least gave Aurie the impression that the professor had believed her, and maybe still believed her.

"I'd better not see those published in the *Herald*," said Aurie.

"And theoretically, how would you prove that?" asked Violet, raising an eyebrow in a taunt. "After all, you've already fed the originals into the golem."

It felt like Aurie had swallowed a bucket of broken glass. The sharp edges of realization burned on the way down, leaving her raw. A curl of flame woke to Aurie's hand.

Violet sneered. "Do it. Let even one little piece of flame touch me and you can be sure the patrons will vote to have you dispelled and removed of your magic. It might even be a blessing. My mother and her friends will own this school soon enough. It's only a matter of time."

Aurie let the flame dissolve. She returned to her golem, limbs shaking. It took a long time to settle down enough to finish her task. Using the proper spells, she linked her soul to the golem. Aurie was able to make it walk across the room, which would have made her proud, because it was the best in the class, but nothing mattered while her life had been reduced to ashes.

TWELVE

Pi woke to Inari pawing at her and whining. The kitsune appeared in pain, shaking her head and grimacing.

"Inari? Are you okay?" asked Pi, knuckling the sleep from her eyes. The clock read 2 a.m.

The kitsune nudged her with her nose to get out of bed. Pi complied, but noticed something different about the collar on her neck. The runes were glowing.

"What's going on?" she asked.

Inari jumped off the bed and pawed at the door, rattling it.

"You have to go that bad? Fine," said Pi, slipping into her pajamas with colorful cartoon ponies on them.

Aurie was asleep on the couch in the common area. She'd been up reading the latest edition of *Herald of the Halls*, which had another round of stories based on the confessions Violet had stolen in the Essence Foundry. Pi placed a blanket on her sister before she left with Inari.

The city was under a deep freeze, colder than normal for December. Despite the enchantments on the rooftop garden dome, Pi rubbed her arms for warmth.

"Did someone leave a door open?" she asked, stepping around the row of combustible orchids.

Inari did not go running for a bathroom break, but stayed by her side glowering at a dark patch on the other side of the garden, so Pi was not surprised when the shadow moved out of the darkness.

"Uncle Liam," she said. "How did you get in here?"

He held his tattooed arm up. The leaves writhed across his arm, revealing a bridge momentarily beneath the canopy. "I'm not without resources."

"What's going on? I mean, it's good to see you. I still have so many questions, but it's late and I was asleep," said Pi.

"Aye, sorry lass, I've been trying to work out the complications that arose from the kitsune bonding with you," he said.

"Did you figure out a way to break the bond?" asked Pi, feeling bad as soon as she said it. Inari looked up at her with puppy dog eyes.

"Not yet," he said. "Until I do, I need to ask a favor."

"Of course, yes, we're family after all," she said.

Uncle Liam shifted on his feet like a boy about to ask a girl to Homecoming. Pi could see that underneath that rough, devil-may-care attitude was a kid brimming with wanderlust trying to make his way in the world. She wished she could have known him when her parents were alive. It would have been a thing to see her dad with his older brother.

"I was going to race her. You see, there's this thing called the Voodoo Run that happens now and again. It's a big race that goes through the undercity. A fair bit dangerous, but that's to be expected with the amount of money on the line. An amount of money that I desperately need."

"I'm guessing you owe someone a lot of money," she said.

"Something like that," he replied, his ruddy complexion growing deeper red.

"You were going to race Inari?" asked Pi. "Like actually ride her?"

"Aye. She's sturdier than you think. Your mount has to be magical and cannot fly," said Liam. "So, since things have gone all pear-shaped, might you race in my stead? I don't know what I'll do if I don't win the Voodoo Run."

Pi didn't know what to say. She didn't know how to turn him down, since she'd ruined his plans; not on purpose, but it'd happened just the same.

"I guess," she said, glancing at Inari. "When is it?"

"Tonight, lass," he said. "Sorry to spring it on you like this. It took a fair amount of maneuvering to get my entry transferred to you. I would have warned you, but I was planning on leavin' town if I couldn't get that done."

"Race? I don't know anything about racing," said Pi, who couldn't believe she was having this conversation in her pajamas.

"Truthfully, you'd be better than me. You're smaller, and you're more learned than I in the magical arts," he said, whistling softly.

"What happens if I don't race?" asked Pi.

The slight wince told her everything she needed to know even before he answered. "Then I go back into hiding."

Only a few short months after learning she had an uncle, she was going to lose him to a freak accident from Inari bonding to her. Part of her felt bad that the only reason she was considering helping him was to learn about her family. Especially since she hadn't created her soul golem yet, a task that grew more daunting the longer she delayed. If she could learn a few things about her history, then maybe she could piece together a picture of who she was.

"Count me in," she said.

He tousled her hair.

"You're my favorite niece," he said, laughing. "Just don't tell your sister."

He threw her a blanket and rope saddle that would keep her on Inari's back during the race. Pi changed into more suitable attire, jamming her pockets with spell components that might come in handy in a race.

On the way across the city, no one gave Inari a second look, and a few people asked about her "big dog," which Pi decided was either self-deception or some sort of magical aura that the kitsune put off. Pi tried to ask about family history, but Uncle Liam was too busy giving her the rundown on the Voodoo Run.

"You ever seen the movie *Ben Hur*?" he asked.

"Is it about being transgender?" she asked.

His green-gold eyes flickered with amusement. "It has a famous chariot race scene. You probably know the movie with pod racing in it that ripped it off."

"I loved that part," said Pi.

"The Voodoo Run is the same thing. Once around the track. Go fast, and try not to let your fellow racers kill you. And watch out for the denizens of the undercity. They can be a bit of trouble as well." His forehead furrowed. "Nice biker jacket. Never heard of the Whirling Dervishes, though."

She glanced down to find her magical leather jacket had changed form again. "Thanks."

They made their way into the undercity by way of the spiral staircase beneath the Goblin's Romp. Big Dave's Town was more awake than the city above it, as if the day-night cycle didn't apply.

After the town, they took the east tunnels to a village called Voodool- and that bordered on an area of the undercity that was affectionately called the Wastelands. It was run by a group of fungusfolk. Uncle Liam warned her not to eat anything in the town, or the spores would turn her into one of them and she'd never leave the undercity again.

The race start area was about as impressive as the village, which wasn't saying much. Voodooland, despite its name, had the feel of an Appalachian town long forgotten after the coal mines had been boarded up. She'd been expecting a New Orleans vibe, but maybe it was like driving through Paris, Texas. Great name, but no relation to the original.

The other racers milled about the start area, which was just a white line spray-painted onto the rock. Pi couldn't decide what was worse, the other racers or mounts. The worst was a nightmarish-looking panther with tentacles undulating from its back standing next to a furry humanoid with ram horns and red demonic eyes. He wore a sword on his back.

"He's your main competition. They call him Goatman," said Uncle Liam.

"Goatman? Couldn't he have come up with a better nickname than that?" asked Pi.

"Says the girl who looks like she's barely fifteen and riding a giant fox," said Liam with an eyebrow raised.

"Point taken," she said.

Most of the other competitors appeared human, except for a lizardman and an individual with giant watery eyes and slimy blue skin. Big Eyes was riding a sleek pink mount with porcupine quills.

A man in a top hat with half a beard made of glowing green mushrooms greeted Liam with a smile and a wave that would have been appropriate in an asylum.

Inari pushed against Pi's leg, so she scratched the kitsune behind the ear. A small whine slipped out.

"Hey, Voodoo Jake, you've got something on your chin," said Uncle Liam to the guy in the top hat.

Voodoo Jake inspected his chin with his fingers, digging them into the mushrooms, making them wriggle.

"Never mind," said Liam, giving Pi a wry grin.

"Is this the competitor?" asked Voodoo Jake absently.

"This is my niece. Pythia Silverthorne," said Liam. "She'll be racing in my place."

"Excellent," said Voodoo Jake. "You're the last to arrive. Take your place with the others."

"Right now?" asked Pi, suddenly realizing this was actually going to happen.

Uncle Liam shoved her towards the starting area. Before she left, she reminded him, "You owe me answers about our family for this."

"Focus on the race," he said. "You're going to need it."

"Great," she muttered under her breath.

She took her position behind the others. Everyone was standing next to their mounts.

Leaning down to Inari, she said, "I hope you're ready for this."

Inari poked her in the neck with her cold nose. When she stood back up, Goatman was staring at her with his red eyes.

"Creepy, much?" she asked him, but he kept staring.

There was no more time for interaction, as Voodoo Jake stepped forward and said, "Racers go!"

The others hopped on their mounts and were off into the darkness before Pi could even register that the race had begun.

Uncle Liam waved at her to hurry. "Go, go, go!"

She climbed onto Inari's back, attaching herself with the simple harness, holding on with her thighs and gripping the ropes with both hands. The kitsune took off at a jog.

"Good luck, Pi. Remember, only first place gets prize money, and I've got a lot riding on this!" yelled her uncle.

"Yeah, like my life," she said, and when she heard a growl from Inari, she added, "Yours, too."

The kitsune jogged after the other racers. The path was lit by glowing fungus cultivated in the shape of arrows every hundred feet. Pi's pelvis bumped against Inari's back at every jarring step.

"Faster," said Pi, trying to goad the kitsune on. The other racers had disappeared into the darkness ahead. At best, Inari was moving at a fast trot. The kitsune seemed to be holding back.

"Come on, Inari. They're leaving us behind," she said, nudging the kitsune's side with her boot.

When Inari didn't speed up, Pi nudged again, and the kitsune stopped suddenly, throwing Pi onto the ground. The impact cut up her palms. Inari was sitting on her haunches, ears twitching.

"What are you doing?" asked Pi. "We're going to lose the race and I'm going to lose my uncle!"

The words echoed in the subterranean cavern. Pi cringed. She'd almost forgotten how dangerous the undercity was.

Inari appeared unaffected by her pleading. The kitsune started walking back the other way. Pi tugged on Inari's fur, but she ignored it.

"What's going on? Did I do something wrong?" asked Pi.

The kitsune gave no answer. Pi blocked Inari's path.

"Please stop. You don't understand how important this is. My parents died when I was little, and I don't know anything about my family. Uncle Liam is my only chance to learn something about them, to see where I come from. If I don't win this race, then he'll have to leave the city and I'll probably lose him forever," said Pi.

The kitsune tilted her head and whined. A sense of overwhelming danger came from Inari. A warning.

"Yeah, I know, the Voodoo Run is dangerous, but it's bigger than that. If I can't figure out who I am, then I can't be a mage in Arcanium," said Pi.

The feeling of danger hit her in the chest like sub vocal echolocation. Inari nudged her hand and nodded back the way they'd come.

"I can't leave, Inari, please. You have to help me. Look, this isn't just for me. There's a lot of bad things going on in the Halls. I don't have time to get into details, but let's just say that me and Aurie are the two mages that know what's going on. If I can't be a mage then I can't stop the Cabal. So please help me," said Pi.

The kitsune hung her head for a moment. The big fox-like creature sighed heavily before turning back around.

"Thank you, Inari!" said Pi, hugging her.

The kitsune shook her head as if saying, "You'll regret it."

Once Pi had resumed her place on the kitsune's back, they took off at a good pace, bounding over obstacles with considerable ease. Pi was surprised how much smoother the ride was now that the kitsune was on board with the mission.

A little ways down the path, a yawning gulf opened up before them. Inari skidded to a stop. When they looked over the edge, it appeared to be a quarry. Pi wondered what they were digging for down here. An old road with worn tire marks went the other direction, but that wasn't the way she had to go. The faint glow of phosphorescent mushrooms could be seen ahead to the right on a thin path that circled the quarry.

Pi created a wisp that hovered over Inari's head, casting light upon the path. Inari stepped carefully onto the ledge. The quarry had multiple levels. Another ledge lay about thirty feet below, straight down.

Pi imagined terrible machines sculpting the earth, dragging whatever precious material had been down there into the light. The darkness of the massive hole on her left had its own gravity that felt like it was pulling her in that direction. Pi leaned towards the stone wall, but the ledge was barely wide enough for the kitsune, and in some sections, Pi had to squeeze her leg to Inari's side to avoid hitting rock.

Pi was wondering how far ahead the other competitors were when an explosion threw them off the path. Her ears rang as they fell. She was disoriented by the concussive blow and closed her eyes for a moment to clear her head, knowing that she was likely going to die when she hit the bottom.

The light wisp was far above her. She squeezed Inari's fur in apology for convincing her to come along, then they hit the ground, slamming Pi's teeth together in a rattling clack. Pi rubbed her jaw, hoping none of her teeth had broken. The impact hadn't been as bad as Pi expected. She looked above to see the light wisp hovering above the path about thirty feet above them.

She peered over the edge into the swirling darkness, swearing that they'd fallen further than the first ledge.

"I thought we were goners," said Pi, climbing from Inari's back. The lower ledge was much wider than the upper path, but only went a dozen feet ahead. She shook her head, trying to get the ringing out of her ears. The impact had hurt, but she knew that they'd been lucky to only get knocked off. The brunt of the explosion had happened ahead of them, probably triggered by the wisp.

The kitsune sat on her haunches, eyes closed as if meditating. Pi dug her fingers into the fur around Inari's neck and gave her a good scratching.

"I don't know what you did, Inari, but you saved us," said Pi. "Now we have to get back up top. I don't suppose you can climb that?"

The kitsune whined.

"I guess it'll have to be me," said Pi, digging into her jacket for a solution. She was still a little dizzy from the explosion, and her thoughts didn't want to connect.

"Be a good spot to be an animalian and change into a bird or something," she said. "Or be a stone singer and chant ladder rungs into the wall. Sometimes I swear Arcanium is useless for practical problems."

The only items she thought could remotely help were a long piece of string and a crumpled-up origami crane that she'd made on the train last week, but after staring at them for a minute or two, she came up empty.

"I think we're going to have to do this the hard way. I'm going to climb up, and maybe I can find a rope or some vines up top," she said.

She made the climb using cracks in the walls where the digging machines had broken stone. It wasn't a difficult climb, but her fingers were raw by the time she reached the top.

Pi looked down to the ledge to find that Inari was up top with her.

"That was fast, and silent. I guess you couldn't climb it with me on your back," she said. "Let's get going. We're so far behind now."

A glowing patch of mushrooms indicated they were back on the path. This time, Pi scanned the way for traps. When they neared the end of the quarry, Pi found a symbol etched into the stone. If triggered, it would explode. They couldn't get past it, so Pi had to disarm it by containing the trigger in a spell matrix while she destroyed the symbol.

Past the quarry, the way opened up. Pi let Inari break into a run, knowing full well that more traps could be ahead, but she had to risk it, or fall too far behind the others.

A quarter mile after the quarry, they found one of the other competitors. Both the man's body and his mount were charred hunks of meat. They stunk like a garbage fire. They took a wide berth and continued into the darkness.

A lake appeared out of the gloom a few minutes later. The brackish water was deathly still. The skeleton of a four-legged creature was piled by the shore. The bones were recent, looking as if they'd been spit there by a great beast. Gouge marks on the rocks indicated large claws.

The path went around the lake, but Pi wasn't excited about taking that way. Inari was bristling with nervousness at the prospect.

"Keep your eye out. I don't think we want to meet whatever's in there," said Pi.

She watched the lake as they took the path. It was better than the quarry, which barely gave room to walk, but the lake seemed more ominous.

They were about halfway around when the water stirred further out from shore. V-lines headed their direction. The presence in the water seemed much larger than a subterranean fish.

There was no way they could outrun it. They were trapped on the shore. When the water broke open, revealing a long slick black shape, Pi conjured a piece of ice and threw it into the lake and yelled, "Freeze!"

The chunk hit the water, turning the immediate area to ice. The emerging creature hit the frozen surface, cracking the ice. She thought it was going to hold until the sheet exploded into snow. Tentacles came writhing after her. Pi fired fire bolts at them, but they ignored her magic.

"Go, Inari, go!"

She ducked the first tentacle, but the second hit her in the chest, throwing her off the kitsune. She landed half in the water.

The tentacles made desperate grabs. She fired more fire bolts, but they seemed to have little effect. A suckered undulating limb grabbed her leg and started dragging her into the water. Pi couldn't blast the tentacle or risk injuring herself.

To her left, Inari fought the other tentacles, trying to reach her. The kitsune wasn't making progress, but at least it was keeping the other limbs from grabbing her.

She threw an explosive seed into the water, hoping to stun the creature, but the impact dissipated on the surface. The tentacle kept pulling until she was halfway submerged. In the deeper waters where the limbs originated, an unholy maw of teeth and slime occasionally surfaced, giving Pi a sneak peek of her impending fate.

Pi pulled the piece of string from her pocket, gave it life, and had it snake back to the rocks. She bound the other part of the string around her waist. The string was fragile, but her magic held, giving her a chance to fight the monster in the water with both hands.

The other tentacles had driven Inari back. If Pi didn't escape on her own soon, the tentacles would converge on her, and they'd drag her into that horrible maw.

Running out of options, she conjured a second piece of ice, this time focusing her faez before throwing it in.

"Freeze!"

The chunk hit the water, sending out shards of frost that collected into a layer of ice. She kept it growing, pouring more faez into her spell, until ice radiated outward, capturing the beast's tentacles.

"Freeze!" she yelled a second time.

The tentacles tried to break free, but she'd built the ice thick enough. Already the brackish water was turning cold.

Pi kicked away the tentacle's grip on her ankle and scrambled out of the water, easily avoiding the other tentacles, which had lost their mobility.

She leapt on Inari's back, and they sprinted away before the thing could break free again. Cold from the submersion, Pi held onto Inari's back and tried to get warm again.

Ten minutes later and still sopping wet, they caught up to the other racers, which surprised her at first, because she expected them to be further ahead. There were six left, including Big Eyes and Goatman. She realized their slowness was because none of the racers wanted to take the lead, exposing their back to the rest of the group. It was a moving stand-off, which had given her an opportunity to catch up.

This was possible because the caverns were wide open, allowing everyone to keep space between them. If and when the track narrowed, they would be forced back together, and the fragile truce would end.

Goatman rode in back on his tentacled panther, his red demonic eyes glowering at her as she approached the back. He bared his teeth and made a gesture of slicing her throat. She moved to the other side of the racers, staying near the cavern wall.

Glances passed between the other racers. Pi sensed that temporary alliances had been made. She caught a nod from Goatman and Big Eyes.

Pi leaned over Inari's back and whispered in her ear, "I hope you're ready to run, because I don't think they like us."

Inari growled her agreement. The decision on whether to hang back or take the lead was forced upon them when the cavern narrowed.

Something flew by her face, narrowly missing her nose. She looked to the left to find Big Eyes closing the gap while reloading a crossbow. He wouldn't miss a second time.

"Go! Go!" she yelled.

Inari bounded ahead, leaping off the wall and a stalagmite to avoid Big Eyes. Pi shot fire bolts behind her randomly to keep him from getting a good shot off.

She was so focused on Big Eyes, she didn't see Goatman coming until it was too late. His blade sung through the air, towards her neck. There was no time to avoid it. She closed her eyes, expecting the end, only to hear a scream of rage from behind.

Somehow, Inari had leapt ahead, saving Pi's life.

"Thank you, Inari," said Pi.

But she didn't have time to relax. Big Eyes and Goatman were hot on her trail.

Inari led them away from the course, leaving the glowing mushroom arrows behind, dodging around stone pillars and leaping ravines. Pi sent fire bolts behind her while avoiding low hanging ceilings.

A crossbow bolt sliced through the meat of her arm. Blood came out in thick pulses. She felt dizzy right away, and not from the blood loss. There'd been poison on the bolt.

Pi slipped her arm out of the jacket. Hot sticky blood ran through her fingers. Spots formed before her eyes, and she had to fight them back. Pi narrowly avoided a stalagmite.

She turned her fingers to flame and jammed them into the wounds, cauterizing the holes. She wasn't bleeding anymore, but poison was still in her veins.

After wiping the blood and charred flesh from her fingers, Pi dug through her pockets for the proper reagents for a general antidote—eucalyptus bark, dried belladonna, and clove—grimacing whenever she moved her right arm.

She didn't have time for proper mixing, so she mashed them together and dry swallowed them, choking on the eucalyptus bark when it got caught in her throat. After a few seconds, the dizziness lessened, but did not go away, which meant her antidote wasn't completely effective. Probably the only thing that had kept the poison from being worse was that the bolt had gone through her arm, rather than lodging in the flesh. If it had, she would have gotten a full dose, and nothing would have saved her.

Glancing around, she realized that they'd lost her pursuers. They'd also lost the trail, which meant they were behind. Big Eyes and Goatman had probably thought she was going to die from the poison and returned to the race.

"Get us back, Inari. We've still got a chance," she said.

The kitsune headed back in the general direction of the racetrack. Pi was worried that they'd gone too far off path until they saw a glowing arrow pointing the way.

Without knowing where the other racers were at, Pi had no idea if they were still in the running.

"Fast as you can, Inari. Fast as you can."

They sped through the caverns. The powerful kitsune kept up a sprint for many minutes. Pi's back ached from the constant motion. She sensed they were nearing Voodooland and the end of the race based on the changing of the cavernscape.

"Come on, Inari," she said to the kitsune, urging her on. "We're almost to the end."

Somehow, the kitsune increased her pace. Pi scanned ahead as they passed through the caverns, twitching at shadows. They were crossing over a ridge when the attack came.

A blade flashed by Pi's neck as Goatman and his tentacled mount dropped from the ceiling. Inari had shifted to the left, saving Pi from decapitation. They leapt and turned.

Pi fired back with a flame spear. Goatman absorbed the spell with his blade, and before Pi could ready a second one, he flung it back at her.

The quickness that had saved them earlier failed. Pi was able to deflect part of the flame spear, but it caught her across the leg. The tail of the flame burnt a gash into Inari's side. Pi fell onto the stone, slamming her elbow hard.

The pain threatened to make her black out. The stench of burnt flesh and hair clogged her nose. She swam though the agony and struggled to her feet as Goatman approached with sword at the ready. Now she knew how he'd so easily killed the other competitors—he reflected their magic back at them with his sword.

Before he could reach her, Pi threw a second flame spear, changing the lexology of the spell.

Goatman easily absorbed the attack, his horns glowing with rage. When he flung the flame spear back at her, it exploded the moment it left his sword, destroying it and flinging him backwards.

She was gathering another spell, when the horned racer leapt back on his tentacled mount and sprung into the darkness.

Pi limped to Inari, who was licking her side where the spear had hit. Raw flesh leaked blood. Pi gave them each a quick repair before climbing back onto Inari. They had no time for a proper healing.

They set off again, much slower due to their exhaustion. Pi kept a watchful eye, but decided that without his spell-reflecting sword, the Goatman would probably race to the end to collect his winnings.

She was proved right when they made it back to Voodooland. The horned red-eyed racer was collecting his gold from Voodoo Jack.

Uncle Liam stood at the finish line, head hung low.

"I'm sorry, Uncle Liam," she said.

"You did your best, lass. You did your best. I'm just glad you're okay," he said.

"What about you? Does this mean you have to leave town?" she asked.

"I'm afraid so," he said, shaking his head.

"What if I lent you some money? How much do you need?" she asked.

When he gave her a figure, she paled. Even if she had that much, she wasn't comfortable handing it over to her uncle, especially since Aurie had warned her that he might have only contacted them for their winnings.

But she also couldn't fathom how he'd set up this race, knowing she'd barely lose, creating the need to lend him money. It didn't seem probable that he could manipulate events that well. She was more likely to have died during the contest than anything else.

"Would it help if I covered the interest? Until I could race again, or we could find another way to pay off the debt?" she asked.

"Are you sure about that?" he asked. "I hate to get you tangled up in my problems. If we can't pay it off, you'll be on the hook too."

"We're family, Uncle Liam. Family means taking a chance sometimes," she said.

For a brief moment, Liam's face broke with emotion, before he bottled it behind his playful stoicism. "You're a good niece. I don't deserve you."

"You can pay me back with stories about our family," she said.

Uncle Liam went quiet, as if he were preparing to deliver bad news. His green eyes reflected a stormy day.

"Aye, lass, aye," he said after a time. "I owe you that and a whole lot more."

He dug deep into his pocket, producing a tarnished gold coin. He placed it in the palm of her hand, which sent a tingle up her arm.

"Soon I'll give you a proper load of answers, but until then, this will have to do," he said heavily. "Now, let's go talk to Voodoo Jake about them interest payments."

Pi didn't move at first. She was staring at the coin. The well-worn raised symbols showed a tree with a crown on one side and a wooden bridge crossing a meandering river on the other. The typography was ancient, predating human civilization. But she didn't need to be a member of Arcanium to know what the symbols meant. The coin was a marker from the realm of Fae.

THIRTEEN

The history of the Court of Three could be found on the internet. As she sat on a simple bench in a waiting room off the main chamber, Aurie wished she hadn't indulged her curiosity, because the history was quite brutal. In the early years of the Hundred Halls, magical misdeeds were more common, requiring punishments that crossed the line on torture, and bordered on murder.

In those days, the jurors evaluated the crime and designed the penalty, which usually invoked the creativity of their magical talents. For the crime of turning a fellow wizard's skin translucent, an offending mage was enchanted with giant insect wings which were ripped off, killing him when the blood loss couldn't be stopped.

Aurie's trial would be simpler. A trial by magic required the demonstration of ability. It had been intended to protect those mages with considerable skill from being litigated by lesser jealous wizards, since uncommon ability was exactly that—uncommon. It felt a little like cheating to invoke the trial by magic, but since Camille Cardwell had tricked her into loosing her magic, Aurie thought it was justified. She wondered if this was how the powerful eventually compromised themselves, rationalizing minor deceptions until they added up to major crimes.

Semyon entered the room in his formal robes. His right arm was wrapped in a cast that had runes covering it.

"What happened?" asked Aurie, standing up.

His forehead wrinkled, waggling his bushy gray eyebrows. "An inconvenience. The bones in my arm were turned to jelly. In a few days, they'll be back to normal."

"You should let my sister and I help you. We've been tracking—"

He cut her off with a wave of his hand. "Enough. You're on trial today. Let's focus on that. It's bad enough with those articles in the *Herald*."

"You could do something about that. Violet stole those stories from me in the Essence Foundry," said Aurie.

"Who says that I'm not doing something? But you should be more careful. If you can let Violet Cardwell outwit you, then how are you going to help me?" he asked.

The rebuke was a punch in the gut. Patron Semyon sighed and put his good hand on her shoulder.

"I realize this is difficult for you, but focus on the trial. It's what is most important right now," he said.

"Didn't we get the Rod?" asked Aurie.

"Let me make this clear for you. Your participation could complicate things. There are forces and magics at work that you have no defenses for. You are forbidden to get involved. If I catch you doing anything else regarding the Cabal, I will remove my support for you on this trial."

"But—"

"No buts. You'll only make things worse. Yes, I know about the Rod, but you got lucky. It was only your parents' preparation that got you through that. This is far worse." He paused. "I have a matter to attend to first, and then we'll get started. It'll only be a little longer."

As the door closed behind Semyon, Aurie caught a glimpse of an elegant blonde woman in stylish robes. Celesse D'Agastine. The patron of The Order of Honorable Alchemists.

Celesse was one of the three patrons that would be presiding over her case. She had to know what was going on between Semyon and Celesse.

The only problem was that the room had been warded against magic. She knew that if she cast a spell out loud, an alarm would sound.

She placed her ear against the door, but it was thick enough she could only hear distant mumbling. Rather than circumvent the warding, Aurie placed her hands over her ears, imagined her wellspring of faez concentrating into her ears, and *thought* about how excellent her hearing was: better than a bat's. She'd never used verumancy before using only her thoughts, but when she pulled her hands away, she winced at the hurricane of air coming out of the vent in the ceiling of the room. It'd worked, almost a little too well.

Aurie placed her ear against the door again, blocking the opposite side with a cupped hand.

"I know you found the archway. Don't lie to me," said Semyon.

"I don't know what you're talking about," said Celesse.

"You're trying to get into Invictus' realm," he said.

She scoffed. "Of course we are. That much should be obvious by this point. Is that what happened to your arm? You should be more careful next time. Or better yet, you should join us while you still can. I wouldn't be surprised if we've got control of the Halls by the end of the school year."

"Not while you align yourself with Malden and Bannon," he said.

"Semyon, sweetie. I'll give you Bannon, he's a wretched man, but Malden isn't as bad as you think he is. Like the rest of us, he recognizes there's a huge risk for all of us if we don't have a head patron. Invictus was as much a symbol as he was a functioning leader of the school. There are a lot of troublesome laws being proposed in governments around the world, including here in the United States. If we don't get order back in the Halls, then we might not have a school. Would you rather go back to the time before the Halls when mages were either tyrants or hunted?"

"If you allow Malden or Bannon to take head patron, then we'll be worse off than that," said Semyon. "They would use the Halls to rule."

"Who's to say that they would become head patron? What about me? I wouldn't be so bad, would I?" she cooed.

The sound of kissing surprised Aurie. Were things as clear between the Halls as she thought?

"I can't, Celesse."

"You used to like fucking me," she said, bitterness threading her words.

"It's not about that."

"You still have a thing for Priyanka, don't you?"

"I don't have a thing for anyone right now. I'm trying to save the Halls. Join me. A few defections would undermine the Cabal's strength. The other halls would rally to my side if a few more major players joined."

"It's too late," she said. "I told you we're not far. I'm sorry, Semyon. You realize you and the rest of Arcanium will be the first example when we win. Malden plans to leave nothing but a smoking ruin."

"We'll see about that," he said.

"Think about your students," said Celesse. "If you join us now, we'll even save this Aurelia, give her a task so easy a child could do it. Think about them. Your students. They're not a part of this war."

Aurie hated herself for hoping that he would agree. For a brief shining moment, she had a vision of Semyon joining them and somehow convincing the others to make him head patron, solving every problem in one quick strike. But even as she had the vision, she knew it was a childish fantasy. Reality was cold calculation, and Semyon's answer did not disappoint.

"Everyone's a part of the war whether they like it or not. I'll sacrifice the lot of them, this girl included, if it means preserving the Halls and thwarting Malden," said Semyon.

"Very well. We'll destroy her to the root to prove our point," said Celesse. "You're a fool, Semyon. We have no more to say to each other. I hope we do not meet in different circumstances. Despite my fond feelings for you, I will not hesitate to strike you down."

"Likewise," he said.

Aurie threw herself onto the bench before Semyon reentered. He was clearly distracted, as was she. *This girl included.* The words bounced around her head. She was nothing more than a pawn in the game, a chess piece to be sacrificed, not even worth a name. From the first time that she'd met Semyon, when he came into her apartment to test her and offer her a spot in Arcanium, she'd thought she was special.

This girl included. He'd said it with no more emphasis than if he were throwing an extra can of soup into his cart at the grocery store. She'd retrieved the Rod of Dominion, and given it to him for safekeeping, and he only thought of her as a minor player?

"Are you ready?" he asked.

In the brief meeting of their gazes, there was a certain amount of measuring, as if they saw each other for who they really were. Aurie vowed not to let his indifference affect her.

"Ready."

The Court of Three was a round room with three high-backed marble chairs facing a simple pedestal at the center, where she would be sitting. At one time, magical chains connected to the floor so the punishment could be handed out without interference from the offending mage. Aurie would be spared that indignity today.

The chairs, for the moment, were empty. Semyon led her to the center.

"Be polite. Any little thing might influence their decision," he said. "When you're done, come see me back in Arcanium and we can discuss how to achieve your task."

His deception burned in her gut. She knew this whole thing was a farce. Semyon left the room, but not before glancing back with a flicker of guilt.

When the others entered, Aurie was not surprised.

Celesse D'Agastine entered first. Aurie refused to allow the woman's pity to affect her. She was the enemy. Aurie glared back.

The next was Bannon Creed in a dark blue tracksuit. He looked at her like every creepy guy on the train ever did, as if she were nothing more than an object to be either desired or thrown away.

The last patron was Malden Anterist. He came into the room hidden by a shifting magical shield. She knew his name because of her sister.

After the three patrons took their positions, Celesse said, "You may sit, Aurelia."

"I'll stand, thank you."

The earlier pity burned away under a cold glare. "Very well."

While Celesse continued, Bannon picked his fingernails with a knife, and Malden sat unmoving. The slight hum of his magical shield made her teeth hurt.

"State your name for the record," said Celesse.

"Aurelia Maximus Silverthorne."

Celesse made a quick motion, as if she were typing in midair. A presence pushed against her skin, made her claustrophobic. Aurie thought for a moment that something was trying to suffocate her, but then as quickly as it'd begun, it was gone.

"It's her," said Celesse to the other two.

"So this is the girl that killed Frank Orpheum," said Malden.

Thinking it was an ambush, Aurie summoned faez to make her escape. Before the first hint of magic could trickle into her, every muscle in her body seized up. The effect was instantaneous and painful.

"Don't worry, my dear," said Malden. "I'm not going to kill you. I just wanted to thank you for ridding us of that preening jackass."

Through the shield, she saw his hand move. A scissoring motion. The agonizing rictus of her muscles released. Aurie collapsed onto the floor in a cold sweat.

Bannon Creed smirked, but otherwise looked bored.

"It wasn't hard to find out how he'd died and what he was trying to achieve once we knew it had happened," said Malden. "Hard to believe he'd let a second-year student outwit him, but he always was an overconfident blowhard."

Aurie almost answered him, until she realized he was fishing for information. He knew she'd been there when he'd died, but not how.

"Hubris has been the death of many a mage," she said.

"Yes. Yes, it has. You know, I remember your sister. Hard to forget an initiate willingly giving up their place in Coterie. I thought I was losing my touch until I heard she went to Arcanium. Such a waste of her talents and ambition. Maybe even hubris. I see you're cut from the same cloth."

Aurie stayed quiet. He drummed on the table with his fingers.

"Was there anyone else besides Frank Orpheum involved with this plot? We might be more lenient if actionable information was shared," he said.

She kept her face as unreadable as possible, which was hard, because she wanted to blurt out Priyanka Sai's name. Was it better to sow derision within the Cabal, or protect her name in hopes of convincing the head of Assassins to oppose them? Zayn had given Pi hope that such a thing could be done last year before he'd returned to his home.

"I see you're thinking," said Malden from behind his shielded form. "Which means there's another person."

"No," said Aurie, right away. "I was just thinking about what he said to me before I killed him."

The three patrons shifted in their seats, though they tried not to appear that interested. Bannon was the most obvious, as he set down his knife. Celesse at least had the decency to give a soft sigh.

"And what was that?" asked Malden.

She had to be delicate. Too strong and they would know it was a lie. Too much information about their plans and they would kill her on the spot to hide their activities.

"He said he was jealous of Miss D'Agastine, whatever that meant," she said.

Bannon's forehead squeezed as if he couldn't quite fit that thought inside his thick head. Malden's shield shifted backwards, unreadable.

Celesse was behind her, so Aurie didn't get to see her face, but the sideways glance from Bannon told Aurie that she'd hit the mark.

"Anything else?" asked Malden. "No other names?"

"No. Nothing," she said.

"If you think of something at a later date, it might help us make our judgment against you," he said.

"I'll try hard to remember, but it might help if I knew what you were looking for," she said.

"You'd know it if you heard it," he said. "And now I must take my leave."

Malden stood, followed by the other two.

"What about the trial by magic? What's my task?" she asked.

"I suppose we should give you one." He sighed. "By the next trials, show us command of your true name."

She'd known it was going to be hard, but this was impossible. But there was no point in arguing.

"How do I know you'll rule in my favor if I can do it?" she said.

He moved behind the shield. A sparkling gold scroll formed in the air. Aurie recognized the magical contract. She read it quickly, checking for hidden clauses, but the whole thing was simple enough that she felt confident in accepting it.

"Search that memory until next time. Another name might go a long way."

The three patrons left the chamber. Aurie slumped onto the bench. She would have to learn to use her true name. They didn't even teach true names until fifth year.

As bad as the task was, the whole thing hadn't been a total waste. She'd learned something about the Cabal. Things weren't as lovey-dovey as it seemed between their Halls. There were cracks to be exploited. If only she knew how. A matter to bring up with Pi.

But her sister was too focused on bringing Ashley back from whatever soulless stasis state she was in. It was probably why she locked herself in her room every night. She was working on a plan to save Ashley. And even if they managed to do that, there was still the matter with their uncle Liam and that fae coin that left them both with more questions than answers. Part of her wasn't surprised to learn they had the blood of fae—if that's what the coin meant—but it didn't change anything.

They needed to knock some of the smaller problems out of the way before they could tackle the big stuff. If she wanted Pi's help, they needed to find the soul thief. Even though she didn't think it was Hemistad, Aurie didn't have a better idea, so it was probably time they confronted him. It was the only way she was going to get Pi's help with the Cabal.

FOURTEEN

A pair of teenagers in heavy coats, board games under their arms, pushed past Pi as they went into Freeport Games. A diorama of a battle between orcs and knights against the backdrop of a towering castle was on display. A couple of kids pressed their noses against the window, making Pi reminiscent of the first time she'd seen it, many years ago when she was younger and believed that good and evil came in convenient, easy-to-spot packages.

These days she wasn't sure if there was such a thing as good and evil, or only varying degrees of self-interest, and that worried her most of all.

When her sister finally arrived, Pi said, "Where have you been? I thought we were going to do this an hour ago."

Her sister had bags under her eyes. "I wasn't finished with the charm. I wanted a little extra protection."

Aurie pulled a chubby cloth doll out of her pocket. The stitching was crude, but Pi knew who she was trying to represent.

"A poppet? Are you sure?" asked Pi.

Her sister turned the doll over. A trio of runes detailed the back.

"I found a hair from him in back. The runes are from the urn that I saw when he summoned his Hunger. I don't think it'll have a huge effect, but at least it'll make our magic more effective against him," she said.

"Or piss him off so much that he rips us limb from limb," said Pi. "I'm not sure if I'm more proud of you or worried. A poppet is pretty dark magic for you, sis."

"It's not dark if I don't use it. It's a backup. What did you bring?" asked Aurie.

"My sparkling wit? Maybe I'll cast some fairy magic on him," said Pi.

"You don't know that's what the coin means," said Aurie.

"Of course that's what it means," said Pi. "And the proof is that I made my soul golem yesterday. I thought about putting the coin into the heart, but decided against it, so I shaved a little bit off the edge."

"I don't trust him, Pi," Aurie said.

"He's family. You know he is," she said.

"I'm not denying that. It's this business with the race and vouching for his debt. I wish you would have talked to me first about that," said Aurie.

"You're not my mother," said Pi.

"This isn't about that! We share a bank account."

"And I didn't give him our account number or anything. Do you think I'm that stupid?" said Pi, heat rising to her face.

"No, but if you get into trouble, do you think I wouldn't give you my half?" asked Aurie.

"I'm not asking you to give me your half. I don't want your money. I just want to help our uncle, or don't you care?" she asked.

"I do care, but what has he done since he's been here? He nearly got us in trouble at the police station, dragged you into the undercity for a race in which most of the other participants were killed, and got you to take on his debt to what I assume are some very bad people. Merlin knows what next!"

"I'd do the same for you," said Pi quietly.

"And I'd do it for you too," responded Aurie, holding out her hand. Pi took it and squeezed. "He might be our uncle, but he's practically a stranger. It's not like Mom and Dad had good stories about him. He was a loner who went in search of power. We don't know who has their hooks in him."

It made Pi mad, not because she disagreed with Aurie, but because she was right. Pi knew it hadn't been a good idea to vouch for his debt, but she didn't want to lose him, even if he was a bit of a mess.

She sighed.

Pi hated when it was like this between her and Aurie, because it turned them into mother-daughter rather than sisters. She didn't want to do that to Aurie—not only because it wasn't fair that she'd had to take care of her, but because it always reminded them that their parents were dead.

"Do you remember that time that Mom screamed at us for breaking that antique lamp she'd brought out of Tehran?" asked Pi.

"Yeah, wow. I literally thought she was going to put a curse on us. She had blotches on her face from screaming. I mean, we did break the lamp, and we knew she was under stress about work, but that was...wow. Everything was weird for a while after..." Aurie went quiet, eyes dark with thought until they gained a mischievous gleam. "So you're saying I'm right? Just like you broke the lamp."

"I'm not saying you're right," said Pi. "And I definitely didn't break the lamp. You pushed me into it."

"You were the last one to touch it." A smile touched her lips, then ghosted away. "Fine. But would you tell me what you're working on in your room?"

A stone turned over in Pi's gut. "I will, but not yet. Soon. We should focus on Hemistad."

"Agreed."

They kept their hoods up and went straight into the back, avoiding the knots of players, who were probably too into their games to notice.

Hemistad was unpacking a shipment of collectibles. When they walked in, he pulled a heavy box off the top. The box had to weigh a couple hundred pounds, but he swung it around as if it contained feathers.

He glanced over his shoulder while he used a box cutter to rip open the packages. "You are not working today."

Since the trip into the undercity, he'd been more blunt. An accent surfaced from time to time, something Slavic, ancient.

"We need to talk," said Pi.

He waved the box cutter, but kept facing the other way. "So talk. I am working."

Pi summoned her courage. "We know what you're doing at night."

"I doubt it." He put the blade into the box, dragging it through the cardboard.

Aurie stepped forward. "We've followed you."

His shoulders slumped. Pi wasn't sure if it was a sigh or exasperation.

"And what do you think you saw?" he asked.

"You're stealing people's souls. We don't know for what, but it's got to stop," said Pi.

Hemistad turned around. Though he was only five-foot nothing, he seemed like he was seven feet tall, a glowering rage of teeth and muscle. When Pi blinked, the impression went away.

"Is this what passes for gratitude these days? I give you money, a job, a safe space, and you come to me with this? In my younger days, no one dared question my judgment, not even a flinch, but now, you come to me with accusations," said Hemistad.

Pi balled her hands into fists. "We followed you into Stone Singers. We saw what you did."

"And I saw what you did to that creature in the cage, back in the undercity. Whatever or whoever it was, you murdered it," said Aurie.

With the box cutter in hand, Hemistad marched up to them. Neither sister summoned magic, knowing that once they did, there might be no turning back.

He shook the razorblade in their faces. He opened his mouth to speak, then sniffed. Before Aurie could stop him, he reached into her pocket, lightning quick, and yanked out the poppet.

"I thought better of you," he said, putting the blade into the poppet, spilling its stuffing onto the floor. "This would have done nothing. Shall I show you what I truly am?"

Behind his black eyes, a furnace of shadow burned with the ashes of past deeds. The feeling Pi'd had when the Hunger had attacked them came through his gaze in malevolent waves.

The moment teetered, tipping one way, and back. Each flare of nostrils, each breath threatened to provoke a fight.

"Ashley was my friend," said Pi, daring the silence. "We were initiates in Coterie together. She gave me her heart when everyone else was trying to kill me, putting her at great risk. She had natural blonde hair like spun gold, a sweet southern accent that carried an ocean of wit beneath, and a wickedly good sense of fashion. I miss her."

Hemistad's bushy eyebrows went up, then down. He sniffed once. "You were there when her soul was taken."

"How do you know?" asked Pi.

The raging furnace behind his eyes cooled. He walked back to the boxes. Set the cutter on the edge.

"You have the stink of him on you," he said.

"Him?" asked Aurie.

"The thief of souls," said Hemistad.

"What or who is he?" asked Aurie.

"Nothing of your concern lest you want to end up like your friend," said Hemistad.

"If he's stealing souls, does that mean that I can get Ashley's back?" asked Pi.

"Forget about her. This is, as the kids say, above your pay grade," said Hemistad.

"Nobody says that, and I don't care who's involved. She's my friend."

An air of sympathy passed across his face. For a brief time he seemed like his old self. "I'm sorry, Miss Pythia. I cannot help you, nor allow you to be involved."

"But our patron trusts us with important tasks," said Aurie. "We can help."

His eyes glimmered with amusement. "You are a skillful liar. But it was Semyon that forbade me to involve you."

"Are you going to tell him that we talked to you?" asked Aurie.

"Not this time," he said. "But if you keep following me..."

"Can you tell us anything about the soul thief? Please," said Pi.

Hemistad cinched his arms around the box of collectibles and headed into the front area without another word.

Pi growled at nothing in particular. "Why won't he help us!"

"He did," said Aurie, "though I don't know if he intended to."

"You're right. Semyon. If he's involved, this has to do with that archway. Which means the thief is working for the Cabal," said Pi. "Do you think that means the archway goes into Invictus' quarters?"

"That's the only thing it can be," said Aurie. "But why would they need souls for that?"

"Souls are potent magic," said Pi.

"But not for that kind of magic. It doesn't make sense," said Aurie.

"So you believe Hemistad?" she asked.

Aurie nodded.

"I don't," said Pi. "At least not everything he said. I believe he's not the soul thief, but he's lying about something."

"What next?" asked Aurie.

"We lay a trap," said Pi.

"And how do we do that? I doubt Hemistad is going to let us follow him any longer," said Aurie. "Plus if we do, he'll tell Semyon, then we're really screwed."

"So far the attacks have been on students from different Halls. We can watch the ones the thief hasn't attacked yet," said Pi.

"That's a lot of Halls," said Aurie.

"Eventually it won't be," said Pi.

Aurie had a funny look on her face. "Celesse said they'd be done by the end of the school year. I wonder if that's how long they think it'll take to get a soul from every school."

"Sounds about right," said Pi. "I wish I knew what this soul thief was. A mage from the Cabal? A supernatural creature? Nothing I've found in the library even comes close."

Aurie had a smug smile.

"You have a source I don't know about? I mean, I've already checked the Biblioscribe," said Pi.

"You didn't check it the way I'm going to check it," said Aurie.

"Did you hack it or something?" A sheen of pride formed on Aurie's brow. "Wait. You *did* hack it?"

"Last year, I realized the Biblioscribe had additional levels of security when I asked it about that book in Semyon's office, *Impossible Magics*. I mean, do you really think that Semyon wouldn't keep everything in there? He's more organized than I am. So I asked about the other books in his shelves, nothing came up. After a few months of work, I was able to break into it. The Biblioscribe doesn't just know the books in Arcanium, but also every other book in the city of Invictus, and every book owned by alumni of the Halls. It's like the ultimate card catalog for magic."

"Is there a book about this soul thief?" asked Pi.

"I don't know yet, but probably. Knowing it's not Hemistad helps me narrow it down. I'll try again when I get another chance. I can't check when there are other students around."

"Until then, I'll work on the map. Maybe there's a pattern to the attacks we can exploit," said Pi.

Aurie grew sullen. "You know there's one place we know he hasn't attacked yet."

"I thought of that," said Pi. "Should we warn the others?"

"It'll get back to Semyon. We can't risk it. If we do anything, it'll have to be covertly."

"They don't have to know why. I think we can make it clear that something is killing students, one hall at a time. It'll make it harder on the soul thief. Give the students from every Hall a chance," said Pi.

"How do we do that? It's not like we can just put an article in the *Herald of the Halls*," said Aurie.

Pi winked. "Why not?"

FIFTEEN

The halls of Arcanium buzzed with tension. A snowstorm had buried the city right after news about the Hundred Halls Killer had been the top story in the *Herald of the Halls*.

Aurie marveled at her sister's ingenious plan of planting the story. During a late-night BS session in the Franklin lounge, a frequent haunt of the third years, Pi had brought up the theory about the killer taking one person from each Hall, knowing that Violet and her gaggle of friends were sitting on the other side of the partition.

So it was no surprise when the story hit the papers a few days later. Violet's propensity to steal from the Silverthorne sisters had turned into a useful conduit for getting information out. The only downside had been the reeking cloud of smugness that hung on Violet like skunk spray, and the constant self-congratulatory comments that she would be on the short list for the Pulitzer because of the story.

Aurie was headed into the initiate wing when a voice boomed out of the darkness, "Who goes there?"

"It's me, Aurie."

Deshawn stepped out of the side passage, followed by Isabella, a petite second year.

"You shouldn't be alone," said Deshawn. "The HHK could strike anywhere. A kid from Animalians got husked right outside of his classroom yesterday. He'd been on his way to the bathroom."

"Animalians? Crap," said Aurie.

"What's wrong? You know this poor kid?" asked Isabella, trilling her R's gloriously.

Aurie couldn't say that she'd been watching Animalians for the past week and had set up an ambush in the location she was sure the soul thief would use. But she'd had a lexology test this morning, and had been studying all day yesterday.

"No, but it's a shame," she said. "How many schools left?"

"Thirty-eight," said Deshawn. "Including Arcanium. What are you doing down here?"

"I need to see Professor Mali."

Deshawn raised an eyebrow. "You in trouble or something?"

"No," she said. "Trial stuff."

"Oh," said Deshawn.

Both of them averted their gazes. Everyone in Arcanium knew the details of her trial by magic. Whenever it was brought up, it reminded her fellow students that she was a dead mage walking.

"I'd better get down there," said Aurie.

"Good luck," said Isabella, though it didn't sound like the second year had much confidence.

Professor Mali's door was open. She was in the middle of casting a spell on a chunk of obsidian on her desk. Sparks flew off the edges of the glassy black stone, eliciting a sigh of disappointment from the professor.

"Come in, Aurelia."

"Problems?" asked Aurie, nodding towards the chunk.

"Obsidian has been disappearing faster than cotton candy at a kid's party around here. I thought there might be an extra-planar reason, but my spells have uncovered nothing," said the professor. "What can I do for you?"

"Do you know when Patron Gray will be back?" she asked.

"I'm sorry, Aurelia, I do not. He's been rather busy lately. Can I help you?"

"It's about the trial," she said.

Professor Mali leaned back in her wheelchair. "Yes, of course. Your true name. How is that coming?"

"It's not. That's the problem. He promised to teach me, but how can he do that if he's never here? It's already January and I don't know anything about my true name. I've tried researching it, but none of it makes sense to me. It doesn't read like a spell, but that crappy self-improvement mumbo-jumbo that you hear on late-night TV," said Aurie.

"I don't know what to say. I don't know when he'll be back," she said.

"You know how to use your true name. Can you teach me?" asked Aurie.

"I'm afraid that's something that Semyon has traditionally taught. While I know how to use my own, I'm not sure how I can help you discover yours. It's a process that takes years," said the professor.

"I don't have years. I have months. Is there anything you can suggest?" asked Aurie.

"I've heard you and your sister know the head of Coterie's real name," said Professor Mali.

"Malden Anterist," said Aurie.

"Yes, that's the one. Do you know why he hides it?" she asked.

"Because names have power? He's trying to keep people from putting spells on him, so he obfuscates his persona," said Aurie.

"But why does Malden do it, but no one else? Shouldn't every patron do the same?" asked the professor.

"I never thought of it like that," said Aurie.

"A child, afraid of the dark, will race through the woods at night, tripping over a tree root in his haste to avoid dangers that don't exist, and in doing so, bust his nose. In a way, a self-fulfilling prophecy."

"So the head of Coterie has given people power over him by worrying about his name," said Aurie.

"In a way. Paranoia is a terrible disease brought about by the shadows cast from the light of one's own soul," said the professor.

"But how does that help me with my true name?" asked Aurie.

"You have to figure that out yourself. What light does your soul cast upon the world?"

"Which name do I even use? Should it be Aurelia, or Aurie?"

The professor smiled in that way adults did when the question was not the one that should have been asked.

"That's up to you," said Professor Mali. "I'm sorry, Aurelia. I know this is frustrating. But there's no spell book that can help you. Everyone achieves their true name through a path of their own divining. The only thing that Semyon can do is to give you a push down that path, but you have to walk it yourself."

SIXTEEN

A helicopter traveled over the buildings, search lights waving. Pi stayed in the shadows of the doorway until the sound of the helicopter was only a faint wah-wah noise. The police were probably searching for the demon that had been spotted in the fifth ward three nights running.

The guy at the coffee shop down the street had claimed he'd seen the demon in the alleyway eating trash the night before. He said it was tall, covered with bumpy gray skin, and had a frog's mouth, and that it ate a rusty lunchbox like a potato chip, belching when it was finished. Pi wasn't so sure it was a demon, but something nasty from the undercity that had come up looking for trouble. But that wasn't why she was in the ward.

She'd been watching the Esoteric Hall, one of the twenty-five remaining schools that hadn't been hit by the soul thief. She'd picked this one to watch because it was small enough that she could nearly watch all entrances. It was also only a half-mile from Arcanium.

With the Protectors' helicopter gone, she made the rounds. Technically, she was supposed to watch for Aurie—who was late—but she didn't think anything would happen in the short time before her sister would arrive. Esoteric Hall was an old Catholic church with colorful stained-glass windows displaying the procession of the cross. There were only a half-dozen members in the Hall, which had to make their existence pretty nerve-wracking, knowing that there was a high chance that the soul thief would target them.

The likeliest entry point into the Hall was a side entrance off an old rectory attached to the church. The other ways in were more visible to the street.

Pi slipped a pair of goggles from her carryall that allowed her to see magical fields. They were the same ones she'd used when she'd broken into Radoslav's delivery box. A field of glowing white lines appeared as the brass goggles settled over her face.

The spell work had been delicate. She didn't want it tripping on a student, or a stray cat, so she'd coded it to trigger when faez was used. Because she couldn't guarantee a student wouldn't use magic in the alleyway behind the Hall, the trap had to be nonlethal, so she'd used a modified book binding glue. Once activated, it would bond whatever was standing on it to the street. Pi had spread the white paste across the entrance area. It looked like moon glow catching wet pavement.

She pulled the goggles off her face and let them dangle around her neck. Waiting was boring. Her calves hurt from standing on the hard street, but she was afraid if she sat down she might fall asleep, so she crouched on her heels and rubbed them, trying not to think about a warm bubble bath.

A cat screech from the block over put her on high alert. She was about to fade back into the shadows when she caught the scent of wet garbage. A shape, tall and lean, hurried past the street near the front of the Hall.

"Dammit."

Pi sprinted down the alleyway, keeping magic at her fingertips. She hadn't forgotten how she'd been duped when Ashley was taken.

The front of the Hall was empty. Pi glanced back down the alleyway to make sure nothing had snuck behind her.

Something was wrong. The hair on the back of her neck was standing at full attention. Pi spun in a circle, examining every ledge and cranny for signs of the intruder.

When she didn't see anything extraordinary, Pi slipped the goggles over her eyes. Faint blotches of leftover faez in little pools ran up the concrete steps and right to the front of the building. There was no guarantee it was the thief. Any of the students could have put a spell on their boots for warmth, or speed, or maybe to ward against foot fungus.

Something put its claws into her leg. Pi let out a scream and ripped the goggles from her face, hitting herself in the eye in the process.

A black cat sat on its haunches watching her. "Mrroew."

"Are you trying to kill me?" she asked the cat.

The answer could have been a "maybe," so Pi slipped the goggles back on to confirm that the cat wasn't a transmogrified student, or other such creature.

"Go away," she said once she knew it was a regular cat, gently shooing the feline.

When it stared back, unmoving, Pi conjured up a puff of air that startled the cat into ambling away.

"I'm missing something," Pi said, looking around the building.

The thump-thump of an approaching sports car with the stereo turned up made her pause until it turned up a side street, fading into the background noise.

She strolled around to the narrow alleyway on the west side, which was flanked by a closed deli. As soon as she stepped into the shadows, Pi flicked her gaze backwards to catch a shape flying at her from above.

A talon narrowly missed slicing her throat open as she threw herself to the ground. Landing on her side knocked the air out of her lungs, disrupting the spell she had prepared. Instead of a vicious ball of lightning, a spray of sparks came out of her fingertips like a Fourth of July fountain.

The shape in the shadows swung a long arm, striking the pavement by her head. She awkwardly fumbled for the explosive seeds in her jacket, but realizing she would be too slow, rolled out of the way of another blow.

Two rolls later, she had her lungs back and sent the ball of lightning seething down the alleyway. The creature dodged, and the crackling energy climbed across its form and the brick wall. Deciding she was too formidable, it fled towards the back of the Hall.

Dizzy and still trying to recover from the attack, Pi stumbled after it.

The only warning she got as she exited the alleyway was the stench of garbage. The hulking gray-skinned creature stepped into the light, roared, and knocked her backwards ten feet.

This time she didn't get up. She couldn't catch her breath. The frog-mouthed creature stalked towards her, smacking its oversized lips.

Without being able to speak, Pi was limited on the spells she could cast. The gestures for a Five Elements spell came easily to her fingers, but as she readied the bolt, the frog-man spat a wad at her hands. The glob of saliva bound her hands together.

The creature grabbed her by the feet as it shook its head, preparing its glistening maw to engulf her. Pi struggled, but the thing had hold of her legs so tight she couldn't move.

"Get away from my sister," said Aurie, standing in the alley behind the Hall.

Pi choked out a strangled "No," but it was too late. Aurie was standing right on the glue field. Whatever spell she was casting triggered it, and like a giant flytrap, the pavement reached up, encasing her in sticky white paste.

The distraction made the frog-mouthed creature pause, so Pi kicked it in the chest. She fell to the ground, landing on her shoulder.

Adding to the confusion, inside the old church an alarm sounded. The creature froze as it strained to listen. A moment later, Pi heard police sirens and helicopter blades.

For a brief moment, Pi cheered, until she realized the involvement of the police could endanger Aurie's existence at the school. The frog-mouthed creature fled the other way in a loping gait.

Pi tried to pull her hands from the spit glob, but it had them fast. Aurie struggled in the glue cocoon. They had to get away quickly, before the Protectors arrived.

She knew a half-dozen spells that would free her hands, but they all required dexterous fingers. While the verbal-only spells she knew had no relevance to her situation. Unless...

Chopper lights flashed over the buildings, reflecting crazy shadows. She was running out of time.

She knew a spell for cleaning hand towels was close enough to modify with lexology, but it was in German, and she hated conjugating other languages.

"*Dreck und Foul sauber das Hände!*"

The word for hands was *hände*, which was similar to *handtuch*, the word for towel.

When part of the glob fell off, she repeated the spell, using more faez the second time.

"*Dreck und Foul sauber das Hände!*"

With her hands unencumbered, she cast the release spell on the glue pod covering Aurie, which released her onto the street. She was free, but the lights of the helicopter were about to fall upon them.

Aurie shouted at the lights, the scent of faez from her verumancy crisping the air. "Falter!"

The spotlights flickered and went dark. Aurie and Pi sprinted down the alleyway before someone could counter her spell. Once they were about three blocks away, they collapsed, heaving and leaning against a rusty blue dumpster.

"That was too close," said Pi, wiping the residue from the spit glob on her jeans. "And I'm going to need a long bath."

"Nice work on the lexology. I thought we were goners. I'm an idiot for missing your glue trap. I saw you in danger and reacted before I thought about where I was," said Aurie, who was still covered in white paste.

"You look like you fell into a tub of Elmer's glue," said Pi.

"You owe me first shot at the bath," said Aurie. "Aughh...what is that smell?"

Pi sniffed her hands. They reeked of rotten garbage.

Aurie wrinkled her nose. "Never mind. You're first as long as I don't have to smell that anymore."

"I'm glad you showed up when you did," said Pi.

"I found a book," said Aurie.

"That's great, but we've got a whole library of them back in Arcanium."

"No. A book on soul stealing. I hacked Biblioscribe's highest security setting," she said. "Do you want to hear where the book is located?"

Pi knew that look on her sister's face. "Why do I assume that this is not going to be pleasant?"

"Because it never is," she said. "The good thing is that you've been in this place."

Pi's heart sank. "Coterie?"

"No," said Aurie. "Bannon Creed's house."

"You've got to be fucking kidding me."

"Would I kid with you while covered in a suspiciously sticky white substance?"

Pi sighed. "No."

"He can't be that bad, can he?" asked Aurie.

"If we don't get caught, no. If we do...we'll wish we hadn't survived."

SEVENTEEN

It took a week to prepare to break into the head of the Protectors' house. The whole time, Aurie wondered if she'd gone completely mad, but the possibility that they might be able to restore Ashley and the other soul-husked students was reason enough to risk it.

They had a bit of luck when they found out that the Garbage Kings were playing the Glitterdome. They were a heavy metal band made of former Stone Singers and Oestomancers, whose shows were part freak circus and part Goth prom, drawing a heavy crowd of unqualified mages. The Garbage Kings had been banned in seventeen countries and twenty-six states due to earthquakes or other unnatural events that had originated in their stage shows. Last year, they'd summoned a minor demon into the crowd and let the wannabe mages battle it. Supposedly, the demon killed seven people before it was taken down, and another twenty were sent to the hospital for significant wounds or faez madness.

Thus, the impending illicit magic use required a larger than normal security detail from Blackstone Security, Bannon Creed's company. Pi had learned that Bannon always oversaw the security when Garbage Kings came to town because he was a huge fan, giving Aurie and her sister an opportunity at the book.

The Blue Line into the second ward was filled with crazies dressed in costumes on their way to the concert. Aurie nudged Pi, who had turned her hair bright red for the evening.

"What about that one?" she asked.

"The kid with the horns? Gotcha," said Pi.

Pi caught the kid's attention and smiled, drawing him in like a fly to honey. The kid wore skintight black transparent leather that creaked when he walked.

"Those real?" she asked.

"Do you like them?" he asked, rubbing the horns. "I did the spell all by myself."

"That's awesome," said Pi, chewing her gum loudly.

"Can you? You know," he said.

Pi put her hand on his arm. Aurie had to hide her face because she was about to burst out laughing. The kid looked like he was about to start humping her leg. Aurie didn't think he'd considered the repercussions of leather during a moment of excitement. He squirmed and shimmied in place.

"Only a little," she said, making a flame appear on her thumb as if it were a lighter.

"Cool," he said, eyes wide with amazement.

"Did you hear about the challenge?" she asked.

"Challenge?"

"Yeah, the Garbage Kings promised a free bone shifting for anyone that can get a picture of themselves doing magic, like anything you want, in front of some ugly-ass building made of glass and steel in the second ward," she said.

"Really? That would be amazing. I'd let them write their names in my bones if they wanted."

"Yeah, totally," she said, smacking the gum louder while pulling out her phone. "Anyway, gotta make a call."

Delirious with ideas, the kid wandered away. They moved to another car and repeated the story. Aurie split off from her sister, picking the less wildly dressed to entertain. They had to ride the same section of track for an hour before they started hearing the story repeated back to them.

With the story successfully planted, they got off the train and circled around to Bannon Creed's house from the opposite direction so they didn't run into anyone who was attempting to get their picture taken. After an hour of watching the security guards in sunglasses and earpieces constantly run off to the south side, they prepared a series of enchantments, including one that would blur their faces on camera feeds.

"Did you get the item from Radoslav?" asked Aurie.

Pi held up a coil of wire.

"That's it?"

Pi shrugged. "He said it would work."

"I probably don't want to know what that cost," said Aurie.

"Nothing, as long as I bring it back."

They sprinted across the lawn to the back of the house. The structure was a glass and steel monstrosity that looked like a glass cage dropped from a great height.

Pi placed the wire against the window in the shape of a circle big enough to step through. When she connected the ends, the glass at the center disappeared. She stepped through, and Aurie followed. Pi yanked on the wire, snapping it into a coil, and the glass resumed its existence.

Two girls in fishnet stockings and body paint lay unconscious on the couches. Dark vials and syringes clustered on the glass table. The nearest girl had a delirious grin on her lips while a glowing tattoo of a snake crawled across her naked chest.

"Where's the book?" asked Pi.

"Give me a moment," said Aurie, pulling out a piece of enchanted vellum. She torched it with a spark of faez, rubbed the ashes on her palms, and blew through them, whispering the name of the book: *Blood, Souls, and Magic.*

A pathway opened in her mind, telling her where the book was located. "Second floor."

Before they could move, a guy in Speedos, wearing a katana on his back, wandered into the room. Pi was about to blast him with magic, when Aurie held her back.

"Look at his eyes," she mouthed.

His irises turned from bright red to the hazy green slits of a cat, before changing to inky black. His jaw hung open. A band of rubber was tied around his upper arm above a line of red blotches.

They stepped past him and moved up the stairs. The moment they stepped onto the second floor, Aurie's wards lit up. A shimmer in the air was the only warning. She stunned the invisible creature before it could attack.

"What the hell was that?" asked Pi.

"Guardian demon," said Aurie. "We better hurry before it wakes up. In here."

They locked the door behind them. The center room had more drug paraphernalia scattered across the tables, including those dark vials she'd seen in the lower floor. Violet liquid bubbled through a series of tubes in a gas titration alchemy lab. It appeared they were distilling a drug from the substance in the vials.

A naked girl was chained to the wall. She had her eyes closed, but was swaying. She was emaciated. Her ribs were showing, and her knees were bony balls that looked ready to snap. Aurie went to investigate the girl while Pi moved to the bookshelf.

"Found the book," said Pi.

At that moment, something heavy hit the metal door, putting a dent into it.

"I guess someone's awake," said Pi.

"Check the book for traps. I'm going to check on this girl."

Pi shook her head. "Not a good idea. We're here for the book. She'll only slow us down, plus I think she's part succubus. Probably harvesting her for tears."

Aurie checked her back: she had wing nubs, but she was mostly human.

"I can't leave her, Pi. She's being held captive."

The demon hit the door again. A couple more and the door would be down. They shared a look, but neither was worried.

"Of course you can't, but you should."

"Just grab the book. Security has to know we're here by now," said Aurie.

Pi cast a few spells on the bookshelves before reaching out. As soon as her fingertips brushed the spine, a white mist exploded into existence around them, filling the air.

As Aurie moved her mouth to speak, she found her lips responding sluggishly. Lifting her arm was like moving it through molasses. The same fearful realization was on Pi's face.

The words finally came out of her mouth a few seconds after she'd intended to say them. "We're slowed..."

"And screwed..."

Pi indicated the helicopter landing on the verdant lawn. The granite fist of Blackstone Security on the side of the helicopter dropped her stomach off a cliff. Bannon Creed.

The demon slammed into the door, breaking the top hinges. It started pushing through the opening.

Aurie pulled a container of salt from her pocket and started kneeling down to make a circle. The weight of each second drew out. Pi slow-walked towards her while casting a spell. Upon resolution, the door tried to repair itself, but her elongated speaking had sapped its effectiveness.

The danger of the slow trap was revealed. Not only could they not move quick enough to escape, but their languishing actions affected their spells, rendering them ineffective.

The door repair spell gave the sisters enough time to get the salt circle around them before the demon barged into the room. It hit the barrier hard, but the sisters were talented enough that it didn't do more than displace a few grains of salt.

"It's not slow..." said Pi.

The helicopter was landing on the south lawn. Sunglass-wearing security guards ran towards the helicopter.

"We have to get out..." said Pi.

The fear in her sister's eyes was shocking. It made their danger more real. But how were they going to get out when they were slowed, could barely use magic, and had an invisible demon trying to kill them that wasn't affected by the slow field?

She had an idea, but needed to be able to speak faster. Aurie put her hands on her throat and used mental verumancy.

"Am I still slow?" she asked herself at normal speed, answering her question in the process.

Aurie touched Pi's throat and repeated the verumancy.

"Oh, thank Merlin, it was driving me nuts not being able to talk. Can we do that with our legs?" asked Pi.

"Let's find out," said Aurie.

She tried to give her limbs speed to counteract the slow field, but quickly came to the conclusion that it wasn't working.

"The field must work on surfaces, or create friction in the air or something," said Aurie. "We can probably use it to speak because that's internal."

"Can we stop analyzing the spell and start escaping?" said Pi, eyes wide. "I really, really don't want to be here when Bannon Creed arrives. I'm serious when I say we don't want to be caught alive."

At that moment, Bannon Creed stepped out of his helicopter, all seven feet of him, in a black tracksuit. His height made children out of his guards. He strode across the lawn towards the house.

"Aurie," said Pi, eyes searching around. "What are we going to do?"

"We're going to let the demon in the circle," said Aurie.

"What? Have you lost your mind?"

"Look at the way it moves around. It's not affected by the field," said Aurie.

Pi couldn't move her head, but her eyes followed the rapid shifting of the shimmers. The demon circled their warding spell, waiting for them to escape.

"Got it," said Pi.

"I'll kick the salt when it's on the side we're facing. Then when the barrier is down, we hit it with a stun spell. Both of us at the same time should do it. Pour everything you've got into it. If we miss, or it's not strong enough..."

"You don't have to tell me," said Pi.

The sisters got into position around the time Bannon was entering the house.

Aurie kicked the salt. The barrier fell away, and as the demon leapt, they hit it with double stuns. She reached down, and as soon as she touched it, she could move at normal speed again.

"We can't drag this thing with us," said Pi, holding her hand on the invisible demon. "Besides, it feels like it has scabs all over its body. I'm really glad we can't see it."

Aurie was feeling around the demon, trying not to think about scabs. "There's got to be something keeping the field at bay. Help me find it."

Somewhere beneath them, the baritone voice of Bannon Creed was speaking to his security guards. Even through the floor, she could tell how angry he was.

Her fingers hooked onto a bracelet on the demon's wrist. There were two of them. Aurie pulled the first off, and as soon as it was away from the demon's wrist, a runed brass bracelet appeared. She slipped one on her wrist and gave the other to Pi.

She tested it by pulling her hand off the demon. Having only one bracelet left her slightly sluggish, but not enough to keep her from using spells.

"Let's get out of here," said Pi, stepping towards the door, but pausing when she heard boots pounding up the stairs. Pi made a series of finger gestures, and the door flew into place the moment before the security guards reached it.

The guards brought spells against the barrier. Pi reinforced the enchantment, layering them so the guards would have to destroy each one.

"I'm getting the girl," said Aurie.

She broke the manacles with a spell, picked the girl up, and thanks to the enchantments she'd cast on herself before breaking into Creed's house, threw the succubus-girl over her shoulder. Her lightness surprised Aurie.

"We can't go back down the way we came," said Aurie.

"Let me handle that," said Pi, pulling out the coil of wire.

Pi made a circle with the wire on one of the second-floor windows. As soon as the ends connected, the window disappeared.

"You first," said Pi.

Aurie stuck her head out the hole. A nice soft piece of grass lay beneath them with no guards in sight. She stepped through the hole. The landing jarred her knees. Pi landed next to her the moment something inside the building exploded, rattling the glass.

"Was that you?" asked Aurie.

Pi winked. "We needed a distraction."

The inside of the building was filled with gray smoke. Somewhere deep inside, Bannon Creed was shouting, demanding his guards find the intruders.

The sisters sprinted across the lawn towards the nearby street. A group of kids wearing Garbage Kings T-shirts were watching the chaos.

Remembering she had a naked girl on her shoulder, Aurie stopped at the teenagers. "You buy those at the concert?"

"Nah, man," said a girl with dozens of piercings. "No tix. Got 'em from a vendor."

"I'll give you two hundred bucks for that T-shirt you're wearing," said Aurie.

The girl glanced at the chaos erupting in the Bannon Creed estate. Flashes and booms echoed from the building.

"Nah, man," she said, pulling it off in one quick movement. "You can have it for free. That's one serious show."

Once they were a few blocks away, they put the T-shirt on the unconscious girl. Pi found a section of cloth in her jacket, and they pinned it around the girl's waist like a skirt.

Aurie didn't completely relax until they made the train station. The concert was still in progress, so it wasn't as crowded as earlier. They sat in the back, with the succubus-girl propped up between them.

"Radoslav going to be mad about you leaving the wire?" asked Aurie.

"Don't worry about it," said Pi. "Anything's better than getting caught. I'll deal with Radoslav."

"The wire won't give us away?" asked Aurie.

"No," said Pi. "Bannon will know it came from Radoslav, but he'd never betray us. Otherwise, he'd have been out of business a long time ago. What are you going to do with her?"

The girl stirred, but otherwise stayed unconscious. "Not sure, yet. I just knew we couldn't leave her."

Pi pulled the book they'd stolen from Bannon out.

"Should we really do that here?" asked Aurie.

"I want to know if it was worth it."

Aurie nodded. She understood her sister's concern. She kept watch while Pi paged through the book, making disgusted noises along the way.

Pi jabbed her finger into the book. "Found it. There were a few other things that can take souls, but this one sounds like our soul thief. It's an elderking, an ancient being that was known for stealing children to eat their souls. There are some allusions to the Pied Piper, as if the elderking's reapings were turned into the tale of the Piper."

"But why one from every Hall? If it eats souls, why would it only take one? Why not eat as many as it can?" asked Aurie.

"I don't know, but there are spells in here that require souls. Pretty sick stuff if you ask me, so maybe that thing isn't eating them, but taking them for magic," said Pi.

"Those vials! That's probably what was in them. Creed's using them for drugs? That doesn't make sense either. I wish I would have grabbed one," said Aurie.

Pi produced a dark vial from a pocket. She stared at it apprehensively. "I grabbed one thinking it might be an expensive reagent."

"Oh Pi," said Aurie, when she realized why her sister was staring at the vial so strangely. "We don't know that it's Ashley in there."

"We don't know it isn't either," said Pi. "I swear if it is, I'm going to burn that fucker's house to the ground with him in it. Leave him nothing but ash and bone."

"Does the book tell us how to catch the thief?" asked Aurie.

"No, but if Bannon has the souls, then that means he knows him," said Pi. "Definitely means the soul thief is working for the Cabal."

"Maybe if we watch his house we'll find out who it is," said Aurie, "though I feel like I'm missing something."

"I saw him," said a voice, startling both of them.

The succubus-girl was awake, eyes clear, cheeks sunken. She sat up, hugging her arms around her chest.

"You saw the soul thief?" asked Aurie.

The girl nodded. "He comes there all the time. Normally I never see him, but once *he* left the door open a little and I saw them. They were yelling at each other about something." Her forehead knotted with thought. "But I couldn't hear it."

"What does he look like? Tall or short? What color hair?" asked Pi.

"Short. He looked like an old man, but both more older than he looked, and not at all. As if he were ancient, but as hearty as a young man," said the girl.

"Hemistad," said the sisters at the same time.

"Yes. That was the name."

"Oh no," said Aurie.

"What are you going to do with me?" asked the succubus-girl nervously.

"Nothing," said Aurie. "Do you have a place to go?"

"Out of the city, somewhere. But don't worry, I'll be fine. I can take care of myself, now that I'm free of him," she said.

The train was rumbling towards a stop, brakes screeching.

"I'm Vale," she said as she hugged Aurie.

She pulled a wad of cash out and shoved it in the girl's hand. "Take this, and good luck."

Vale stepped to Pi and gave her a long kiss. The succubus-girl tickled her fingers along the shaved side of Pi's hair. When she pulled away, Pi rocked on her feet with a grin on her lips.

They waved at Vale as she disappeared into the crowd.

"What now?" asked Pi as the doors whooshed closed.

"We stop Hemistad."

EIGHTEEN

Pi paced across the common area between their rooms, rubbing the fae coin between her forefinger and thumb. The side with the cross caught her fingernail in a pleasing way, keeping her from interrupting Aurie while she read aloud from a book about fairy monsters.

"...the Erlking or Elderking looks like a bearded giant or goblin-elf, depending on its mood. It was once a fae lord that made a deal with a demon in exchange for power, only to find out the contract was flawed, forcing it to feast on the souls of children for all eternity."

She slammed the book closed. "That sounds like Hemistad."

Pi squeezed the coin in her fist. "Not like it matters. He hasn't been seen at Freeport Games in the last week. It's like he knew we'd figured out that he was a liar."

"I don't think so," said Aurie thoughtfully. "Bannon Creed doesn't know we stole the book, so Hemistad can't know that we've figured it out. And I've been thinking about that night in the undercity, when I made the runed cage. That might have been the demon lord he'd made a pact with. Maybe the Cabal have offered him a chance to break his curse in exchange for the souls."

"It seems like a waste to stir up this much trouble so Bannon Creed can get his rocks off on soul-infused drugs," said Pi.

"I'm glad it wasn't Ashley's soul in that vial," said Aurie cautiously.

It'd taken some work to figure those things out, but they'd worked together to do it.

"It means there's a vial somewhere with her soul in it. If we can find it, we can restore her." Pi paused, concerned about how her sister might react to what she had to say next. "You know there's a spell in *Blood, Souls, and Magic* that should be able to heal Annabelle. We have enough soul left in that vial."

"Pythia," said her sister, her voice dripping with disappointment. "We can't do that. What if we can find the rest of that soul and restore that student? I can't make that choice."

"It'd go a long way towards redeeming your name in the *Herald of the Halls*," said Pi. "In a head-to-head poll with a zombie Nixon, I think you'd lose."

"The only thing that matters is learning how to use my true name, which I know nothing about," said Aurie, staring into her hands as if they might hold answers.

Pi hated seeing her sister like this. The trial by magic was rapidly approaching. Semyon was supposed to help, but like Hemistad, no one had seen him.

She could see how the impending doom was sapping her sister's energy. Often when they were studying together, she'd catch Aurie staring off into space. She knew what Aurie was thinking: why should I bother studying when they're going to take my magic?

"We could leave the Halls," Pi blurted out, startling her sister.

"What?"

"Vamoose. Adios. Get the hell out of here. Why stay and have your magic taken?" asked Pi.

"Semyon will come back," said Aurie. "He'll come back and show me how to use my true name."

"I want to believe it as much as you do, but he doesn't care about you, Aurie. You told me what he said at the trial, *this girl included.* We're pawns in this game—why should we play by their rules anymore? There are other ways. We can find a patron like Uncle Liam did. Maybe we could ask him if we could meet the dragon he's pledged to."

"Mom and Dad would kill us if they heard you say that. I know you remember their lectures about how the Hundred Halls are the only responsible path for a proper mage. If we didn't have the Halls, the world would end in chaos," said Aurie, pain wracking her expression.

"Mom and Dad are dead," said Pi. "If you let them take your magic, you'll be as good as dead too. It would break you. Then I'll have no one left."

"You'd have Uncle Liam," said Aurie. "I'd bet you'd prefer him anyway."

"That's not fair, Aurie. You're my sister. I'd do anything for you. I just want some stories from him, that's all," said Pi.

Aurie's lips curled in anger. "Stories? That's all? You nearly got killed in his stupid race and then vouched for his debt with notorious gangsters. Don't bullshit me, Pi. That's more than just wanting to hear a few stories."

"Stop pushing me away! You're just doing this because you're giving up," said Pi.

Aurie stood up. "I'm not giving up. I'm doing everything I can to survive, but I can't do it your way. I can't circumvent the system to get what I want. If we do that, none of it matters. Even the patrons of the Cabal follow the rules when it comes to the school. I knew what I was doing when I asked for the trial by magic. I'm not giving up. I'm still fighting, even if it means I go down swinging."

Pi wanted to believe in her sister's earnestness, that everything would be okay. She wanted to believe in hope, wanted to believe the good side would win, but her illusions had been shattered the day their parents had died. Looking at her sister was like looking at a dead person who didn't know they were dead.

Before she could say anything, a low growl came from her room, followed by a stack of books collapsing.

"What was that?" asked Aurie, moving towards the door.

"No, don't go in," said Pi, rushing to stop her sister. She'd forgotten to lock it when she grabbed the book they were reading.

Aurie pushed her way in before Pi could stop her. Pi didn't want to have to explain to her sister how she'd been lying to her this whole time about Inari right on the heels of their fight.

"I can explain," said Pi.

Aurie spun around, a confused look on her face. "Explain about what? Harboring a ghost or something?"

Pi slipped past Aurie. The room was empty. The stack of books had definitely fallen, but there was no sign of Inari. The kitsune had been here ten minutes before.

"Shit."

The window was closed. They'd been in the common area, so there was no way she could have gotten past.

"What's wrong, Pi? You look like you forgot an important step to a dangerous spell," said Aurie.

"Something like that," said Pi.

The closet door was open. She swore she'd closed it earlier. Pi stuck her head in and slid the clothes to the other side, expecting to find a hidden portal, but the only thing she found was a cedar wall. She was about to give up when her boot kicked a pile of pebbles.

Closer inspection revealed they were obsidian. There was a pile of the glassy black stone shoved into the back of the closet.

Aurie stuck her head in. "Is this what you're hiding? That you're the one stealing all the obsidian?"

"It's not me," said Pi, frustrated.

"Sure looks like it."

Pi raced out of the room with Aurie on her heels. She stopped and listened for Inari. She couldn't have gone far, right?

"What's going on, Pi? You're acting really strange," said Aurie.

Pi ignored her sister. She knew the obsidian was the key to Inari's escape, even if she didn't know how. After retrieving a piece from the bottom of the closet, Pi cast a finding spell on it to locate the pieces that it'd been connected to. The spell was originally intended for finding lost pages from old books, but a bit of lexology made it work for her.

The spell tugged in two directions: one back in her room, the other deeper into Arcanium. Pi took off with Aurie right behind.

A howl sent a chill through Pi's gut. She knew exactly where it'd come from: the main library. She leapt down flights of stairs in her haste. She knew she'd pay the price later.

The lights in the library were out. The Biblioscribe was strangely blank-faced.

"What is going on?" asked Aurie in a forced whisper.

Growling echoed from deeper in the shelves. Pi couldn't figure out what the kitsune was doing until a familiar wave of vertigo staggered her.

"The soul thief," said Pi. "Stay together."

It was here in Arcanium, stalking someone in the shelves, which meant that Inari had either come to help or fight it.

Together the sisters moved through the stacks. Something dashed through the shadows at the far end. They ran after it.

Inari yipped from somewhere behind her. A wave of vertigo hit her again, leaving her incapable of moving. More shouts and barks came from different directions. By the time she looked up, Aurie had moved further into the library.

Another scream, followed by a shout, had Pi running while yelling, "Aurie! Aurie!"

Crossing a main path, Pi was tackled onto the ground. Pi almost unleashed her magic until she recognized her attacker.

"Deshawn, get off me. The soul thief is in here," she said.

"I know," he said, looking remarkably flushed. "I heard something, and when I turned, a shape moved out of the darkness. I felt everything going dim until a huge dog tackled the shadow."

"It's a giant fox," she said.

"How do you know?"

"I saw it."

A moment later, Violet burst out of the shadows. Pi almost blasted her with magic. The blonde girl looked like she'd seen a ghost. Her hair was messed up and her silk shirt disheveled.

"What's going on?"

"The soul thief is here."

Violet glanced over her shoulder.

"What do we do if we find it?" she asked.

"It doesn't matter," she said. "We need to find Aurie."

To Pi's surprise, Violet joined them in the search for her sister. They ran up and down the shelves whisper-shouting Aurie's name. Pi feared the worst. The library was deathly quiet. No more bouts of vertigo intruded.

"Aurie!" she shouted, wanting the reassurance of her sister's voice.

When no answer came, Deshawn sent up a halo of expanding light. A dark-haired girl lay fallen at the end of the row.

A tortured "No" slipped out of her lips. It was Aurie. She'd been soul-taken. Pi's face went numb with the thought of losing her sister.

Pi knelt by her sister's side. When her fingers touched warm flesh, rather than the cold stone of a body without a soul, she was relieved.

Aurie groaned and rolled on her back. She had a bruise forming on her temple.

"What happened?" asked Aurie groggily.

"I was going to ask you that."

"It was the soul thief," said Aurie.

Pi touched Deshawn on the shoulder. "Get Professor Mali. The Hall needs to be alerted. I'll take my sister back to our room so she can rest."

"I'll go with him," said Violet, lips tight with concern.

Deshawn ran off after the professor. Pi lifted her sister up, and together they made their way back to their room.

"I thought you were a goner," said Pi.

"I thought I was too," she responded. "I thought the soul thief was ahead of me. I was going to knock him through the wall with a force spell, then the world shifted and turned, and I didn't know which way was which."

"He gets in your mind somehow. That's what happened with Ashley and me. I bet she walked right to him. He split us up by getting me to stop."

Aurie made a noise. "I thought you were with me the whole time. It wasn't until I turned and saw him coming at me, did I realize that you weren't there."

"So you saw him?"

"Yeah," said Aurie. "Hemistad for sure. The light fell on him just right. It couldn't be anyone else."

"How'd you get away?"

"I didn't. It was like I'd accepted my fate. I was ready to lose my soul when something large and four-legged leapt over me, knocking me in the noggin on the way over. Is that what the growling was in your room?"

"It is," she replied. "It's a long story, but I have a kitsune named Inari bonded to me, though if she escaped the room, I don't know where she is."

Pi helped her sister to the couch in their common area. She was going to grab a bottle of water from her mini-fridge when she noticed that Inari was lying on the bed, head on her paws, looking directly at them.

"That's Inari?" asked Aurie.

The kitsune whined in a way that could be interpreted as an affirmative.

"You can teleport, can't you?" said Pi.

Inari whined again.

"I'm guessing you need the obsidian. That's where it's been going. You're teleporting around the house, stealing it."

The kitsune hid her face with her paws apologetically. It was adorable.

"I'm not mad, Inari, just trying to understand," said Pi. "Whatever reasons you stole it, you saved my sister. Thank you."

Inari gave an affirmative bark.

"I think you've got a lot of explaining to do," said Aurie.

"I will, sis. After we get you patched up, and explain things to Professor Mali. I'm sure she's going to want to know what happened."

Aurie raised an eyebrow in Inari's direction. "You gonna tell her everything?"

"Only what she needs to know. That we stopped the soul thief," said Pi.

"What about that it was Hemistad?" asked Aurie.

"Not now," she said. "Not while everyone else is around. They know we work for him. We don't want to give them the wrong idea. We'll explain later when we have time."

"I guess," said Aurie reluctantly.

Pi shut the door on the giant fox and replaced the wards and locks she'd forgotten the last time. Before the locks had been to keep Inari in, as much to keep everyone else out. But knowing that the kitsune could teleport changed everything.

She was wondering if Liam had been completely honest with her about the reasons he needed the kitsune. Pi had her suspicions that it was related to his debts. As soon as she could track him down, she was going to confront him about his plans. A task she was not looking forward to, since it would only prove everything that Aurie had warned her about Uncle Liam.

NINETEEN

The map room had a heaviness that hadn't existed before. On Tuesdays and Thursdays, Aurie crossed through it on her way to Alchemy of Ink classes, but today she couldn't help but hold her arms against her stomach. The soul thief's attack on Deshawn had reminded her fellow students that they weren't as safe as they thought they were in Arcanium.

Some of the younger students speculated that foiling the attack meant that Arcanium was safe now, but Aurie and most of her fellow third years didn't think that. The only one who seemed to act like nothing was wrong was Violet.

"It feels that way to me, too," said Pi as she walked into the room, nodding towards Aurie's crossed arms. "I've been wondering if it's the map, reflecting the tension of the Hundred Halls, the monster attacks, the general sense of foreboding in the city."

"I've only noticed today," said Aurie.

She hugged her sister to ward away that feeling.

"It's been that way for months," said Pi, wiping away an errant strand of hair. "I've been coming here to find patterns in the attacks."

"Eleven Halls left, including Arcanium," said Aurie. "The *Herald of the Halls* is having a field day with the coverage. I overheard Violet talking about how sales have never been as good. Leave it to the Cardwells to profit on misery."

"I don't know how you don't lay the biggest curse on her. I'd have given her a case of lava crabs by now." Pi hovered her hand over the map of Invictus on the wall. "Have you figured out a pattern? Is that why you asked me to meet you here?"

Aurie checked to make sure no one else was in the room, then created a privacy bubble around them. No one would be able to hear what they were talking about.

"I think Violet knows something," said Aurie.

"How to match her shoes with the skins of dead babies?" offered Pi.

"Probably, but not that. Back in the Essence Foundry. She said something that I forgot about in the aftermath of her recording me. She said it at the beginning of class: *my mother and her friends will own this school by the end of the year.*"

"If I were her mother, Violet would be the last person I'd tell about my plans. But I get your point. The Cardwell household has knowledge about what the Cabal are planning to do. What are you suggesting?"

"I don't know," said Aurie. "That's why I wanted to talk to you."

"Why not in our room?" asked her sister.

Aurie didn't know how to say it, but the look on her face must have given it away.

"You don't trust Inari," said Pi, crossing her arms. "Pretty ungrateful of you."

"I'm being cautious. Something's not right about your new friend. Why does she need a collar of glowing runes? I researched those things. They're not associated with good magic. Controlling demons and that sort of thing," said Aurie.

"I'm way ahead of you," said Pi. "Trust me, I didn't sleep a wink the first few nights she was in my room. But now? She saved my sister from having her soul ripped out. I'm good."

"If we wanted to get the information out of Violet, how could we do it?" asked Aurie.

Pi's face went through contortions. "Are you asking if we should torture her? I mean, I will, if it gets us answers, but I didn't expect that to come from you."

"I don't want to torture her," said Aurie. "Even if I was willing to do that, which I'm not, we'd only be alerting the Cabal that we know their plans, which would only ensure that they change them."

"You know we're not going to have an easy time of it if we keep following the rules," said Pi. "The other day, I was watching a documentary on Caesar. He said, '*If you must break the law, do it to seize power; in all other cases observe it.*'"

"But we're not going to seize power," said Aurie. "We're trying to keep the Cabal from taking it."

Pi paced across the map room floor. "What if we are? There's no head patron anymore. If we don't take it, then they will."

Aurie couldn't believe her sister was suggesting that they claim the Hundred Halls for themselves. They weren't even alumnae yet.

"I've always thought that Semyon would take it like he did the Rod of Dominion. We only need to block the Cabal," said Aurie.

"I'm not disagreeing with you, sis. I'd prefer that someone with more experience be the head patron. Semyon would be as good as anyone. Maybe even Professor Mali. She's strict but fair. But what if we're not given that choice? What if it comes down to one of us?" asked Pi.

The world seemed to shift under her feet. Aurie couldn't imagine having that responsibility.

"You could do it," said Pi, startling Aurie out of her thoughts. "Don't let yourself think anything else. You have it in you. It's not probable, but you have to be prepared to grab it if you must to keep it away from the Cabal. I know I am."

The first thought that ran through Aurie's head was that she wouldn't trust her sister with the position of head patron. She was so shocked and embarrassed by this thought that she turned to look at the map, lest her sister catch the expression.

"I'll...I'll think about it," said Aurie. "But what do we do for now? How do we get that information out of Violet?"

"There's a spell I know that might work," said Pi. "Well, I don't know it, but I know where it is. It gets you into someone's dream. If we're careful, we might be able to interrogate Violet without her knowing it. I'm sure I can get her to talk."

"No," said Aurie, "I'll do it. I know her better than you do."

"Are you sure? I figured you wouldn't want to do it in case you got caught," said Pi.

"What does it matter? Semyon's not here, and I'm likely to get kicked out after my trial. Better for me to take the risk," said Aurie.

"Well," said Pi, scrunching up her face. "It's not completely safe. If the dreamer figures it out, they can attack your mind, turn you into a blithering moron if you're not careful. You're pretty defenseless while you're in there."

"When can you get the spell?" asked Aurie.

"Tonight if necessary," said Pi. "I'll need a couple of hours to acquire it, but Violet won't be asleep until later anyway. The astronomy lounge isn't far from her room. We could reach her from there."

The desire to get a sneak peek into Violet's mind was strong, even without the need for information. They'd clashed so many times, Aurie wanted to know what was going on in that girl's head.

"Think she'll have any protections?" asked Aurie.

Pi gave a dismissive shrug. "This isn't Coterie. Nothing she can put up will be enough."

"Let's do it," said Aurie.

Pi clapped her hands a bit too gleefully for Aurie's taste. "Awesome! *Dooset daram.* I'll see you back in our room before midnight."

Until her sister returned with the spell, Aurie paced her room. It felt wrong to invade someone else's dream, but the risks of not doing it seemed worse. Decisions like this seemed so clear and easy for her sister. Aurie envied her lack of doubt.

When Pi returned, they sequestered themselves in the astronomy lounge, putting up wards on the door so no one could enter. They left a note that explained they were taking sensitive readings with the telescope and couldn't be bothered.

The spell was difficult, but not out of her range. She set it so she'd be in Violet's dream for an hour. It made her drowsy right away. Aurie settled on a cushioned bench and concentrated on the room above, focusing her mind on Violet. If the spell worked, she'd "wake up" in Violet's dream.

The next thing she knew, Aurie was in an expensive house filled with tacky gold wall decorations. The carpets were so white she thought she was walking on cushioned air. She almost forgot what she was there to do until she heard a childish cough.

Aurie peered through a doorway, careful not to be seen. A younger version of Violet, hair nearly white and formed into a stylish bob, sat at the kitchen counter scribbling in a notebook, nodding her head to the music in her headphones. She wore a boarding school uniform with a patch on the vest.

From the other direction, Camille Cardwell entered the kitchen in a blindingly white tennis outfit. She approached the counter and, to Aurie's surprise, ripped the page from Violet's notebook.

Startled, young Violet nearly fell off her stool. She yanked her headphones out.

"Mother, I'm sorry. I was just taking a break. Only for a minute. My brain was tired," said Violet.

Camille slapped her daughter across the cheek. The slap was a shotgun blast through the kitchen.

"Don't you lie to me," said Camille, holding up the paper, which displayed a detailed pencil drawing of a dragon in mid-swoop. "This doesn't look like a minute or two. I told you to sit at this counter and focus on your homework. Did I say anything about doodling? Did I?"

"No, Mother."

"Then why in the fuck are you doodling? Do you realize how embarrassing your B was last year? And this is normal school. Not the Hundred Halls. Do you think that kind of attitude will get you far in Alchemists?"

"No, Mother."

"And why not?" she asked.

"Because magic is dangerous. One mistake could kill me, my friends, my teacher, or my mother," said Violet, hate-filled gaze flicking up to Camille's face.

"If you cannot be perfect, then I won't allow you to join Alchemists and embarrass my name," said Camille. "I was the top student in my year. Those experiences molded me into who I am. Remember, the *Herald* was a two-bit rag that my uncle owned before I took it from him."

Aurie understood that when Camille said "took it from him," she meant it literally. She wondered if her uncle was still alive.

The abuse went on, and though it was insightful to the mother-daughter relationship, it wasn't helping with the current predicament. Eventually, Camille stormed out of the room. Violet was choking on her sobs, clearly fearful of her mother's return.

Using the malleability of the dream state, Aurie changed herself into the older version of Camille in a dark blue pantsuit.

When she walked into the kitchen, young Violet stifled her sobbing like a frightened mouse trying to avoid a soaring hawk.

"Violet," said Aurie, and in hearing her own voice, cleared her throat and tried again, concentrating on the memory of the mother, hoping the dream would fill in for her inadequacies at mimicry.

"Violet. How are your classes in Arcanium coming?" she asked.

The young Violet appeared confused. Aurie held her breath as she waited for her nemesis to remember that she wasn't a twelve-year-old boarding school student, but a member of the Hundred Halls. The transformation took the blink of an eye. Sitting across the counter was the Violet that Aurie knew, wearing a stylish peasant dress complete with a necklace of pearls, though in the presence of her mother, she appeared unsure, like a beaten dog cringing at the foot of her master.

"What do you want, Mother? You don't care about Arcanium," said Violet, eyes flickering with caution. Taking the guise of her older self had come with more self-restraint, the carved mask of a person practiced at deception, but it was clear to Aurie that Violet hated her mother.

"I care about your success," said Aurie.

Violet scowled, staring at her as if she were trying to see through the illusion. Aurie realized her mistake. Camille would never say that. Aurie chose her next words carefully to not upset Violet's expectations.

"The plan requires you to hide in plain sight," said Aurie.

"So there *is* a plan," said Violet, getting off her stool.

"Yes," said Aurie. "We need you to find out what Semyon's up to."

A look of relief rose to Violet's face like a wave of euphoria, before turning hard, unbelieving. Before Aurie could breathe, Violet was standing before her, lips snarled.

"Who are you?" she demanded.

"I'm your mother," said Aurie, backing against the middle island. She'd only been in the dream for fifteen minutes, tops. If things went wrong now, she'd be stuck with Violet for far too long. Aurie searched her mind for something else to say, but came up blank.

A knife appeared in Violet's hand. The lights flickered, and the room warped around them as if they'd stepped into a budget horror film. If Violet figured out who she was, she could do a lot of damage before Aurie could leave the dream.

"You're not my mother," said Violet, pressing the tip of the blade into Aurie's stomach.

The illusion of Camille overtop was fading. Aurie tried to prop it back up, but it was Violet's dream, and she held the power.

Violet's expression was slowly moving towards understanding. This was going all wrong.

"What the fuck do you think you're doing?" asked Aurie, channeling Camille as best as she could.

Unfazed, Violet stared at the knife. She was clearly contemplating shoving it in. The attempt to startle Violet back into submission had gone too far. The illusion was maintained, but Aurie was at risk of getting murdered anyway, a chilling realization.

"Violet," she said, holding a level, but forceful tone. "Sit back down. Do your homework."

The lights went back to normal, and the knife disappeared.

"I'm sorry, Mother," said Violet with her head down.

Aurie gained an insight to the nature of their relationship. She'd been operating based on her experiences, but those were irrelevant here. Despite all the charities, and the public service that Camille had performed over the years, she was not a pleasant person, even to her own daughter.

"I assume you know the real reason you're in Arcanium," said Aurie.

"Because I failed you," said Violet, matter-of-fact.

"Yes," said Aurie, and for a moment, she choked up. Aurie always had the love of her parents. Even after death, that love was real. That the basis of Violet's existence was that she was a disappointment to her own mother was tragically awful.

Aurie knew what she needed to do to get the information she needed, but the cruelty of it gave her pause. What made it worse was that Violet, though the age that Aurie knew her now, was wearing the short hair bob and the boarding school uniform that she'd been in earlier. She was, at her core, always that twelve-year-old girl frightened of her mother.

"What do you know of our plan?" asked Aurie. "Tell me now, or I will get out the truth potion. I need to know how much risk we have with you in Arcanium. If you do not disappoint me, then I will be merciful."

The normally pale girl turned even whiter, until she was almost a translucent ghost, confirming what Aurie had suspected. Camille wouldn't have told her daughter anything.

"I...I..."

Aurie growled, putting heartbreaking menace into her words. "Tell me the fuck now. Or I will leave you in the wilderness for an eternity."

"I overheard a few things, nothing more. I swear I can keep a secret," said Violet, trying to be as small as possible.

"Tell me," said Aurie.

A part of Violet seemed to realize that this could be a ploy, but the presence of her mother squashed free thought. She complied as only the beaten can do.

"You were on the phone with someone. I didn't hear who, I shouldn't have been listening, but I know the soul thief works for the Cabal and that you need the souls to get through Invictus' portal. Something about trying to match an imprint," said Violet.

Aurie knew instantly how they were using the souls. Since Invictus had been the head patron, he had a connection to every Hall. In a way, every student had a part of Invictus in them, even after death, because of these links. It was the whole reason the patron system worked. The Hundred Halls was Invictus, and Invictus was the Hundred Halls.

Since Hemistad was an Erlking, the Pied Piper of old, he could only take the souls of the young. As people got older, their souls became more attached to their bodies. Everything made perfect, terrible sense.

"Mother?" asked Violet.

Aurie resumed her scowl. "Do you know where the portal is?"

"No, Mother. I swear. I don't know. And even if I did, I wouldn't tell anyone."

"You just told me about what you overheard," said Aurie, crossing her arms.

This did a number on the poor girl. Aurie almost regretted it. Her face screwed up in both horror and apology, the two emotions fighting with each other as she sputtered out, "I was just doing as you asked."

"I will allow it," said Aurie. "This time."

Violet crouched meekly on her stool.

"Violet," said Aurie, and the girl's face came up, hopeful. "Keep your head down. Let no one notice you. With this information, you've become a weak link."

Violet nodded precisely. "Yes, Mother. Understood."

Aurie marched out of the room. As soon as she was out of sight, she collapsed against the wall. She hated herself for what she'd done.

When the hour was up, Aurie woke back in the astronomy lounge. Pi was crouched on the couch like a gargoyle, the purple tips of her hair swaying as she leaned over Aurie.

"How did it go?" asked Pi.

Aurie sat up and rubbed her eyes. She felt like she'd woken up from a nightmare. It'd been a good thing she'd gone in and not her sister.

"I got what we needed," said Aurie, then she explained what had happened in the dream.

Afterwards, Pi sat back on the couch. "Wow. What a fucked-up relationship. I almost feel sorry for Violet. Almost. Do you think her mother really had her put in Arcanium as punishment?"

"Whether or not it's true, Violet believes it," said Aurie. "We have to remember that it's Violet's impression of her mother."

"It can't be that far from the truth," said Pi.

"I'm not denying that."

Pi picked up the tome that contained the dreamspell. "I should get this back to its owner. What do we do now?"

"We need to find the portal," said Aurie.

"We need to find Hemistad," said Pi.

"I bet if we find one, we find the other. And the souls."

Pi grew teary-eyed and fiddled with the watch on her wrist. "You know, once they get the last soul, Ashley's a goner. They'll use what they need to get through the portal, and the rest that fucking Bannon will snort up."

"We've got time," said Aurie, rubbing her sister's shoulder. "We can figure this out."

Pi wiped a tear from her cheek. "They probably picked Ashley because of me. It's all my fault. If I hadn't been friends with her, they never would have taken her soul."

"It's not your fault, Pi. Don't you ever think that," said Aurie.

Pi grimaced, holding back the emotions that were building up like floodwaters behind a dam. Her whole face was wracked in pain except for her eyes, which were hard and focused.

"I'm going to stop them, whatever it takes," said Pi.

"We have to be careful, sis," said Aurie.

"Fuck careful, they took my friend," said Pi, eyes bloodshot. "And I don't want to lose you."

"We'll figure it out," said Aurie. "We'll stop them somehow. But we can't lose ourselves in the process. Remember what Mom and Dad taught us."

"I remember," said Pi, then she looked away.

Aurie realized it was a mistake to bring up their parents. It wasn't what they'd taught them that her sister remembered, but that they'd been killed because someone else had more power.

TWENTY

The Goblin Romp hadn't changed since her last visit. Seedy bars kept the character of their customers, and this one was the same. Pi could taste the stale beer on the back of her tongue even before she'd reached the front door.

The bouncer barely gave her a second look as she marched in, a far cry from the first time she'd entered the Glass Cabaret years ago, when the bouncer there had seen her as an ingénue. Nearly three years in the Halls had changed her. Though she still wore her hair in punk styling, the rest of her felt different, older.

As she suspected, Uncle Liam sat at the bar, a glass of whiskey captured between his hands.

"You're planning on leaving town soon," she said, hopping onto the stool next to him.

He glanced up at her, before his head sunk back down, a mountain of self-pity weighing him down.

"The best problems are the ones you can run from," said Liam.

"You can't run forever," she replied.

He waved at the bartender for another glass, and after receiving confirmation, downed the drink in front of him with the practice of a serial drunk.

"That is patently untrue," he said. "And I'm the proof of that."

"The whole race thing was a scam," she said, jabbing her finger into his side.

He raised a curious eyebrow at her. "Kill me then. I deserve it."

"A few days ago, I went back to negotiate with your creditors. It didn't take much digging to uncover that there was no debt. You got me to sign up for interest payments that don't exist," she said.

He lifted his glass in mock salute. "You got me. It seems you got the clever side of the family."

"How would I know?" she asked.

"Noted."

He put two fingers up. The bartender poured two glasses of Jameson, sliding one of them towards Pi. She shoved it over to her uncle Liam.

"I don't drink," she said.

"A noble stance," he replied, "but I suggest taking up a cheap way to self-flagellate, or you'll drown in bills when you regret the things you do for power, forcing you to sign up for another tour of duty whenever your bank account hits a fat goose egg."

Pi wasn't sure if she pitied her uncle, but the display had removed the scales from her eyes.

"Is that what happened? You went too far and couldn't come back?" she asked, not only because she was curious, but because she was worried about her own trajectory.

"Something like that," he said, spinning his glass, making the ice clink together.

"You owe me a story," she said.

"It's complicated."

"Bullshit," she said, pulling out the fae coin. "What the hell is this then?"

The way he smirked at the coin revealed the truth.

"It doesn't mean anything, does it?" she said. "You gave it to me to get me to shut up."

"There's that cleverness again."

"Is it even really gold?"

He gave a half-shrug that felt like a middle finger to Pi. "Maybe enough to get you a Starbucks coffee with all the toppings."

"Why won't you tell me anything?" she asked.

He went quiet, tapped his glass a few times. "Because I don't know any stories. Nothing you want to hear. I left the first chance I could, never looking back. Honestly, I didn't know your dad that well, definitely not your mother."

She sensed a real honesty from him that she hadn't been getting before.

"So this has just been a con," she said, putting her hand on the glass of whiskey before shoving it away.

"You'll do a lot better if you understand that all of life is a con," he said. "From morning to night, we're all trying to convince each other that we matter, that anything matters. Even your Hundred Halls is a con."

"What does that mean?"

He snorted. "It's not about teaching. It's about control. They own you."

"Fuck you," she said bitterly. "I don't believe that."

"Yet, you do."

He tapped on the bar as if he were playing a piano, before spinning towards her. "I've got a story for you. It's not about your family, but it's about me. Sorry. I know you want to hear that you're related to bloody faeries or djinns or maybe you're a secret princess or other such bollocks, but this is the cold hard truth.

"Once I was offered a hefty sum for completing an onerous task that someone else didn't want to do. When the doing was done, I went to collect my fee, only to learn that he wasn't going to pay me."

"You got conned," she said. "What did you do?"

"I learned my lesson. Kept my eyes open and didn't believe anyone, especially when I wanted it to be true. Think of this as a favor. One of those life lessons, growth, and all that blah, blah, blah."

"No wonder Mom and Dad didn't talk about you," she said. "You're a selfish asshole."

"Selfish assholes live a lot longer than wide-eyed do-gooders," he said.

"That was your brother!"

He appeared repentant for his remark. Swirled his glass once before throwing back a swallow. "You want to know who you really are, but what if you don't like what you find?"

She knew he was talking about himself, but the warning for her wasn't unheeded.

"I've got my sister," she said defiantly, hopefully.

He nodded. "Maybe that'll be the difference. There was no one but me."

The pain in his eyes made him older than he was. His mistakes had aged him in ways she couldn't yet comprehend. Then she recalled the way the bouncer hadn't batted an eye at her on the way in. Proof that even she'd changed more than she thought in three years' time. What would another twenty bring?

Uncle Liam dug into his pocket and threw some crumbled bills on the counter.

"Did you come all this way just to scam me?" she asked.

"No," he said. "But when the opportunity arose, I couldn't let it pass. Old habits. I'm sorry I'm not who you thought I was."

Pi watched him leave, positive that she'd never see him again, which was a good thing. She supposed that despite the feelings of frustration upon learning the truth, the con had been instructive for her. She might be a little more jaded, but hopefully a little wiser too. It wasn't like the Cabal was going to take it easy on her and Aurie because they were still students. If they got in the way, they'd get squashed like insects. As for Uncle Liam, she was certain that his ways would catch up to him eventually. She hoped she wouldn't be around when it happened, because it would be tragic.

TWENTY ONE

A gondola floated through the air far above their heads on the way to the Spire. Aurie jabbed her thumb in that direction as they strolled down the Boulevard of Griffons.

"Next year we'll get to ride in one of those," said Aurie.

The thought of soaring through the sky brought a smile to her lips. Pi, on the other hand, looked away, darkness clouding her expression.

"What? Don't tell me you don't want to ride in one," she said.

"It's the first week of May, there are only a few Halls left for the soul thief, and you don't know a thing about your true name. How can you act like nothing's wrong?"

Her sister's disappointment was like a funeral shroud. Aurie glanced to the blue sky rather than meet that conflicted gaze.

"Because if I dwell on it then I can't get anything done. I have to think about what might be possible rather than what is likely," said Aurie.

She knew the smile she wore was propped up and ready to collapse at the first stiff wind, but she refused to be maudlin about her fate.

They turned onto Copernicus Avenue. Their destination was a retired alumnus from Aura Healers named Dr. Finegold that did forensic analysis for the police department. When Aurie had contacted him, she hadn't given any details except that it was for an Arcanium project. If they could find out where the rest of the souls were being stored, they might be able to save Ashley.

"We should leave the Hundred Halls—"

"No," said Aurie. "I told you, I'm not doing that."

"You're going to die then," said Pi.

"I'm not giving up. I've been doing research. Patron Semyon isn't the only one who can teach me how to use my true name," she said.

"Oh?" asked Pi, with a hopeful arch of her eyebrow. "Another professor? A summoned imp or something?"

"Not exactly," said Aurie.

"What?" asked Pi as they ran across the street.

"I found some videos online, and a message board where people can discuss their progress," said Aurie.

"This on a Hall website?" asked Pi, perplexed.

"No," said Aurie, shaking her head. She'd been trying to show her sister that she was trying, but it felt like it was only making it worse. "It's a place, you know. It's given me some good hints, more than I had before."

"Sounds like a 3 a.m. infomercial if you ask me," said Pi as she pulled her arms around her chest in self-comfort.

Aurie reached out to put her arm around her sister, but pulled away instead. She hated seeing her sister like this, but she didn't want her to throw her chance at graduating from the Hundred Halls away.

"Where would we even go? If we left," said Aurie, only to cheer her sister up.

It did the trick, because Pi's face lit up like a sunrise. "Anywhere we want. We've got enough gold in the bank to last for years, at least until we can find a new patron. Though if I had to pick, I think I'd want Paris first.

It's not like we couldn't make money. The two of us working together would be a force of nature. I hear there's an ancient vampire sorcerer that lives there, taking students every couple of decades."

"I don't want to be a vampire," said Aurie.

"It's not required," said Pi, "or at least, I heard it's not. There are other options. I have a spreadsheet of them. Really, we could go anywhere."

She wasn't sure why she'd never realized it before, but it hit her like a thunderbolt. Pi was only staying in the Hundred Halls because of her. If she failed the trial and had her magic ripped from her, Pi would leave the next day, bitter and alone. A dangerous combination for a mage of her ability. Leaving now would preserve not only her magic, but Pi's humanity. For the first time, Aurie actually thought about leaving the Hundred Halls, not for herself, but for Pi.

"Paris would be nice," said Aurie, trying to think about the upsides, but the look of concern on Pi's face brought a follow-up question to Aurie's lips. "I thought this would make you happy."

Without moving her lips, Pi said, "It does, but that's not the problem. I think we're being followed. Don't look."

"I wasn't going to," said Aurie.

"Really?"

"Fine," said Aurie. "But it's hard not to."

"Let's keep going and try and lose him," said Pi.

They walked briskly for a few blocks, heading away from Dr. Finegold's neighborhood. After turning a corner, they stepped into a used bookstore called Page Turners and hurried into the shelves, but didn't go so far that they couldn't see if anyone went by. No one passed the front of the store while they watched.

"Are you sure we were being followed?" Aurie asked.

"I'm pretty sure. I mean, the way the guy looked right at me, then turned his head as if he knew he wasn't supposed to make eye contact. It just felt wrong. I caught a glimpse of him in the storefront windows following on the last block, but after that, I don't know," she said.

"What did he look like?"

Pi scrunched up her face. "Bulky, thick neck, crew cut. Think high school linebacker who let himself go after the glory days."

"That would be the stereotypical Protector," said Aurie. "Which probably means he's a cop."

The attendant walked by, so they acted like they were checking out books. Aurie grabbed a tattered copy of *Pride and Prejudice* and held it open. Pi had the latest Stephen King hardcover.

"We should abandon the soul vial and get the hell out of here," said Pi. "It was a long shot to find the source anyway."

"No way," said Aurie.

"I don't want to lose you, sis. If the cops caught us with that, you'd be screwed, not only with the authorities, but the Halls," said Pi.

"Don't you want to get your friend Ashley back?"

"I'm deluding myself to think I can bring her back," said Pi. "And if you're serious about what you said back there, about leaving the Halls, why mess around with this any longer? It's not like everything isn't stacked against us."

It would be easy to leave. Damn easy. Aurie and Pi against the world. It sounded good in her head. She wouldn't have her magic ripped out of her head, and she could keep an eye on Pi.

"I'm not ready to give up yet," said Aurie. "We're almost to Dr. Finegold's. Let's sneak out the back. I'm sure we can get to his house without being seen. And if you see that guy again, we'll dump the vial and go back to Arcanium."

"If we do that we're leaving, right?" asked Pi.

"We can talk about it. A serious talk. I may not have any choices left," she said.

Pi squeezed her arm. They found a back way out of the bookstore. Bypassing fire alarms using magic was trivial. It led them to a back alley. They cut through a few yards to reach the neighborhood of fixed-up brownstones. Every fifth house or so was a little more run-down than the others, but the number of Lexuses and BMWs on the street indicated it was a neighborhood on the rise.

Pi hit the doorbell on Dr. Finegold's door. An annoying buzzing sound echoed inside the house. They kept an eye on the empty street until Dr. Finegold arrived.

He had white-gray hair, a pair of reading glasses perched on his nose, and he wore a sweater over a tie. He looked like the kind of doctor that performed house visits and enjoyed talking with his patients.

"Aurelia?" he asked.

"Yes," she said. "And this is my sister, Pythia."

"Remarkable names. The Oracle of Delphi?" Pi nodded. "And you, Miss Aurelia. Caesar's mother?"

"No. Marcus Aurelius," she said.

"How fascinating," he said. "Your parents sound like interesting people to give you such names. I'd love to meet them."

"I'm sorry, they're dead," said Pi.

"Apologies, how crass of me," said Dr. Finegold. "Come in, come in. Making you stand on the porch and bringing up bad memories. I've really lost my manners."

The living room was warm and inviting. An antique rocking chair was a minor throne for a tabby cat, while an old player piano displayed a roll of music paper.

Pi went straight to the piano and tinkled the keys. Dr. Finegold watched approvingly.

"Do you remember our neighbor back in Philadelphia? Didn't he have one of these?" asked Pi.

"The guy with the mangy dog and the prosthetic arm? Yeah, I re-member. Mom would bring him muffins on holidays, wheat with walnuts, if I recall," said Aurie.

"Bleah," said Pi, then remembering they were in someone else's house, blushed. "I'm sorry. I just haven't seen one of these in a long time."

Dr. Finegold offered them a seat on the couch. He took the rocking chair after scooping up the tabby cat, whose minor protest amounted to a halfhearted mrroew.

"Have we met before?" he asked. "I swear I've seen your face."

Aurie's gut turned over. She had to assume that he read the *Herald of the Halls*. If he'd already made up his mind about the events earlier in the year, there was no use asking for his help.

"No," said Aurie. "Unless we met you when I was younger. My dad was in Aura Healers."

"Really?" asked Dr. Finegold.

"Mom was in Arcanium, and our dad was in Aura Healers, though he was much younger than you. I doubt you knew him, but his name was Kieran Devlin," said Aurie.

His eyes widened with surprise. "I didn't have privileges at Golden Willow, but I was at a few conferences with your father. I read his paper on using simulacrums to safely remove certain curses, tricking the magic into thinking that it hadn't changed. Remarkable thinking, brilliant really, easily his best work. It was a great loss to the medical profession when he passed."

Aurie never knew what to say in these situations, so she gave a tight-lipped smile and nodded her head. It was safer than commenting, which would only draw more discussion.

Dr. Finegold seemed to sense their discomfort.

"You said something about a project?" he asked, leaning forward.

Pi pulled out the vial and handed it over. "We're trying to figure out where this came from."

He wore the cheery expression of a professor about to demonstrate his excellence. Dr. Finegold set the dark vial on the wooden table, and after releasing the tabby from his lap, cast a couple of spells. His expression quickly changed.

"This isn't an Arcanium project. Where did you get this?" he asked, deadly serious.

Pi looked to her, so she tried to answer without giving too much away.

"We found it," said Aurie. "We know what it is. It has to do with the whole soul thief thing going on at the Hundred Halls. We've lost some friends to it, and we want to help stop it."

Dr. Finegold went unnaturally still. The look he gave them left Aurie with serious doubts. When she caught Pi's attention, her sister gave her a head nod towards the door.

"And why haven't you taken this to the authorities?" he asked calmly.

Aurie knew her inability to answer right away wasn't helping their cause. When her answer finally came out, she realized it sounded worse than saying nothing at all.

"We thought they were too busy to worry about the soul thief. They haven't caught him yet, have they?" she said.

"I see," he said.

With the vial in hand, Dr. Finegold said, "I'll be right back."

Almost as soon as he was gone, Pi whispered through gritted teeth, "He's going to call the cops. We should get out of here. *Now.*"

An aching need to flee filled her limbs, but Aurie pushed it away.

"I don't know, Pi. If we weren't going to give him a chance, we shouldn't have come here," she said.

Pi looked ready to run out the door. She fidgeted like a toddler in church.

"I have a bad feeling," said Pi.

Aurie kept staring at the doorway, expecting Dr. Finegold to return. The longer he was gone, the more she wanted to agree with Pi.

She was about to cast verumancy on her ears to find out if he was on the phone to the police when Dr. Finegold returned.

He took one look at their expressions and said, "I did consider calling the authorities, if you're wondering. Especially with all the coverage of you in the *Herald*. Yes. I didn't recognize you at first, but once we were talking about your father, I remembered where I'd seen you."

"What made you change your mind?" asked Aurie.

"Two things really. The first is that I can't imagine the apple falling that far from the tree, and second, I've known Camille Cardwell from charity events in the city. Everything she does is calculated for her benefit, so I read those articles with a healthy dose of doubt. But before I tell you what I know about the vial, I need to know how you acquired it and what you're planning on doing with it," he said.

"We can't tell you the first part," said Aurie, shivering when she thought of what she'd seen in Creed's house. "I'm sorry. Let's just say that it's for your safety. The second is exactly what we said. We lost a friend to the soul thief and we're trying to stop him. We think we know who it is, but it's bigger than that. He's working for the Cabal."

"The Cabal?" he asked skeptically.

"Alchemists, Protectors, Coterie, and Assassins. Those four want to take control of the Hundred Halls now that Invictus is dead," said Pi. "We want to stop them."

"And how is this soul fragment going to help with that?" he asked.

"It's complicated," said Aurie. "We're trying to find where they're keeping the rest of the souls. We want to put them back in their bodies, and stop the Cabal in the process."

"Isn't it their right to take control of the Halls now that Invictus is gone? Those are the oldest Halls in the university, along with Arcanium, of course. It would only seem natural," he said.

"Doesn't stealing the souls of their students to accomplish this kinda show you how they might rule the Halls?" said Pi, arms spread wide.

Dr. Finegold pushed his glasses up his nose. "Excellent point. Just trying to keep an open mind."

"Which is usually how these assholes take control," said Pi. "Look, do you know anything or not?"

"Dr. Finegold, I'm sorry for my sister's rudeness, but it's been a tough semester," Aurie said.

"No, it's quite alright. I'm sure you're under a lot of stress. I assume you haven't had your trial by magic yet?"

"It's in a couple of weeks," she said.

Dr. Finegold handed the vial back to Aurie. "I don't know anything about soul magic, so I wasn't able to learn anything about that, but the vial itself has some traces of concrete dust on the bottom, but it didn't take magic to learn that. It helps to be observant."

"Concrete dust could be anywhere," said Aurie. "Can you tell us anything about the dust in particular? Where it might have come from?"

"Not without more advanced equipment. I'm afraid I don't have the right tools here. You really need a mass spectrometer, which isn't as exciting as a spell, but would give you a more precise answer. At least enough to narrow it down. And I'm afraid the only spectrometer I know that can give you the level of detail you need is in the police headquarters," said Dr. Finegold.

Aurie's next question was interrupted by a knock on the door. Pi glanced around the corner and then ducked her head.

"It's that guy that was following us." Pi pointed at Dr. Finegold. "You called the police, didn't you?"

He held his hands up. "I swear I didn't. I told you that I believed you. Didn't you just say he was following you? He might just be stopping by to ask if I've seen anyone. Remember, I do work with the department on a professional basis."

Aurie shoved the vial in her pocket. "Either way, we should use this as an opportunity to leave. Do you have a back door?"

He nodded. "I'll keep him occupied. If you go out the alleyway to the north, the next street runs into the train station about five blocks up."

"Thank you, Dr. Finegold," said Aurie.

"Good luck."

They crept to the back door. Aurie waited for a moment. She wanted to hear what Dr. Finegold had to say before she left. When he made no mention of them, she slipped out the back, following Pi.

The alleyway was exactly as Dr. Finegold said. As soon as they hit the street, Aurie found it hard not to break into a sprint. They fast-walked the five blocks. When the tall letters from the train station came into view, she started to relax.

They cut through the parking lot, holding hands. Aurie didn't see them coming, but felt Pi's grip tense up, heard the spell forming on her sister's lips.

A big-bellied man in a Protector's robe stepped out of a Buick right in front of her. She called faez to shape into a spell, but he shouted, the Voice of Command scrambling her thoughts.

More officers surrounded them. Pi knocked one down with a stun spell, but another tackled her to the ground.

Rough hands grabbed her. Cold shackles were placed on her arms, deadening her access to faez. She was slammed against a car, the air knocked from her lungs. A large hand pressed her face against the window.

On the ground, things were worse for Pi, who was fighting against them like an angry badger. They hadn't quite gotten the spell-dampening shackles on her yet, and Pi was managing to get out little spells that only did enough to enrage the cops. The fat officer who'd tackled her punched

Pi in the face and the fight was over. Her sister went limp.

"Stop hurting her!"

Aurie recognized Protector Cox from the day they'd rescued Uncle Liam.

"Got that little nasty witch," said Protector Cox, then he stuck a fat finger in Aurie's face. "Go ahead and give me a reason to put you down."

The aura of faez was thick around him. Aurie held her tongue.

"That's what I thought."

Protector Cox dug into her pockets and pulled out the soul vial. "Well what do we have here? It seems we've caught the soul thief."

TWENTY TWO

When they'd been living in the section eight apartment back in the thirteenth ward, Pi had bought a bottle of vodka from a neighbor once. She'd been curious about why people drank.

Aurie had declined joining her experiment, giving her a disapproving eyebrow raise before returning to her spell book. So Pi sipped from the bottle alone.

The first hour was unremarkable. Pi felt her face warm, but not much else, so she increased her intake. By the end of the second hour, she was shooting sparks from her fingers and annoying Aurie with her random pronouncements like "we owe a real debt of gratitude to the first person who ever decided to try cheese" and "the best astronauts would be tinker mages because they could fix anything on a long journey."

By the end of the night, half the bottle was gone, and she spent the rest of the time puking in a trashcan while Aurie rubbed her back. The next morning her head had felt like it was being slowly crushed in a vice.

Lying on the floor of a concrete jail cell with a pair of spell-dampening manacles on her wrists, Pi felt worse than that night. At least she'd known the hangover would eventually go away.

She lay on her side, wearing an orange jumpsuit, knees to elbows in the fetal position, mostly so she wouldn't throw up. There was no doubt that she had a concussion, an affliction she could cure with a simple spell, but without access to her magic, she had to ride out the symptoms. So Pi filled the time with thoughts of how she could pay Protector Cox back for slugging her in the head.

They didn't come get her for what seemed like weeks, but was probably only a couple of days. Because she had magical ability, a Protector led her to the interrogation room, pulling her along by the manacles. He was surprisingly skinny for an officer, had a large beak nose, and seemed quite annoyed at having to drag her along.

"Is my sister okay?" she asked.

"Shut up," he said.

"I just want to know if she's alright," said Pi. "I'm not asking for secret intel."

"I said, shut the fuck up," he said, bulging his eyes at her.

"Dick," she muttered under her breath.

He glared at her and pushed her into a room with a one-way window. Pi stepped over a permanent warding circle around a table and two chairs, one on either side. The walls were covered in runes.

As the Protector hooked her chains to the table, she said, "I know what you do in here. I bet you leave the perps in here, summon a demon into the room, and let them freak out."

The way he looked at her confirmed she was right. Beak nose left the room.

While she waited, Pi put her head on the desk and tried to catch some sleep. She woke to Protector Cox kicking the table.

"Wakie, wakie," he said. "We sure are gonna have a lot of fun."

"You've got a sick sense of fun," said Pi.

He slapped his hands on the table. "Don't think I don't remember what you and your sister did to me when we arrested your uncle."

Pi didn't think there was any reason to tell him that it had been her uncle Liam that had put the spell on him, so she kept her mouth shut.

"That's what I thought," he said. "Not so tough now that you're in here."

"What do you want to know? I'll tell you anything, just so I don't have to smell you anymore," she said.

The brief moment that he tilted his head to sniff was worth the pain he inflicted once he realized she'd been messing with him. He placed a fat finger on her arm, whispering a spell, and her body convulsed with agony.

When it was finished, she felt like she'd run a ten mile race in under five seconds.

"I made your muscles tense up, every last one of them," he said. "If I do that a few more times, the body gets so worn out, you'll get cramps even when I'm not casting it on you."

"You are aware that you haven't asked any questions yet," she said.

The next thing he said made her go cold with fear. "Who said I'm going to ask questions? Maybe I'm just going to get my revenge for your little stunt. It's not like I can't make up a plausible story for my report. We caught you and your sister with the soul fragments, not to mention we're pretty sure we can link you to the dead student in Esoteric. What more do we need to know?"

Pi checked the room for cameras. She couldn't see any inside the room.

"We don't use cameras here," he said. "That's entirely too inconvenient for times like this. The official story is that the magic interferes with the electronics, but you and I both know that's bullshit."

"What happens at the end of this?" asked Pi.

Protector Cox squinted at her. "You're a cagey one. The official story will be that you and your sister confessed to the crimes and we take your magic away permanently. But the real truth is that you're going to be a guest of Bannon Creed's for a long, long time."

She didn't think it could get any worse, but hearing Bannon's name was more terrible than the days of torture she was likely to endure.

"Yes, you understand now," he said. "Creed is unhappy that you and your witchy sister broke into his house and freed a pretty valuable item from his collection, and I mean pretty. Now, I have to say, I'm impressed that you were able to get into his house, but impressed is not the word I would use for Mr. Creed. As we say back in Brewton, he's madder than a snake that married the garden hose."

"Creed's a sick fuck," said Pi, more to herself than Protector Cox.

"Don't worry, little darling. He wouldn't waste a good mage like you on petty sexual favors, especially one that works for that slippery Radoslav. What he is going to do is offer you a deal. If you release yourself from Arcanium, and bind yourself to him, he'll go easy on your sister."

Pi's mind whirled with the possibilities of revenge at a later date, until Protector Cox chuckled knowingly.

"I see that look on your face," he said. "Here's a little something you might already know, since you've already been bound to two patrons. Each one holds the reins of patronage a little differently. In the Protectors, Bannon Creed has complete control. I could no more act against him than cut off my own head."

"I didn't realize I could still transfer to another patron," said Pi.

"Any longer and the process would kill you. The fact that you've already done it once helps, but I hear it's very painful," he said, smiling.

"If I agree, what happens to my sister?" asked Pi.

"Then we take her magic, and put her in jail for life," he said. "Of course, she has to confess to the crimes of being the soul thief."

"That's not much of a deal," said Pi.

"You don't have much to bargain with," said Protector Cox.

"So the Protectors get credit for catching the thief, Creed gets me as his personal mage, and my sister gets to live," said Pi, the words hollow to her ears.

Protector Cox clicked his tongue. "You've got the right gist of it."

"And the alternative?" she asked.

"Do I really need to spell out the alternative?" he asked.

"No. I guess not," she said.

It wasn't like the world wouldn't accept that Aurie was the soul thief. The *Herald* had been priming the public all year that it was her, and technically, neither of them had to be alive.

But she couldn't leave her sister to die in prison, because that's what would happen if she had her magic taken. Better that they survive together, even under difficult circumstances. As long as they were alive, there was a chance of getting away later.

"What if we both bound ourselves to Creed?" asked Pi.

"The pair of you would be quite a boon, but she wouldn't survive it," said Protector Cox.

"Don't underestimate my sister," said Pi.

He rubbed his chin. "I'll take your offer to Creed. No guarantees, but it's better than the alternative, right?"

After he left, the beak-nosed Protector led her back to her cell. The headache was still with her, but her circumstances made the pain irrelevant. There was no way she could allow Creed to get control over her and Aurie. She had to find a way out. But how? She had no magic, her magical jacket was in the evidence room, and there were dozens of mages outside that would stop them, even if she could get out of the room.

This was why she sought power, to keep things like this from happening. Having a voice meant nothing in this world—the only currency that mattered was power, and now she'd be handing it over to Bannon Creed.

Once she was bound to him she'd no longer be able to act. She knew thoughts of revenge were foolish, as a man of his peculiarities didn't survive this long if pissed-off underlings were able to put a knife in his back. Once she was under his control, her life would be over.

Pi promised herself that if she escaped, she wouldn't play by their rules anymore. Even the Halls were shackles that bound too tightly, chafing her wrists until they bled. The only thing the Halls had to offer was protection from faez madness, because the knowledge of magic was omnipresent in the world. Maybe she could bind herself to Radoslav. Hell, she already owed him three more years of service, why not permanently enlist?

But if she did that, she knew that it would strain her and Aurie's relationship. Pi was under no illusions that as sisters they would be together forever. She wanted that to be the case—Aurie was the most important person in her life—but looking around at the world, seeing how power and relationships changed people, put wedges between allies and family, she knew that their close relationship was a tenuous thing.

Aurie wouldn't forgive her if she left the Halls, even if she stayed in the city and worked for Radoslav. That was the price of following your heart, that it might hurt the people you love because it went against their expectations.

None of this mattered, because she wasn't going to be free, she was going to be bound to Creed, and if she was lucky, so would Aurie. But Creed would never allow them to be together. He'd send one or the other to another part of the world, keeping them apart until they couldn't remember each other's faces.

Pi pushed her palms against her swollen eyes, the pain of impending separation incoming like a speeding train. No matter which way she turned, the world was conspiring to cleave them from each other, and how could she resist it? It seemed the only way they would be together was if they went out in a blaze of magic, tearing it all down so someone else, someone luckier than them, could start over.

Eventually Pi slept, and because there was no external light to tell her what time of day it was, she couldn't tell if it'd been an hour or a whole evening. The concrete floor didn't help either as she never completely felt rested.

When Protector Cox entered, she sat up against the wall.

"You're one lucky little witch," he said. "Mr. Creed has agreed to your offer. He'll be arriving tomorrow to bind you to him."

"What about Aurie? I'm not going without my sister," she said.

Protector Cox clucked his tongue at her as if she were a disobedient hound.

"You don't get a say in when and what things happen anymore. Be glad he accepted the arrangement. If you're lucky, and you perform well for him, you might find service to Mr. Creed a fine use for your worthless life."

"But he promised to take her too," said Pi.

"And he will," said Protector Cox. "After she confesses to being the soul thief and is sentenced. The judge is a personal friend of Mr. Creed, and will accept the arrangement that she be bound to him. We can make something up about the difficulty of removing magic from a mage of her ability. The public will believe anything if you repeat it enough times."

"What if I don't agree to bind myself to him anymore?" she said.

"I hope you do that, missy," he said. "I hope you do. I've seen him break a mage like a wild horse, and it is a fine thing to watch. You do that. You defy him after he's agreed to *your* deal and we'll see how that works out."

Protector Cox left the cell, leaving Pi stewing in her thoughts.

In less than a day she'd have to give up her connection to Arcanium and, in a way, her sister, then bind herself to Bannon Creed, the worst of the Hundred Halls. Pi knew there were no guarantees that Aurie would even agree to join her in Protectors.

It was hard not to think about how close she'd been to convincing Aurie to leave the Halls. Had things gone a little differently, they could be on a flight already, headed for parts unknown.

Pi squeezed her fists together. The worst part about it was that she couldn't talk to Aurie. If she knew what her sister wanted, it might be easier.

She put her hand to the wall and reached her mind out towards Aurie, wishing she could speak with her. The need filled her like a blossom of blinding white light.

"*Dooset daram*, Aurie. Please, what should I do? We're trapped in here and I don't want us to die. Whatever happens, it would be better if we could be together. I could withstand anything by your side."

For a moment, she felt a connection, another mind brushing against hers. Aurie? But then it was gone, a breeze caressing her desires, but amounting to nothing. She'd been deluding herself. There was no way she could contact Aurie. She was stuck in this cell, and her sister in the other, and it was likely that they would never taste real freedom again.

TWENTY THREE

No one had come to see Aurie in five days. She marked the time by the patterns of the jail, rather than the frequency of her meals. She'd figured out by the second day that her food came when someone remembered to feed her, rather than on a set schedule.

By listening to the different voices of the guards, and when they changed, she'd determined that they worked on a three-shift schedule. When she heard the gruff voice that complained that his kids didn't listen to him, she knew the morning shift had come.

She also felt a slight temperature difference on the wall opposite the door during that time, which she assumed meant it was on the outside of the police building and was taking sunlight from the east.

None of these things were going to help, that much she knew, but it was helpful to keep her mind occupied with something other than her and Pi's situation.

That they hadn't come talk to her worried Aurie that they were focusing on her sister. She wished she knew what was being asked, and hoped they weren't treating her too roughly.

Aurie remembered a time when they were at their third foster home, when the man of the house, a concrete worker who spent his evenings at the bar resenting that his wife had taken them into their house, would wind himself up. By the time he got home, his cheeks were ruddy with rum, primed like a trigger wire looking for a fight. Never one to back down, Pi would push his buttons until he threatened to beat her, but he never did because he was afraid of her magic. So instead of hitting her, he would keep the temperature in the house freezing in the winter so they had to wear coats indoors, or only give his wife enough money to buy food for herself, leaving them hungry.

Aurie stole food from his lunchbox, getting up early in the morning before he left for work to give it to Pi. She couldn't steal too much, or he'd notice, so she'd usually remove one slice of ham, leaving the rest on the sandwich, or take only the apple, or bag of chips. When she'd give the food to Pi, she always told her that she'd eaten her share already so she wouldn't try to give her half. To combat the constant ache in her stomach, she would eat crumbled up paper, imagining that it was strips of fruit. Eventually, his wife had them moved to another foster home.

On the sixth day in the jail, her door finally opened. Aurie was ashamed of the relief she felt upon seeing another human face, even when it was the heavy jowls of Protector Cox. He wore smugness like a cloak, which meant that whatever they were doing with Pi was going well. She vowed to not be so easy.

"Get up," he said. "Follow me."

He took her to an interrogation room that had permanent protection circles etched into the floor. She wondered if they questioned the demons or otherworldly creatures they captured or they were meant to intimidate. She wanted to study the runes on the wall, but Protector Cox slammed his meaty fist on the metal table.

"Confess," he said, lip twitching with amusement.

"Confess what?"

"Confess."

"I don't understand. What's going on? Where's my sister?" she asked.

"Confess," he said, then after a few moments followed up with, "The prisoner has declined to confess."

He grabbed her arm with lightning reflexes, a surprise for a man of his size, and attached an amulet to her wrist, right below the manacles.

She only had a second to study the runes on the amulet before Protector Cox spoke a command word and the world disappeared behind a curtain of pain. The agony was so abrupt that she couldn't breathe, and when her need for air finally overcame the overwhelming experience, she gulped in desperate heaves.

Eventually Protector Cox released her from the pain. Aurie quivered on her chair, wiping the spit from her lips.

"Confess," he said.

She squeezed her eyes shut.

When he spoke again, it made her flinch, which was most worrisome. She was being conditioned.

"Confess."

She had tears in her eyes. "Fuck you."

"Confess," he said, then, "The prisoner has declined to confess."

The pain resumed.

This pattern went on for many cycles. By the tenth or twentieth, she lost count; the word *confess* brought an anxiety that choked away thought.

Eventually, they took her back to her cell. They'd put a cot in her room, a reminder that they could be generous as well as spiteful. Aurie hated herself for sprawling across the thin mattress as if it were a queen's featherbed.

The next day, Protector Cox led her to the interrogation room. He set the amulet on the table, but did not put it on her.

"You won't last forever," he said. "No one does. Confess to the crime of soul stealing. If you do, the judge will be lenient."

"Tell me what's going on with my sister," she said.

Protector Cox rubbed the edge of the table. "She already made a deal with Mr. Creed. She'll be joining his service tomorrow."

"You lie," she said.

It wasn't so much a grin on Protector Cox's lips, but a slow baring of the teeth, like a predator reminding its prey of their relationship.

"Your sister believes that she's made a deal with Mr. Creed for both your and her service. He has no interest in you. He's far too aware that your personality wouldn't be a good fit. Your sister, on the other hand, has connections with the maetrie, and has a bit looser ideas on what is possible.

"Tomorrow, you will go before the judge and confess your crimes. If you do so, your death will be quick and merciful," he said.

"I thought you said there would be leniency? What if I refuse to admit something I didn't do?" she asked.

He smirked. "There are things worse than death. Yesterday was a taste of what we can do while you're in our custody. Imagine that every day from now until I don't know when. You see, these trials, especially one as sensational as this one, could last years."

"I'm not afraid," she said, even though she was.

"I almost believe you," he said. "And that's why Mr. Creed has excellent judgment. You would defy him to the very end, and no matter how powerful you are, it's not worth the risk. But here's why you're going to confess. If you don't, Mr. Creed will ensure that your sister does not have a pleasant experience in his service."

Her resolve melted away. She was willing to endure a lot of terrible things, but not that.

"I can see you're coming around to our thinking," said Protector Cox. "We both know that your sister can do quite well under Mr. Creed's leadership. If she's worked for that snake Radoslav, why not a member of her own species? Despite all you've heard, Mr. Creed is not that bad."

Aurie was going to remind him of what she'd seen in his house, but decided that for a guy like him, those would be positives.

"She will, of course, mourn you. We'll claim that the judge double-crossed us due to political pressure. It will take a few years for her to get over your death, but once we start putting her to work, those memories will fade. They always do."

As much as it pained her to admit it, she knew this was true. Pi was a survivor. She'd joined Coterie first rather than Arcanium, and had only come around after the incident with the Rod of Dominion. Pi's happiness was more important to Aurie than anything else.

"Can I think about it?" she asked.

"You have until the morning," he said. "And whatever you decide, don't surprise us later by changing your mind. We don't like surprises."

Back in her cell, Aurie curled up on the cot. She didn't think about her decision, because that had already been made the moment he'd made the final threat. Instead, she thought about when she and Pi were kids, hiding under a blanket fort in their room, telling each other stories about what they were going to be when they grew up.

They wore cotton pajamas, the kind that made you feel like you were getting a whole body hug. A flashlight would be propped against a book, casting weird shadows across the uneven ceiling. Sometimes they painted each other's toenails and the fort smelled like nail polish.

She didn't know if she should be happy that she'd gotten to spend so much time with her sister, or sad that their lives had ended up as they did. As those kids in the blanket fort, they'd been certain that all would be right in the world, that good prevailed over evil, that they and their parents would live to ripe old ages.

Aurie mourned the illusion as much as her upcoming death. She hoped they would give her one last chance to see Pi, give her a hug, tell her how much she loved her before she was put to death. She would honor the agreement, tell Pi that she did her best, no matter what the result. It would be better that way.

Aurie wondered what those two little girls would think about where they were today. They wouldn't believe it, of course. No one really understood the flow of history, even their own.

She curled onto her side, imagining that she was holding Pi beneath that blanket fort, fingers entwined, hair tickling her nose, heart thumping away like an alert rabbit. Though she was holding her sister, in a way, it felt like Pi was holding her. They were two broken towers leaning against each other while the storm raged around them, trying to knock them over, while they had to find the strength to keep themselves up.

At some point, she remembered whispering to her sister, telling her everything was going to be okay, that she would find a way to survive, and that maybe in the far future when Creed had forgotten what he'd done, she would get her revenge for the both of them.

When she heard her sister answer, Aurie thought she was dreaming.

"Why wait to get revenge?" asked Pi.

"Wha—?"

She had to clear her eyes to know if she was really seeing her sister standing in her orange jumpsuit over the cot. It wasn't until she saw Inari standing behind her that she understood.

With tears in her eyes, Aurie threw her arms around Pi.

"Creed was going to let me die," said Aurie.

"I should have known better," said Pi.

Aurie grabbed her sister by her shoulders. "No. I don't mean to make you feel guilty. You were doing what you had to do. And if it ever comes to that, something awful, live your life the best as you can."

"How about I not choose what's behind the door that reads something awful," said Pi.

Remembering the kitsune, Aurie turned to Inari and gave a short bow. "Thank you, Inari." Then back to Pi. "How did she know to get you?"

"I was missing you so badly, wanting your advice on what to do, I reached out with my mind. Inari must have been listening. She appeared in my cell moments later," said Pi.

"Good," said Aurie. "Let's get out of here."

"Not yet," said Pi. "We need to get our trinkets. I'm not leaving my jacket here. Assuming that's okay with you, Inari."

The kitsune placed her head under Pi's hand, so she scratched the creature behind the ear.

"How can she jump us there if she's never been here?" asked Aurie.

"She can read their minds and understand the layout," said Pi.

"Let's go then."

The jump gave Aurie vertigo, but it was nothing compared to the pain from the day before. The storage room was dark except for a couple of thin windows with steel grates over them near the ceiling that let in street lights. After searching the boxes, they found one with the label of "SIL-VERTHORNE."

They changed in the darkness while Inari watched them from her haunches. It felt good to have her comfortable jeans and sleeveless cotton hoodie on rather than the scratchy orange jumpsuit. They left the prison gear in the box.

Pi gave her leather jacket a hug before she put it back on. While she was doing that, Aurie started going up and down the aisles reading labels.

"What are you doing?" asked Pi. "We need to get out of here before someone finds us."

"I want the soul vial," said Aurie. "And a chance to use the mass spectrometer on the concrete dust. We've got to figure out where they're keeping the rest."

"I thought we were going to leave the Hundred Halls," said Pi. "After what we just went through, we'd be stupid not to. It's not like they won't come get us if we try and return to school."

"If we expose the real soul thief, then they'll be forced to clear our names," said Aurie. "Please, Pi. We're the only ones that can help them. What's the point of learning magic if we can't help people?"

Her sister gave an embarrassed shrug of the shoulder. "I'll do it because you asked, but I'm not getting captured again. Next time I'm not holding back."

"I don't think Creed's the type to give second chances, so that's probably wise," said Aurie.

Pi let out a breath of relief and joined Aurie in the search. They found the soul vial in a ziplock bag with the date written on it.

Inari got them to a pitch-black lab room in the basement. After feeling around in the darkness, they found a switch. The lights buzzed on, revealing a large room with multiple tables full of chemistry equipment, a chemical shower in the corner, and other machines set around the room. There were also signs of magical investigations: a protection circle, bins full of reagents, and other magical devices, like a runed puzzle box.

The mass spectrometer was a machine the size of a desk. Pi tapped on it.

"Do you know how to use this?" she asked.

"No, but I'm sure we can find the directions somewhere," replied Aurie. "You look while I get the dust off the bottom of the vial."

While she didn't know anything about a spectrometer, Aurie was skilled with chemistry equipment due to her experience measuring reagents. She found bright blue plastic gloves, pulled the vial from the bag, and using a fine brush, knocked the white speckles of dust off the bottom into a small bowl.

"Is this it?" asked Pi, holding up a pamphlet she'd removed from a desk drawer.

Halfway across the room to join her sister, Aurie heard the door open. She threw herself to the ground at the same time as Pi.

"Hello? Anyone in here?" asked a male voice at the door.

Aurie had caught a glimpse of Protector robes before she hit the ground. Inari was lying behind a desk, so none of them were currently visible. The only problem was they weren't near Inari, so they couldn't jump out easily.

"What's going on? I know I heard voices," said the Protector.

It sounded like a gun had been unholstered. Bullets were faster than magic.

"Frank? Jessica? If you two are fucking over there, just tell me and I'll leave. I won't say anything," said the Protector.

Pi and she exchanged glances. They had to get back to Inari before the Protector came further into the room.

Aurie got on her belly to see beneath the tables. A pair of black boots were moving around the tables. In about ten seconds, the Protector would see Inari and then the two of them.

The click of a radio, followed by static and the Protector's voice whispering, "I'm going to need backup in the lab. Something or someone is down here. Hopefully Smith didn't leave an imp loose in here again."

Inari started crawling towards them, keeping her paws flat and haunches low. The man was moving around the desk. He'd see them any moment. The soul vial was sitting on the table, along with the dust she wanted to analyze. Aurie reached up and snatched the vial off the table.

"I saw that," said the Protector.

The next few seconds seemed to take forever. The Protector's heavy boots slapped against the tile as he ran around the corner. Pi reached Inari first, sliding across the tile. Aurie could see the top of the Protector's head, and his gun. She lunged forward, sliding on her belly. When her fingertips brushed Inari's fur, the world shifted around them.

They were back in their room in Arcanium.

"That was too close," said Pi, hugging Inari.

Aurie examined the soul vial in her fist. "We didn't get any answers. Do you think we can go back another time?"

"Are you crazy?" asked Pi. "You know they'll have guards now. We're fugitives."

"Possibly."

Pi shook her head. "We won't be able to go back, and it doesn't matter. I promised Inari I'd let her go after she helped us escape."

"Are you sure that's wise? Didn't Uncle Liam warn you not to?" Aurie asked, then when Inari whined at her, she added, "Sorry. Shitty of me to say that after you saved us. But she could be a big help to us in stopping the soul thief."

"Aurie, I promised. And I don't think she's dangerous," said Pi. "I think that was just another part of the con. I'm pretty sure that Uncle Liam was going to use her to break into the Invictus bank, the same place we keep our money. I found an enchantment on the fae coin that neutralizes wards. I bet he was hoping I'd put it in the bank since it's gold. And remember that day they picked him up? He was near the bank. It makes sense. He's exactly who you said he was, a liar and a cheat. He was only here for the gold."

"I'm sorry, Pi. I know you wanted him to be better than that. I guess it's a good thing he wasn't around when we were kids. Did he ever tell you anything about our heritage?"

"Nothing. So I guess we're plain ol' red-blooded humans." Pi put her hand on Inari's back. "I'm going to let her go. I promised."

"It's your choice," said Aurie. "I'm grateful that Inari saved us."

Pi nodded soberly and started removing the collar. Once she had unhooked the latch, the runes stopped glowing. The kitsune shook her head as if the collar had been crimping her neck.

Aurie watched as Pi gave the kitsune a big hug. Inari bent her body in the semblance of a bow.

A message of thanks was projected into her mind.

"Goodbye, Inari."

In a blink, the kitsune was gone, leaving the two sisters alone.

"What now?" asked Pi.

"We stop them," said Aurie.

"How? We don't even know where they're at," said Pi.

Aurie put a hand to her chin. "Actually, I think we do."

"What?"

"The concrete dust," said Aurie. "I think I know where it's coming from, and you do too."

"Aurie, stop being clever and tell me."

"The statue of Invictus. They've had the museum and gift shop under construction all year. Which means you know what we'll probably find there," said Aurie.

"The portal."

TWENTY FOUR

The statue of Invictus had been under construction for the entire school year. Pi found the information online. She also found nothing about their escape from the city jail, which confused both of them.

"Why didn't they put out a press release about capturing us?" asked Aurie.

"That's easy," said Pi. "If Creed was going to get me to sign up for Protectors, he couldn't very well pin being the soul thief on me. I assume they would have announced it as soon as they had your confession."

Aurie's face drained of color. "No, that's not it. They weren't going to say a word, but I was going to die, just the same."

"I don't understand," said Pi.

"Check how many schools are left that haven't had someone taken by the soul thief. I think they've been keeping track on the *Herald* website," said Aurie.

Pi pulled it down out of her favorites list as she said, "I still feel icky every time I check this." The count was on a banner on the front page. "Camille is a sick lady. Only three schools left—ours, Justicars, and the

Blue Flame."

"Tragedy sells," said Aurie. "They would have given me to Hemistad, taken my soul to complete the halls. Can't exactly announce you caught me if you're going to kill me shortly after. We need to take this information to Semyon. I know he forbade us to get involved, but it's too late now, and he needs our help."

"It's not the best of ideas," said Pi. Aurie made a face, and she added, "But...if we're lucky, he's already stopped the Cabal and we're safe to return to our regularly scheduled studying. Finals are next week and all."

"I've never in my life been more excited about the prospect of finals," said Aurie.

"Don't lie. I've read your diary," said Pi, then mimicked her sister's slightly lower voice. "Dear diary, only one hundred and thirteen days until finals, how will I survive the wait?"

Aurie rolled her eyes, and it made Pi feel a little better that her sister could maintain her sense of humor through this. They headed down to the waterfall, avoiding their fellow students, since they didn't want to get anyone else involved. Which only made Pi wish she hadn't sent Inari away, but she was trying to do the right thing. The smarter decision would have been to make Inari help them until they caught the soul thief, but part of her had wished that Aurie would give up the idea, and the two of them could flee the country, especially since their names hadn't been plastered over the city in the newspapers. If anything went wrong, she was sure that could happen anyway.

The creature in the pool showed no sign of surfacing when they crossed the invisible path. The whole place felt muted. Pi worried what they'd find on the other side.

The passage to Semyon's living quarters was closed, with no signs to indicate when he might return. Pi was taking a step towards the waterfall when a dark shape hurried through.

Pi sent a bolt of flame when the person appeared.

"Deshawn!" cried her sister.

He ducked beneath the flame, barely keeping from falling into the pool.

"What the devil?" he asked, stumbling onto the stone, knocking the singed hair from his tight fro. He was wearing a black runner's jacket, though he didn't look sweaty.

"Sorry." Pi cringed.

"Where have you two been and why are you wound so tightly?" he asked, pushing his sleeves up.

"Don't tell him," said Aurie.

"We need his help," said Pi, right away. "Look, if you want to do this, let's do this. At the very least, we need Arcanium to be on high alert."

"Why's that?" he asked.

"Because the soul thief still needs one of us," said Pi. "They were going to use Aurie, but we escaped."

"Holy hells, who had you?"

"Long story," said Pi. "And we don't have time. But no one should be wandering the halls alone. Are you looking for Semyon?"

"No," said Deshawn. "He left Arcanium a few hours ago. Looked in a hurry."

"Do you know where he went? Or anything strange about him?" asked Aurie.

"Professor Mali went with him," he said. "They left in a taxi van, which was weird."

Pi and Aurie shared a look.

"The Cabal must be monitoring the Garden Network," said Aurie.

"You're assuming that he's going after them and not just getting the hell out of here before they take over," said Pi.

Deshawn kept looking back and forth between them. "What are you two talking about?"

"Look," said Pi. "The Cabal is trying to get into Invictus' quarters so they can take control of the Halls. Patron Semyon and Professor Mali are likely going to stop them, or try anyway. We're going to help."

"Are you two nuts?" he asked.

"Probably, but we don't have a choice. If we can't prove they're behind stealing the souls, then they'll pin it on my sister," said Pi.

Deshawn rubbed the back of his head. He seemed to be processing it. "Man, that's fucked up. What do you need me to do?"

"Rally Arcanium. Get everyone together in one place so they can't take anyone," said Aurie. "The auditorium or something like that."

"What about you two?" he asked.

"We're going after them," said Pi.

"Won't you be giving them what they need? They can take one of you?" he asked.

"We don't have a choice," said Aurie.

"There's always a choice," Pi said to her sister, but she could see that she wasn't going to change her mind. She could always count on her sister to be more stubborn than a petrified mule.

"I hear Paris is lovely in the spring," she added as a taunt. Aurie stuck her tongue out.

Deshawn left to gather the other students of Arcanium. Afterwards, Aurie turned to her.

"What are we going to do about Hemistad? We can't take him, which means we can't really stop them," said Aurie.

"So you're saying facing the leaders of the Cabal isn't bad enough?" asked Pi.

"Yeah, basically."

"Some of the books I was researching made mention of spells that were used to combat the erlking, but I never found any. If you give me a little bit, I can check the library," said Pi.

"Good idea. I'll grab a few things from our room," said Aurie.

The Biblioscribe was a brass golem that contained information about all the books in Invictus, though mostly it was used by students for the books in the Arcanium library. The Biblioscribe had a serene, but comical look on its metal face as if it were contemplating monkeys stuck in Chinese finger traps.

"Biblioscribe," said Pi. "Are there any spells involving an erlking in the library?"

The brass golem blinked once to show it was thinking. "No, Pythia. There are no spells on erlkings in the library."

She hated the way the golem said her name. Pi-THEE-a. "Okay, my brass monkey, are there any spells about herlakings, or hellequins?"

"No, Pythia. There are no spells—"

"Got it," she said. "We don't need a dissertation each time. Just a simple yes or no will do."

"Affirmative, Pythia. I will not give a dissertation each time, but a simple yes or no."

Pi sighed. She paced about the room, trying to remember the many books she'd read about the subject. A snippet from *Leaves of Fae* bubbled up that linked erlkings to elf kings. At the time she'd thought it was a translation error, but she was desperate. The only problem was imagining Hemistad as a withered old royal elf.

"What about spells involving the elven kings?"

"There are one hundred and thirty-seven spells involving elven kings," said the Biblioscribe.

"How many in the library?"

The Biblioscribe blinked twice. "Fifty-seven."

She didn't have time to go through the books. A project like that would take a couple of days with no guarantee that any might work.

"How many of those spells have to do with soul magic?"

"Zero."

Pi kicked the desk. "How many of those spells can be used against an elven king?"

"Eighteen."

Hope bubbled in her chest. "How many could I master enough to cast tonight?"

The Biblioscribe tilted its head. "I cannot ascertain the level of your ability, Pythia. That is beyond my function."

"I'm asking the wrong questions," said Pi. "How many of those spells require being in Fae to cast?"

"Eighteen."

Pi slammed her fist on the table. Maybe this wasn't going to work.

"Wait. Biblioscribe. What about the Pied Piper? Are there any spells related to the Pied Piper?" she asked.

"One."

Before she allowed herself to cheer, she asked, "Is it in the library?"

"Affirmative."

Pi kissed the brass golem on the forehead. "Thank you!"

She ran through the stacks until she found it. The tome was falling apart. It appeared to be a scholarly work about the Piper. She quickly paged through until she found the spell, whose purpose didn't immediately suggest itself to her. Rather than dissect its meaning, she ripped the page from the book and stuffed it into her jacket for later.

Before they left, Pi checked the street outside the drawbridge for signs of the police or Creed's men. A few thick-necked guys with crew cuts were milling about acting like they were tourists.

"Could they be any more obvious?" asked Aurie.

"Unless it's a trick," said Pi, not trusting anything after her experience in the jail.

"How do we get out? Based on what Deshawn said, we can't use the Garden Network, even if we could get into Semyon's quarters," said Aurie.

"We need our own Garden Network," said Pi. "Which gives me an idea. Do you think we can use the carryall? The one we put the mini-portal in?"

"We can't fit through that small space. It would take expanding it. Which would make it unstable. Could as easily blow up, killing the both of us. But even if we did that, we'd need someone to take it out of Arcanium, and we don't want anyone else to risk themselves."

"Let me call Hannah. Tinkers was hit a few months ago," she said.

"Won't that look suspicious?" asked Aurie.

"Leave it to me," said Pi. "You work on that carryall."

When Hannah arrived an hour later in a Gus's Pizza shirt with a pizza warmer in her arms, Pi greeted her at the door, standing in the shadows so no one could see her.

"Do you own that?" asked Pi.

"The perks of being poor enough for too many part-time jobs. I kept the warmer for keeping dragon's blood hot when I need to make Bellet's Lifting Pistons," said Hannah, pulling a pizza out of the insulated package.

"You actually brought a pizza?" asked Pi.

"I didn't want them to question my authenticity. I will, of course, require a tip," said Hannah with a grin.

Pi handed her the carryall. "It's all I've got on me."

"Where do you want me to put it?" asked Hannah.

Pi thought about asking her to take it to the statue, but that was on the other side of the city, and she didn't want Hannah to get involved. Last year with the contest had been bad enough.

"The train station will be good enough," said Pi. "Just stick your hand through and wave us in. We'll do the rest."

Hannah nodded, stuffed the carryall into the warmer, and skated back over the drawbridge. Pi watched from the shadows until her friend had safely left the area before returning to her room with Aurie.

When she arrived, the room was bathed in golden faez. The raw magic tingled across Pi's skin.

"Is this a good idea?" asked Pi. "You know this could react badly with all sorts of things."

"It's the best I could do to open the portal wider. The faez gives the obsidian a cushion as I widen it; otherwise the whole thing threatens to collapse, which will lead to an explosion." Then she added with an exasperated sigh, pointing towards a wipe board with equations hastily scribbled across it, "Look, I did the math, and I'm at least fifty percent certain I did it correctly."

"A coin flip, great. And how are you going to maintain the faez matrix and crawl through it?" said Pi.

"Very carefully."

A little while later, a shimmering silvery disc appeared on the desk where they'd anchored the portal, and a manicured hand with skulls painted on the fingernails shimmied through.

Pi climbed onto the table. "I can't believe I'm doing this."

While she crawled forward, Aurie stretched the portal wide enough for her to fit. When she stuck her head through the silvery disc, the world spun around her. The vertigo nearly made her collapse, but she kept going, knowing that delaying would only invite calamity. Her head came out in a dingy room with yellowed walls. The smell of urine hit her immediately, followed by a muted flush. With Hannah's help, Pi pulled herself through the portal and into the women's bathroom at the train station.

"Oh, god, I need to wash my hands now. I touched the floor," said Pi.

"Sorry, it was the only place I could find for privacy."

Despite Pi's experience with magic and regularly seeing impossible things happen, watching her sister crawl through the carryall was unnerving. The fluctuating portal was stretching her sister like silly putty, while the strain of maintaining the faez field was evident from Aurie's expression. When her hips had passed into the train station bathroom, everything grew wonky. Suddenly, Aurie faded in and out, followed by the smell of burning canvas.

Without thinking about it, Pi grabbed Aurie when she became solid and yanked her through. Aurie hit the tiles, and the carryall started sparking and humming.

"Get out!" yelled Aurie.

The three of them ran out, right before the mini-portal exploded. Smoke leaked out the cracks in the door. No one was directly outside, but they heard people yelling from around the corner, so they went the other way.

They reached the train. Pi and her sister jumped on before the doors closed, waving to Hannah, who gave them two thumbs up as encouragement. Approaching sirens wailed, and the train sped away from the station towards the third ward and the statue of Invictus.

TWENTY FIVE

A second-story cafe was the closest Aurie and her sister could get to the statue of Invictus. Despite the late hour, tourists milled about the square, directly outside of the covered scaffolding, snapping pictures. Helicopters roamed the air above the city like angry hornets.

Pi tapped on the window. "I see four police officers in the square and I recognize that at least one of them can use magic."

"I think that lady on the bench is a fifth," said Aurie. "I saw her nod to one of the others when he walked by."

"Do you think it's a trap for us?" asked Pi.

"They're probably just being careful," said Aurie. "If tonight's the night they take control, they want to make sure no one interferes. It's probably more for Semyon than us."

"How do we get in there? We can't just sit here all night and watch," said Pi.

Aurie ran her hand through her hair, trying to think. "We need a distraction."

"I don't think the pizza trick will work again."

She was staring at the statue when she heard Pi cursing. As soon as she saw what her sister was looking at, she added her own invectives. A pair of robed Protectors marched someone with a hood over their upper body towards the building like a condemned man. Tourists averted their eyes as if they instinctively knew not to acknowledge it lest they be grabbed next. *Is that how the normals see mages?* Their cowardice angered Aurie, though she knew they had no power to stop them. This was quickly followed by self-condemnation as she remembered she was hiding out in the second-story cafe, safely hidden from prying eyes.

"I recognize that jacket. That's Deshawn. He must have tried to follow us," said Pi. "They probably grabbed him as soon as he left Arcanium."

A wave of guilt hit Aurie. "Why can't people just listen to me? Now he's complicated things."

"You know we're not required to follow your lead unless we want to, and clearly Deshawn wanted to help," said Pi.

"Is now really the time for this?" asked Aurie, exasperated. "We need to get in there before they husk him."

Pi gave her that look that made Aurie feel like she was losing her sister one comment at a time.

"Pi, please."

Her sister's expression softened. "Let's focus on getting in there. Dooset daram."

"Dooset daram. What if we went in spells ablazin'?" asked Aurie.

Pi laughed incredulously. "I like the idea, but I'm afraid we'd have collateral damage."

Memories of the beginning of the year in the Enochian district slapped Aurie across the face, draining her of emotion until she was cold. Pi reached out and touched her arm.

"Sorry, sis. I didn't mean to bring that up. But we're going to have to face some risks if we're going to do this. People might get hurt, most likely us, but it could be people who have nothing to do with this. It's the price of caring."

Aurie tried to shake Annabelle's face from her vision, but she could only see her pigtails bouncing as she ran around the fountain, a giggle at the edge of her lips ready to burst forth like bubbles.

"Why is shit like this so complicated?" asked Aurie.

Her sister at least had the decency not to answer.

"We need to get in there. I wish there was a spell for invisibility." Aurie paused. "Are there any demons that can help us?"

The look on Pi's face was part surprise and part concern.

"I know a few. Spells I've memorized for emergencies," said Pi. "Though it's not going to be pretty. We don't have much to offer."

They moved to a nearby street, upwind of the statue. Pi produced a woody chunk of tangled leaves from an inside pocket.

"Keep people from bothering us," said Pi.

Aurie put up a couple of subtle spells that would unconsciously divert people away. It was a risk with the Protectors so near, but they had to take chances.

Using a paint marker, Pi drew a protection circle on the sidewalk, leaving the dried sagebrush in the middle, and waited until the street was clear to start the summoning spell. After a minute of chanting in Infernal, a scaly imp, no taller than a bucket, appeared. The minor demon had red beady eyes and a toothpick sticking out of its mouth.

"Howdy, cowgirls," said the imp with a western accent. "Been a long time since I've been in these parts."

Pi made a scooping motion with her hands as if to say that it was Aurie's show.

"I have a deal, demon," said Aurie. "If you're interested."

"Call me Bart," said the imp. "Black Bart."

"We need your help, Black Bart," said Aurie. "I know imps have a talent for fire, but I need smoke, that's why we summoned you."

The imp craned its little head. "This is the *ilithadrihilcth*." It was the Infernal name for the City of Sorcery. "It'll take a pretty penny to get me to interfere here."

The imp's comment made Aurie want to question it further about what it meant, but she knew they were exposed on the sidewalk. If someone called 911 about a demon sighting, the cops would descend on them like locusts.

"What's your price, Black Bart?" asked Aurie.

The imp glanced around, finally laying its red eyes on her sister. The coy smile on its leathery lips made Aurie shiver. Pi's eyes grew wide with concern, even before the imp spoke.

"Oh, she has all sorts of fingers in her pie," said Black Bart, "like wires on a puppet, some you don't even know you have. I smell fate on the both of you, and I wants a taste. Give me one strand on that pretty little head of hers."

"Fuck no," said Pi, right away. "No way am I giving that creepy little Doc Holliday a single hair."

"Doc Holliday," hissed the imp. "I knew him, knew him well. Had an air of faez to him."

"Pi. We need his help," said Aurie. "I can make smoke, but we need enough to fill that whole square, give us a chance to sneak in. Time's wasting."

Her sister spun away, clearly trying to contain her rage. It was no small thing to willingly give a demon piece of you, especially a strand of hair.

Pi spun towards the imp, jabbing her finger in his direction. "What are you going to do with it?"

"Nothing," said Black Bart, eyes burning red. "For now, anyway. Mayhap in the future I might need a favor from the pair of you, fate-twisted as you are."

Aurie knew enough to ignore such comments about fate, especially from demons. They liked to act like they knew more than they did. There was no such thing as fate, only probability and self-fulfilling prophecies.

"Pi..."

"Fine," said Pi, plucking a hair from her head, but not handing it over. "Promise first. Make the deal, and I swear if you screw me over, I'll feed you to Pazuzu."

The imp squeaked with fear at the demon lord's name. The fact that Black Bart took the threat seriously said more about what was going on in the infernal lands than anything else.

"I promise," said Black Bart, crossing an "X" over where a heart would be on a human. "You want smoke, I'll give you smoke so thick you won't be able to see your hand in front of your face."

With great reluctance, Pi handed over the hair. Black Bart gave them a solicitous wink, and got right to work on the pile of sagebrush.

As smoke billowed from the summoning circle, Aurie grabbed her sister's hand and started marching towards the square.

"How bad is he?" she asked.

"Who?" asked Pi.

"That demon," said Aurie.

"He caused the shootout at the O.K. corral, if that's what you're wondering. I hope that was worth it," said Pi.

Before they reached the square, a wave of smoke enveloped them, flowing like a river towards the statue. Aurie imagined the towering figure of Invictus sticking out of the fog.

The smoke made her eyes burn, forcing her to squint. Aurie could see her sister, but not much else. Shouts and odd noises rang through the haze, rising and falling, sounding like they were right next to them.

One of the Protectors, who had to be within twenty feet, shouted,

"Freeze!"

Her legs wanted to seize up due to the magic of his voice. Together, they yanked their legs forward as if they waded through molasses. They were able to get away, but only because the Protector hadn't used his voice in their direction.

A gunshot rang out, followed by screams of panic. The sisters reflexively ducked.

"What the hell," muttered Pi.

They hurried forward, right as someone large barreled into them. Aurie was knocked backwards. The big man had a purse in his hand. An opportunistic thief had used the smoke as a chance to steal a purse. The thief ran off into the smoke, leaving Aurie alone.

"Pi?" she whispered, wishing they'd come up with code names. Any nearby officers would surely know their names if they heard them.

"Aurie," came her sister's voice, further away in the smoke.

Aurie was creeping forward in the direction she hoped was the building when the sound of boots slapping the pavement made her turn to protect herself. One of the Protectors in robes appeared. Both of them were surprised, but he acted faster.

"Freeze!" he yelled.

Aurie was hit with the full brunt of his magic. She felt like his voice had encased her in ice.

Though her body was frozen, her lips could still move.

"Aurelia!" she shouted at him, trying to use her true name to break the spell.

The Protector flinched, worry crossing his gaze like clouds, then when he realized the magic had been too weak to break his hold, he laughed.

"I caught one," he called into the fog.

Before long, she was surrounded by four officers. The smoke was thinning. She could see further than ten feet. The older female officer who'd been on the bench and had lost a purse to the thief pulled her gun out and switched off the safety.

"Did Bannon say to bring this one in dead or alive?" she asked the others. It was clear she was the one in charge of the guard detail.

"I don't think he cares since they've got their last donor," said the Protector who'd captured her. "But if you're going to do it, you'd better do it before the smoke clears."

"It'll be a lot easier to find the one with the short hair if this one is out of the way," said the female officer.

Then she put the gun to Aurie's head.

TWENTY SIX

When the thief ran into Aurie, Pi was knocked away and spun around, until she didn't know which direction she was facing. She made random steps until she realized she was only making things worse.

A shape in the smoke ran past, but it didn't notice her.

"Pi?"

Her heart leapt in her chest at hearing her name spoken from her sister's lips. But it sounded far away. She must have moved in the chaos.

"Aurie."

As soon as the name left her lips, Pi cringed, realizing how stupid it was of her to use her sister's name, after they'd escaped from the precinct.

She made it three steps closer to her sister when a Voice of Command cut through the smoke. Pi got hit by a glancing blow. The left half of her body was unresponsive. She felt like she'd slept on her arm and leg and couldn't feel them anymore.

"Aurelia!"

Her sister tried to use her true name. Pi felt the magic in her voice. She was surprised at how far Aurie had come in learning the technique, especially without guidance, but it wasn't enough. Soon after, other voices converged on her sister.

She heard the female officer discussing shooting Aurie. *NO!* Pi strained against the immobility of her left side, but she couldn't break the magic. Her left leg was trapped. Pi reached out with her right, tried to drag her body across the concrete, but it wouldn't move more than a few inches.

The smoke was fading. Through the haze, shapes started to appear. If one of the officers turned in her direction, they'd see her.

The shot that rang out was like a hammer blow to her heart. Pi nearly gave up then and there. What was the point of going on without her sister? The only thing that got her to move was the thought that Deshawn was inside. With a trembling hand, she pulled a paint marker from her coat and imbued her frozen limbs with verumancy to combat the officer's stun-magic.

As she dragged her waking limbs towards the building, the smoke fading to wisps, Pi knew there was a darker reason to go into the statue. Revenge. Revenge on those responsible.

She slipped past the tarps and shimmied along the wall until she found a door, locked but not insurmountable. She made light blossom around her with the snap of her fingers, but it was cold, so cold, and she found she hated the light. She went on.

The building beneath the statue contained a gift shop and museum. Pi had come through an emergency door to rows of glass shelves filled with glass globes and bobble-heads. She picked up a globe, and the snow inside fell around the miniature Stone Singer hall. The motion activated colored lights inside which alternated sides of the stone flower.

She set it back down and walked past the globes with detached numbness. What frivolous junk. Is that what the normals thought the Halls were about? Didn't they realize the power to warp the world was contained in the city? If they did, they'd never let the Hundred Halls remain.

At the end of the row, Pi collapsed on the floor, sobbing. The urge to flee had dragged her this far, but now that she was, at the moment, safe, her bones dissolved beneath her. Pi heaved, her forehead bumping the floor.

She didn't delude herself with regrets of Paris, or escaping. She knew that Aurie would never have agreed, would never have left the Halls, and it had cost her life.

Pi lay on the floor for a long time. Only when a door opened in another part of the building did she douse her light. Past the wax statues of the original five patrons, a group of people moved.

She recognized the voices from outside. The officers were headed down a set of stairs. Though it was hard to see across the animatronics figures and display boards, the glimpse of her sister's face was enough to send waves of emotion through Pi.

Aurie!

Pi could hardly believe her eyes. Her heart thundered in her chest, her ears. Pi wanted to scream her sister's name, but restrained herself, limbs shaking.

"Oh, Aurie," she whispered. "I thought I'd lost you. I'll do anything to get you back. Just you wait. Stay alive, don't let them hurt you."

The urge to race to the stairs and take them on right then and there was hard to contain. The tears that had come so liberally before from heartache still came, either from happiness or the wild swings of emotions. She wiped them away using the sleeve of her jacket.

A couple minutes after they left, a strange vibration reached her through the floor. It lasted about a minute and then went away. She waited another few minutes to see if the officers would come back, and when they didn't, Pi went to investigate. Her senses were on high alert, tingly with anticipation and the faez she kept at the ready.

The staircase had signs indicating that it wasn't meant for tourists, but it wasn't blocked off. If she hadn't seen her sister taken in that direction, she wouldn't have thought to go down rather than up. Pi'd been under the impression that the place they were hiding was inside the statue, but maybe she'd find an elevator or other such entry method.

The basement was dark except for flickering emergency lights that buzzed. She wished she had something in her hands, a wand, or gun, something to focus the energy inside her.

A maintenance tunnel went about fifty feet before it opened into a storage room filled with shelves of electrical parts, wires, motors, and materials to keep the animatronics running. The detached head of Bannon Creed stared at her from a middle shelf. Pi flicked it in the forehead with a fingernail.

The back area had a generator room that smelled like diesel. None of the engines were running currently, but she assumed that's what had created the vibration she'd felt.

She was about to go back down the maintenance tunnel looking for hidden passageways when she noticed an archway covered in runes. The bricks had been replaced with obsidian sheets connected by unseen wires, probably inside the wall. The archway didn't lead anywhere, just about ten feet further before ending in a stone wall, but that wasn't the point. If she could activate the portal, she could go wherever it took her.

Pi didn't think this was the way into Invictus' tower, but something else. Maybe an entryway, or other hidden realm that Invictus used.

Studying the runes revealed multiple layers of protection. She was halfway to understanding their purpose when a light bloomed in the direction of the maintenance tunnel, followed by the soft echo of voices.

Pi hurried behind the massive generator, but kept the inactive portal in view so she might learn how to pass through it.

As the voices neared, she thought they sounded familiar. She craned her neck and leaned forward on the greasy motor, right as a hand went around her mouth.

TWENTY SEVEN

The gunshot deafened her left ear. Her neck stung from the blast, but she was alive. Aurie opened her eyes to find Uncle Liam with his hand on the officer's arm, holding it up. She stifled her surprise.

The other officers glared in his direction, but seemed to tolerate his presence. No one had made a move for their guns.

"Mr. Creed prefers the young lady alive," he said, the leafy tattoos on his arm glowing with magic.

The older woman's mouth wrinkled with distaste. "That's not what he told me. And who are you to give me orders?"

A twinkle formed in his eye while a Cheshire Cat grin spread across his face. "Oh, come on, lass. Are we still bitter about that little misunderstanding?"

When she didn't move, he whistled a little tune that placated their anger, softening their expressions until they were cow-like.

She backed down, pulling her gun down to reholster it. Uncle Liam patted her on the shoulder.

"There, there."

"I don't know why he keeps you around," said the officer, face wracked with confusion. It was clear they were aware that he was affecting them, but they couldn't figure out how. Since he hadn't targeted her with his magic song, she was able to see him for what he was. She was angry at herself for not realizing it sooner. The fae looks, the tattoo with a bridge beneath an autumn canopy, the whistling that accompanied his use of magic.

"For times like this," said Uncle Liam. "We're taking her inside, so button her up so she doesn't start any mischief."

While the officers put regular handcuffs on Aurie's wrists behind her back, Liam's role became clear to her. Seeing him in person, knowing what he'd done, made her sick to her stomach. And it wasn't just what he'd done in the Hundred Halls. If she didn't have her hands behind her back she would have clawed him across the face.

"You're the soul thief," she said, hoping to provoke a reaction from the officers.

None of them gave her comment any attention; in fact, they seemed to be averting their gaze as if that would remove culpability.

"Sorry you have to find out this way, lass."

Her heart burned with the thought that they had falsely accused Hemistad. He'd been true to his word.

"You weren't going to race Inari. That was another lie. You were going to use her to get into the Halls with stronger wards."

His nostrils flared. "Not sure how that troublesome kitsune turned the tables on me, but she did. In the end, except for taking a hair bit longer than planned, the result was the same."

"So we're *not* related."

His gaze went dark. "Was nice while it lasted. Been a long time since I've had family. Speaking of, where's your sister? I can't imagine she's far."

"She left the city," said Aurie. "Gave up on the Halls, and now she's headed to I don't know where. Which is a good thing, since you tried to kill her in the undercity to get the kitsune back."

Liam lifted her chin with his finger, staring directly into her eyes. "You're a good liar, a really good one. That bit about the race, while true, was meant to distract me from the first part. But remember, I'm better. Been doing it much longer than you. But that's okay. Since we've got you, I'm sure she'll turn up eventually. I know you sisters wouldn't abandon each other."

He winked and pushed her towards the statue, which Aurie could see now that the smoke had faded. She hoped Pi had the good sense to leave, but knew that she was likely inside. As Liam had said, they would never abandon each other.

Two officers went inside the building with them while the woman in charge and a fourth officer returned to the square. Aurie was led down stairs, and through a long maintenance tunnel until they came out in a storage area that smelled like diesel.

Liam turned the generator on, then moved to a runed archway with obsidian casings lining the underside. This had to be the archway that Semyon had been talking about with Celesse. The purpose of the generator wasn't clear, but Aurie had no time to think about it.

"Gather around, lads and lasses, I don't want to leave anyone behind," said Liam.

Realizing that as soon as they took her through the portal, she was unlikely to come back, Aurie spoke to the two officers.

"You don't want to do this. He's the Pied Piper," she said. "Murderer of children from ages past. I understand you're doing what your boss wants, as this is a Hall matter, but why are you working with him? He's the worst serial killer of all time."

The worried glances told Aurie that they didn't know the true extent of the being in their midst, but neither looked ready to challenge him.

"Stories get exaggerated over the years," he said.

"You murdered a hundred kids at this school," she said.

He held up a finger. "Not murdered, and not quite a hundred, yet. Just liberated them of their souls, which after a little bit is borrowed, can be safely put back."

"Liar," she said. "Creed's using them for his sick toys."

"What their boss does with them is not my problem." He snapped his fingers in her face. "Enough talking. Travel time."

He placed his hand against the stones in three locations, lighting up specific runes. When he finished, a silvery portal appeared in the archway.

"Hold tight, and walk together," he said.

The two officers, Liam, and Aurie went through the portal. They came out in another basement. Two sets of stairs went up in different directions. A muted car honk, followed by distant sirens, reached her.

"Are we in the statue?" asked Aurie.

"Aye, lass."

"But why have a portal? Why not just walk upstairs to get inside?" she asked.

None of them seemed to know why, and it appeared they hadn't asked this question themselves, because they all pondered it.

"Alright, lads," said Liam. "You can take her from here. Up the stairs, down the hall, up another set of stairs, and you'll find your boss. He'll be more pleased than an Irishman drowning in beer. Upsie-daisy while I fetch the other one."

He disappeared back through the portal, leaving Aurie alone with them. She hadn't planned anything, but sensing she would have no better opportunity, she kicked the nearest officer right between the legs. He doubled over, collapsing to his knees.

The second reached for his gun, but Aurie was faster. She funneled a dozen spells' worth of faez into her voice.

"Aurelia!"

The blast of magic stunned the officer, knocking him backwards, but not unconscious as she'd hoped. She was getting better with her true name, but the majority of her magic had failed to convert itself into useable force. But she had no time to contemplate what she'd done wrong and fled towards the staircase.

She'd never run up stairs with her hands behind her back before, and she misjudged a middle step, slamming chest first into the last three steps. Behind her the groans of the officers rallying themselves sent fear into her limbs, numbing the pain.

The next level had crisscrossing hallways with multiple doors. A faint humming was coming from somewhere nearby.

Aurie regained her feet like a newborn foal, picked the nearest door, and backed against it, using her hands to work the knob. She slipped into the dark room and locked the door, after which, she rolled onto the floor to slip her handcuffed wrists beneath her until she could shimmy them to the front. With her hands in front, she could work limited magic, assuming the spell didn't require wild motions.

The sound of boots passed the doorway, then after muffled speaking, backed up. The handle rattled. Aurie held her breath until the officers left.

She knew she didn't have much time. Once they found Bannon Creed, and after he finished yelling at them, they'd come searching for her.

A wisp of light revealed she was in another generator room, except this one had no roof. It was like an elevator shaft. Bound cables went up through a tube in the center, while a metal ladder was attached to the outside of the tube. A whiff of faez permeated the space, the source of which she could find no obvious answer.

Aurie considered going back out to see if she could leave through the portal, but knew that it was unlikely. Based on Liam's actions, and the fact that they'd all had to touch him, there seemed to be some limitations on who could use it.

"The ladder it is."

Going up stairs with handcuffs behind her back was one level of difficulty, but climbing a ladder was a whole different challenge, even with the handcuffs in front. Since the rungs were further away than the spacing of the two cuffs, she had to move her hands from one rung to the next together, leaving the ladder for a precarious moment, untethered from its support. If she missed a rung, or her fingers slipped off, she would plummet to the bottom.

After the tenth rung, her hands were sweating. She tried rubbing them on her shirt, first one hand and then the other, but it was slowing her down, and she didn't want to be caught on the ladder when they figured out she hadn't gone up the other way. It would be too easy for an agitated officer to point his pistol up the shaft and bring her down.

The wisp followed her as she went, which was a blessing and a curse. By the fiftieth rung, she couldn't see to the bottom, and her labored breathing hid any noises. If they returned, she'd never know until she took a bullet to the leg.

Aurie was starting to worry that the ladder wouldn't come out anywhere, that it would go until it reached the top, while the wires would go through the ceiling to another room. But peering through the gloom above her, she could see that the shaft opened up into a larger space.

She must have been leaning too far back to see because the next rung skipped off her fingers and she fell back, the darkness of the shaft sucking her downward. She was going to fall, so she did the only thing she could think of to get back to the ladder.

With a turn of the head, Aurie imagined the force of a giant invisible hand pushing her onto the ladder and yelled, "Aurelia!"

The impact knocked her back, allowing her to grab a rung, upon which she clung to catch her breath. Aurie didn't rest long, since her shout had announced her location. The officers, and possibly Bannon Creed, couldn't be far behind.

Forearms shaking, Aurie focused on the remaining stretch of ladder, even when the door far below her was kicked open. She dismissed her light, which only made the climb worse, as she couldn't see the next rung and had to rely on her muscle memory.

Shouts echoed upward, demanding that she stop or they'd shoot. Aurie ignored the command and focused on the remaining rungs. If Bannon joined them, he could bring her down with his Voice, and there'd be nothing she could do about it.

When a bullet zipped past her head, Aurie made the last few desperate lunges, like an earthworm on speed, and threw herself into the room.

"You'd better come back down here," yelled the officer.

After catching her breath, Aurie leaned towards the hole. "Go fuck yourself."

The exact purpose of saying that was unclear to even Aurie, but it felt good after the long climb. She shook her forearms, trying to get life back into them.

"I'd like to see those Crossfit people do that," said Aurie between breaths.

A quick check of the little room revealed no obvious exit. There was a slot that the wires went through in the ceiling, but it wasn't wide enough for her to fit and she wasn't ready to open it further using magic in case there was a large power source attached. Faez could trigger unshielded electrical equipment.

"You'd better come down," said the officer. "Or things are going to get much worse."

"For you," muttered Aurie.

She heard them conversing below in quiet voices, but not what they were saying. The next voice that echoed up the shaft was another she recognized, and one that turned her hands into fists.

"You're the little bitch that broke into my house, aren't you?" said Bannon Creed. "Come on down so we can talk about it."

"So you can take my soul and add it to the others? I think not," said Aurie.

"By all means, stay up there," said Bannon. "I don't need you since I have your friend."

"I'll fry these wires of yours, damage whatever it is you're planning," yelled Aurie.

"I doubt it," said Bannon. "Unless you'd like to be a char of human flesh."

Another voice interrupted Bannon, and once again, Aurie couldn't make out the words.

"I'm afraid your chance to leave has passed," said Bannon. "I'd love to climb up there and teach you a lesson, but I have another matter to attend to. You, however, will not be leaving anytime soon."

A vial was unstoppered, and the overwhelming smell of chemicals rose up the shaft, making her eyes burn. The air pressure in the room made her ears hurt, and wind came rushing into her little room, whistling out the crack in the ceiling.

Aurie summoned a wisp further down the shaft. She didn't understand what was changing the air pressure until she realized that the floor was rising. The substance looked like the rubberized spray foam used for insulation, and it didn't appear to be slowing down.

Already she was finding it hard to breathe and was so dizzy that her vision was going cross-eyed.

Aurie beat on the walls, finding they were made of hardened steel. Only a thin gap in the ceiling was allowing any air to escape.

The handcuffs were getting in her way. "Aurelia!"

When the first shout didn't work, she tried two more times, until the chain was weak enough to break by pulling the cuffs apart.

Her wisp was chased into the room as the foam neared. She fired a small fire bolt into the material. A section turned black and released an awful black cloud of chemicals that burned her exposed skin. Not only would she not be able to burn through it, but it'd likely kill her from fumes before she could get through.

When the foam crested into the room, it had to fill a larger cavity, so its upward speed slowed, giving her more time. Aurie coughed and kicked the steel wall.

The black smoke made her eyes puff up until she couldn't keep them open. Aurie stumbled around the room, trying to keep her feet on top of the foam, but it kept overtaking her shoes. She felt like she was sinking into a vat of melted gum.

Aurie jumped onto the wires, pulled herself towards the ceiling, and put her lips to the crack to catch breathable air. Before she had time to wonder if she could hold herself in the air, the foam bumped against her shoes. She was out of time.

TWENTY EIGHT

The hand around Pi's mouth was cold. She thought about biting it until she heard the voice in her ear.

"Shhh..."

Amid the diesel fumes and her own stark-white fear, she sensed an air of autumn.

Uncle Liam!

Slowly, he pulled her deeper into the room, past the engines to the deep shadows. He didn't press as tightly, but kept his hand over her mouth until they were behind the generators. When she wheeled on him, he held his hand out and his expression was one of caution, so she swallowed her question.

From the room with the archway, Hemistad's gruff voice rang out. "Are you prepared?"

The next voice surprised her even more.

"As ready as I can be," said Semyon. "No going back after this, but they've given me no choice. I just hope we don't destroy the city in the process."

"So you know why he kept this place?" asked Hemistad.

Pi could only assume the "he" in this case was Invictus. But why was Semyon working with Hemistad? Unless he didn't know what was going on. She was further conflicted by her uncle Liam, standing in the shadows with her. He was studying her for a reaction.

Should she yell for help? Was Uncle Liam trying to help her or was Semyon in trouble?

The wealth of options left her immobilized. Eventually, the generators surged, a portal was formed, and Semyon and Hemistad were gone, for better or worse.

"What are you doing here?" she asked.

"I saw you and Aurie head into the smoke," he said. "I wanted to help, make up for being an asshole earlier."

She studied him, looking for the reason for the lie. "Bullshit. You couldn't have seen us go into the smoke. I was watching."

It didn't come out as forcefully as she wanted. His lip twitched.

"Call it familial intuition. I was in the area, sensed something wrong," he said with a soft whistle.

Pi pushed him in the chest. "Get away from me. Get out of here. You're nothing but a liar. I don't know what your con is, but I'm not buying."

He was wounded by her words, tucked his chin to his chest, and walked towards the maintenance tunnel. She watched him, waiting for the inevitable comment, a last-ditch effort to reel her in.

Liam turned, a ghost of a smile hiding at the corner of his lips, impish and wild. His ruddy hair seemed longer, his eyes greener.

"What if I told you the truth?" he said. "The real truth."

"I knew you were going to do that," she said, moving to the archway to study it. "Always one more level to the con, isn't there?"

"No, lass. For real. There are things I ain't been tellin' ya to protect you," he said.

"Tell me quick or get the hell out of here," she said. "I've got to get in there and save Aurie."

He glanced to the archway. "What if I told you that I know how to get in there? You were right before, I didn't see you go into the smoke. I've been down here, watching them come and go into whatever that place is."

"Why are you so interested in it?" she asked, suspicious.

"The kind of people going in there have valuables," he said. "Things that might help me out of my mess. Whaddaya say? You don't even have to believe me. You just have to trust me to get you in there. We can go our separate ways if you want."

Between the runes and the story from Semyon about losing the bones in his arm at the archway, she knew it was unlikely she'd stumble upon the solution to activating the portal. If she wanted to save Aurie, she was going to have to hold her nose and let him help.

"Fine," she said, motioning towards the archway. "But hurry up, and I swear if you do anything, I'll turn you into a bug."

He looked properly mortified, but once again, she didn't believe him. Once a liar, always a liar in her eyes. She just wished she'd seen it sooner, or that Mom and Dad had warned them what a shit-show he was.

Uncle Liam approached the archway, reached under the bricks, and touched them in a certain order. The generators surged and the silvery portal formed. He reached his hand out, and together they stumbled through.

"Which stairs should we take?" asked Pi, seeing the two options.

Uncle Liam made a half-hearted gesture towards the stairs on his side. His reluctance to suggest a direction made her question his intent, so she picked the side nearest her. As her foot touched the first stair, she reflexively checked the time on Ashley's watch only to find it stopped.

"What the...?" she muttered, remembering the last time the watch stopped was when Ashley got husked by the soul thief. Pi threw herself to the side as Liam lunged at her back. She blasted him with magic, knocking him across the room.

"You lying fucking liar," she said, advancing on him with fists at her side. A rage like she'd never felt before coursed through her veins. "Everything's been a con, even the uncle thing. I see it now. The race was to get rid of me, and Inari, I guess she was a tool or something. I'm going to make sure not another lie comes out of that mouth."

The smirk on his lips put a hitch into her stride. He wasn't intimidated by her, was maybe even excited by the prospect of combat.

"You're a good lass, you know. I was actually enjoying being your uncle, what with all the brooding and family story thing. I never had to work so little for a con. Yeah, things went all pear-shaped with the kitsune. She was supposed to make this job take a lot less time, but no matter now. I'd say I'll be sorry not having you around, but you're going to be with me for a long, long time."

Pi threw a blazing solar spear at him. He grabbed it out of the air. The white-hot shaft sizzled in his hand, but otherwise appeared not to harm him.

"You're going to have to work a lot harder to hurt me," he said. "I'm jacked up on souls, so I got power to burn. Almost nothing on this planet could hurt me right now."

Screaming in rage, she let loose with everything she had: more spears, explosive seeds, a crippling curse, an eye bite spell.

The leaves on his tattooed arm glowed, and he knocked each spell away, just as he'd said he would. Liam gave her a chilling smile and advanced on her. Pi knew that battling him would have as much success as a toddler trying to wrestle with an adult, so she did the only thing she could think of—she ran.

TWENTY NINE

With the foam filling the room, Aurie rescued the purple paint marker from her front pocket, pulled the lid off with her teeth, and wrote "weak" on the walls. Then she gave the steel a firm kick. The impact sent a jarring reverberation through her hip, forcing her other foot deeper into the foam. She yanked it out, but by then the foam was so deep there wasn't enough room to maneuver for another kick.

"Aurelia!" she yelled, hoping to blast through the wall with her true name.

The only thing she succeeded in doing was deafening herself, as the shout filled the ever-smaller room.

She slammed her fist into the wall, bloodying her knuckles as she fought to keep her eyes open. They were nearly swollen shut from the fumes.

She didn't know what kind of material the walls were made of, but they seemed to resist magic. Before she could try anything else, the foam climbed up her feet, capturing her ankles. Aurie struggled against the foam as it pushed her into the ceiling. She dropped the paint marker, which rolled across the foam and disappeared as if it'd fallen into a cloud.

Desperate for air, she stuck her lips into the opening where the wires went out. Even that was barely enough as the fumes crowded out oxygen, leaving her with black dots before her eyes.

She thought about unleashing her magic, all of it, but knew she'd only immolate herself, and likely kill everyone around her. As much rage as she had for her situation, she couldn't let go, fearing another event like with Annabelle.

Aurie pounded her fist on the ceiling. She lacked materials she could use for spells. Arcanium had taught her many skills, but conjuring an answer out of thin air was not one of them.

Unless she used the foam itself?

As the last remaining air of the room was filled with foam, she held her breath, steeled herself against the burning of her eyes, and shaped a section of foam before her. The whitish material stung her flesh, but she formed it into a snake-like appendage. Then she poured faez into the foam-snake, whispering lies and truth magic to give it function, hardening it, and directed it into the gap where the wires left the ceiling.

The foam-snake pushed through the hole, coming out on the other side, but rather than extend upward, she coaxed it to widen, fatten itself like a python digesting a full-grown pig.

All this effort put a strain on the remaining air in her chest. She wanted to open her mouth, suck in a breath, but knew the chemical-filled air would knock her out.

It wouldn't be enough, as the foam wasn't stiff enough, so she added heat, trying to solidify it. At first she didn't think widening the hole would work, but then the foam-snake crystallized.

Through the tears in her eyes, she watched the foam turn yellowish-black like an aged concrete cylinder. Once she knew she could change the density, she poured everything she had into expanding it until the steel ripped open like a flower. When it turned to dust, Aurie pulled herself through the hole as the foam tugged on her lower half.

Escaped, she collapsed on the roof of the structure—which was still inside the statue—and worried that the foam would keep coming and push her off, but it seemed content to have filled the shaft and room. Breath came in gasps. Her lungs burned from the fumes, and she could only see out of a small slit in her eyes.

A few spells she'd learned at Golden Willow reduced the swelling, and the fresh air rejuvenated her thoughts. For the first time she was able to examine her surroundings. Based on the shape of the inner walls, and the faint traffic noise outside, she confirmed that the structure she was perched upon was high above the main floor inside the statue. It appeared this structure had been placed in the statue for the object above her head.

The wires from the shaft ended in a three-foot-diameter silvery ball about ten feet above Aurie's head, suspended by wires from the shoulders of Invictus. It reminded her of those static electricity generators that made your hair stand on end when you touched it, but she didn't think it was wise to touch this one.

The sounds of people talking reached her, so Aurie crawled to the edge. Fifty feet below, a meticulously organized alchemy lab was arrayed in a semicircle facing a runed archway like the one in the basement.

A woman was pouring a shimmering green substance into a volumetric flask. Aurie wasn't surprised when she saw the red-white-and-green patterned couture jacket and heavily hair sprayed blonde coif of Camille Cardwell.

But she was surprised when she saw who was handcuffed to the wall in Deshawn's black running jacket—Violet Cardwell. She was limp against her chains, bound and gagged.

A confusing cocktail of sympathy and anger burned through Aurie. Because Arcanium had resisted the attempts of the soul thief to take one of their own, Camille had volunteered her daughter. Aurie imagined it'd only taken a phone call to get Violet to leave the safety of the Hall. Had she not seen inside Violet's dream, she would have found it hard to believe that a mother would do that to a child.

The towering Bannon Creed ducked through the doorway into the room.

"Has that fae prick returned yet?" asked Bannon.

"I haven't seen him," said Camille. "Any word from your team? Have they captured any other Arcanium students?"

"If they do, you'll be the first to know, but if it's not before Liam returns, we're moving ahead with the plan. The longer we wait, the more we risk interference," said Bannon.

From the same stairway that Bannon had used, Semyon Gray and Hemistad appeared.

"Interference? Happy to oblige," said Semyon.

"You're nothing but a paper tiger, old man," said Bannon.

Semyon adjusted his tweed jacket. "Wonderful suggestion. Does Celesse know you're cheating on her?"

Camille crossed her arms. "She's got no backbone. No vision about what we can accomplish."

"Even if it means sacrificing your daughter," said Semyon. "I knew you could stoop low, but not this low."

Camille turned away and started fussing with her jacket.

"I hope you're aware of why Invictus created this place," said Semyon.

Aurie looked around for a way to climb down, but there was no obvious path. If she could sneak down, she might be able to help Semyon and Hemistad when it came to fighting, which it almost certainly would. Aurie quietly started the spell that she'd used to climb Invictus' tower.

"I'm not a fool," said Bannon. "He had many secrets, but this one wasn't hard to find."

"You clearly don't understand the danger if you're tampering with it. You could kill us all with the wrong spell," said Semyon. "This place is connected to the wells, it provides protection for the city. If it's damaged further than it already has been, the wards will fail."

"It was necessary to gain entry to this place," said Bannon. "I'll repair the dragon well once I've got control."

That Camille had doused her at the beginning of the year had been no simple act of revenge, but a piece of a larger plot. Bannon wanted the wells of magic damaged. The guilt that Aurie had been carrying all year turned to anger at the thought it was Camille's fault she'd lost control.

"Don't you understand you could unleash a horde of demons?" asked Semyon.

"I don't care about a few demons and neither do you," said Bannon. "We've got the power to control them, so why should we care?"

"One demon, yes. A hundred, possibly. But thousands, maybe tens of thousands? Too many would die. It's not worth the risk," said Semyon.

"You shouldn't be so timid, old man. Control of the Halls is worth the risk. There'll be some collateral damage, but in the end, we'll win and I'll be the hero for saving the world. Who knows, maybe I'll have a statue built in my honor afterwards," said Bannon.

"What if Pazuzu, Lord of Storms, leads that horde of demons?" asked Semyon.

Aurie nearly flubbed her spell in surprise. That was the demon lord Pi had summoned years ago to get into Coterie of Mages.

"Impossible," said Bannon. "Invictus banished him a century ago. I'm not even sure you have the skill to perform that ritual."

"A few years ago an enterprising mage summoned him. It wasn't the full demon, but an aspect. That summoning weakened the bonds he was held by," said Semyon. "So please, heed my warning. I will walk away from here if you promise to end this."

"So you know it will work," said Bannon, grinning.

"Of course it'll work, but you'll tear the wards until they're nothing but frayed threads. This archway wasn't meant to be traveled in this way. It's only here as a conduit for the wards," said Semyon.

"Walk away, Semyon. Take your little hunchbacked friend and leave," said Bannon.

"We're not leaving," said Semyon, pulling a piece of paper from his jacket. He folded it with precise movements like a martial arts grandmaster going through his forms, his gaze staying on Bannon the whole time.

"You can't beat me here," said Bannon, pushing up his sleeves and advancing. "My magic won't hurt anything, while yours could trigger what you fear most."

"That's why I brought him," said Semyon, gesturing to Hemistad, who had been silent during the discussion.

Bannon Creed had barely acknowledged Hemistad, but as the owner of Freeport Games stepped forward, the head of the Protectors tilted his head as if he was starting to recognize him.

Without further discussion, the two flew at each other with the rage of two rams, hitting each other at full speed. Creed drove Hemistad backwards through an inner wall. They crashed into another room, only the sounds from their battle escaping.

Semyon set a little origami tiger on the ground and whispered to it until it grew to full size. Camille pulled a vial from her jacket—the bright green mixture she'd been brewing earlier—and threw it down her throat like a shot of whiskey. Her flesh transformed into iron.

The paper tiger leapt at iron Camille, who knocked it away with a fist, denting the side of the tiger. The tiger shook its head and the dent popped out, whole and new.

While the battles raged, Aurie finished her spell and started climbing down the side of the inner tower. Looking over her shoulder, she watched as Semyon formed a second origami animal with lightning quick fingers.

He was so focused on his paper that he didn't see the shadow move up behind him. The soul thief, the person she'd once thought of as her uncle Liam, fell upon Semyon like a sudden wave.

"No!" screamed Aurie, descending as fast as she could.

Semyon Gray collapsed against the floor as shadows from Liam's hands writhed. He tugged the soul from Semyon's body like stiff taffy, a sheet of inky blackness poking from his neck. He had his boot on Semyon's lifeless body, yanking and pulling. It was like he was trying to pull a thick sheet of fabric through a small hole, and the more it came out, the worse Aurie felt, since she was connected to Semyon through his patronage.

When Liam gave a hard tug, Aurie nearly lost her grip. Twenty feet up, still too high to jump.

"Come down here, dear girl," said Camille, crumpling the paper tiger in her iron fists. "See, Violet, you won't have to make your sacrifice after all."

Aurie turned her head to tell Camille off when another yank on Semyon's soul knocked her unconscious.

THIRTY

The lower section of the statue was a maze of rooms which Pi tried to lose herself in. She threw herself into a dusty spare bedroom that was barely above a prison cell and locked the door, not that it would stop Liam.

The worst part was that she didn't even know if Liam was still behind her. As far as she knew, he was standing right outside.

As she leaned against the door, trying to catch her breath, she admonished herself for not seeing who Liam really was. A con within a con within a con. He'd been the soul thief the whole time, and she hadn't seen it.

"I'm not giving up," she gave herself a pep talk. "Just a moment to catch my breath and then I'm going after Aurie."

It felt ludicrous. Her magic hadn't even put a mark on Liam. But why would it? She knew what he was now—a fae lord, cursed and thrown out of his realm for dabbling in forbidden magics. He was the Pied Piper of Hamelin. The soul thief.

But none of that hurt as much as knowing he wasn't her uncle. He'd taken Liam's name, used it for whatever games he was playing. Their real uncle was probably dead in Siberia as her parents had thought.

A crash from the floor above startled Pi. It sounded like two rhinos in battle. As she turned the handle to leave, the ceiling gave way, and Hemistad and Bannon Creed crashed into the room.

Pi didn't know what kind of magic they were using, but it registered as a corona of heat and light surrounding them as if the pressure was squeezing the air itself into releasing energy. Bannon drove Hemistad backwards into Pi. She threw herself across the room to avoid being crushed.

A hole had been knocked in the wall. Pi scrambled on her hands and knees towards it. When Hemistad threw Bannon over his head, Pi dove through the hole to get out of the way.

As she climbed the flights of stairs, a wave of vertigo passed through her. The connection with Semyon was weakening somehow. Pi instinctively knew that Liam was the cause. Older souls, especially one like Semyon's, were too embedded to be removed, but Liam could damage her patron permanently.

Through fading vision and wobbly legs, Pi ran through the halls and up the stairs. The scene before her was disorienting, as it defied her expectations. Liam was pulling on Semyon's lifeless form as if he were a rubber doll, an iron-skinned Camille in her red-white-and-green couture jacket battled a giant paper tiger, and Violet—not Deshawn—was chained to the wall.

Where was Aurie?

She saw Liam preparing for another big tug, so she lowered her shoulder and charged him like a bull, slamming into him as her consciousness was knocked for a spin.

After losing her sight for a moment, Pi struggled to her feet like a newborn foal. Liam advanced on her.

Out of the corner of her eye she saw Camille moving towards another body—Aurie!—but had no time to help.

"Which one do you want?" asked Liam.

"Take that one," said Camille. "This one is mine."

Camille Cardwell lifted Aurie's body by the neck and slammed her against the wall, crushing her throat. Aurie fought against Camille's iron grip, but she might as well have been trying to punch a statue.

"Sorry, lass," said Liam, the tattoos on his arm glowing with autumn fire, "it ends here."

Pi was preparing one last volley of magic when she heard a low growling from behind Liam. He straightened and turned to find Inari bristling behind him. The fox-like kitsune lowered her head in preparation to leap.

Liam strode forward, confidence in every motion. "You can't hurt me, you fucking rodent. I made sure of it, because I knew you'd come back eventually."

Inari leapt at the same time as Liam. As soon as they touched, they both winked out of existence.

"Thank you, Inari," said Pi, before she turned to help her sister.

She threw a force bolt at Camille, knocking her away from Aurie, who crumpled onto the ground, holding her throat. Pi took two steps forward, and Camille threw a glob of liquid. The missile flew unerringly at Pi, forming a cocoon around her when it hit.

Pi fought against the sticky matrix, but it held her fast. She tried using magic, but she had no way to move her fingers to cast a spell, and even if she could, her access to faez was weakened by what had been done to Semyon. It felt like she'd drunk two bottles of cold medicine.

Camille used the same trick on Aurie, who hadn't fully recovered. Then Camille stumbled to the alchemy table, hastily combined ingredients, and downed the mixture with a shaky hand. Her iron skin faded until her flesh was pink again.

"Where is that damned Liam?" she asked.

"He's gone," said Pi, glancing to Semyon's motionless form. He wouldn't be getting up anytime soon, and it appeared that neither would her sister, whose chin was against her chest. "Far, far away."

A rumble came from beneath them. The battle between Hemistad and Bannon still raged. A secret smile grew on Camille's lips.

THIRTY ONE

The tinkling of vials woke Aurie, followed by a stabbing headache and an ache in her neck where Camille had choked her. Through the stiff matrix of webbing around her, Aurie saw her sister in a similar cocoon, Semyon motionless on the floor, and Violet still chained—but awake—on the wall.

Aurie studied the runes on the archway. They were as much a warning as an instruction manual. It didn't take long for Aurie to figure out what Camille was doing.

"Don't do it," said Aurie. "It won't work unless you have the full hundred."

Camille's head snapped to the right, but she kept working. "Don't tell me what to do. Once I get in there, I won't have to listen to any of you anymore."

The desperation in her voice concerned Aurie more than anything. Desperate people could do anything. It was clear she didn't like having to work with Bannon, but had held her nose to get to this point.

Though it was hard to see Pi beneath the stiff webbing, Aurie made eye contact with her sister, enough to know she wasn't hurt. But it appeared Pi was working on something, and was trying not to be noticed.

"Are you sure you want that responsibility?" asked Aurie, hoping to keep Camille occupied. "You heard what Semyon said. The barriers between this world and the infernal one have been damaged. It'll be your task to beat them back. Are you sure you want that?"

"Semyon was just trying to scare us into listening to him. All lies. I know what I know, and I know it's true. You can't persuade me otherwise," she said.

"Listen to her, Mother," said Violet, who'd spat the gag out of her mouth.

"Quiet, traitor," said Camille. "If you would have only put Alchemists in the book, you wouldn't be in this mess. You'd be safely in your Hall right now preparing for finals."

The wounded gaze on Violet's face revealed the truth. She had put other halls in the book during her Merlins, which had given Semyon a chance to pick her. She wondered if he'd known about the relationship between mother and daughter. It almost seemed cruel to have driven a wedge between them, but then again, Aurie had seen inside Violet's dream. She'd probably been looking for a way out.

Violet muttered something, which sounded suspiciously like "Fuck you, Mother," but Camille was too busy finishing the potion to notice.

The final mixture, a combination of ninety-nine souls, distilled for the imprint of Invictus, defied sight. Like a black hole, Aurie couldn't really look right at it, as space seemed to warp around the liquid.

The heavy scent of faez leaking into the room made Aurie wide awake. She sensed the power of the potion and the warding of the statue would not mix well.

"Can't you feel it?" said Aurie. "You'll upset a delicate balance. You're more likely to kill us all than succeed."

"A chance I'm willing to take," she replied.

At that moment, Bannon Creed stumbled into the room, his blue athletic outfit torn to shreds.

"Did you kill it?" asked Camille.

"No, but I wounded him enough that he had to flee. There will be no more interference," he said, toeing Semyon's still form with his boot. Then his gaze rose to what Camille was holding. "Nice of you to prepare that for me."

The insinuation in his tone revealed that he knew Camille had turned on him. He took a step forward.

"You're too late," she said, and threw the soul potion down her throat. The effect was immediate. It was like a supernova exploded from her chest. Power raged through her body. It was hard to look at her. Aurie wasn't sure how her mortal cage could hold it.

Bannon leapt at her with arms wide. Before he reached her, she extended her hand in a lazy motion. Without touching him, he was thrown through the wall. He did not come back out.

Her display of power reacted with the wards. Quivering bolts of electricity connected between Camille and the silvery ball on the tower. She shrugged them off and marched towards the archway.

Aurie knew she had one chance to stop her. She used her true name to crack the cocoon, tearing it away in chunks that crumbled to dust. Then she called on faez, not only hers, but the well of power beneath the statue. When Camille had dosed her with that heroic potion, she'd taught Aurie how to access the well.

Before Camille could reach the archway, Aurie threw a force bolt that would have knocked a hole through a battleship. It stopped Camille momentarily, but she kept going, and all the while, the tower grew more excited, throwing crackling electric-faez streamers in all directions.

When Aurie realized there was no way to stop Camille from entering the archway, she turned her focus on the wards. Whether or not Camille succeeded in gaining Invictus' realm, the wards of the city would be damaged. Aurie turned that power inward, reaching her arms around the protections that were slowly coming apart.

"Mother, stop!" yelled Violet.

Camille touched the archway, creating a feedback loop that spun towards explosion. Aurie dug deep, throwing herself in its way, using herself to shield the wards, to shield the others in the room. The world was ripped apart as the statue filled with flames.

THIRTY TWO

The power unleashed nearly blinded Pi, even though she had her eyes closed, like the shadows burned into the walls after an atomic blast. Spots and glares filled her vision.

The impact weakened the cocoon enough that she could finish the job with a quick spell. Pi fell to the ground, and ran immediately to her sister. Flames crackled around the room, awoken by the exercise of power.

A quick check of Aurie's pulse revealed that she was alive but unconscious. While Aurie had kept the tower from exploding, her connection with the well of power was keeping the reaction going. If Pi couldn't get her sister out of the statue, it wouldn't matter that they'd been saved.

Camille had been obliterated in the blast when she'd touched the archway. Miraculously, her daughter had survived, though she too was unconscious.

She checked on Semyon, finding him barely alive. Whatever Liam had done to him had placed him in a stasis-like state. It was like his soul had been loosened from his body, but left inside the shell. It seemed something only time would heal.

A quick check of the room revealed no exits besides the archway in the basement, which she didn't know how to activate and was unlikely to stumble upon the answer.

"Think, Pi. How do I get us out of here?"

The walls of the statue had absorbed a significant blast and had held, which meant it would be impossible to breach them using magic.

At last, she came upon the ruins of the alchemy table. The cabinet that held the ninety-nine vials of souls had been damaged. Many were broken, leaking life-essence. A small number were intact, minus the amount that Camille had taken, so she slipped those vials into her jacket. The remaining were either empty or had too little left to give hope.

When Pi found the vial marked Coterie, she openly sobbed. The vial was unbroken, but it'd been half-emptied. Probably turned into a drug for Bannon.

With tears in her eyes, she collected the half-filled vials. There were a dozen left. Coterie. Oculus. The Daring Maids. Pi touched each one with reverence.

The spell that she'd ripped out of the book in Arcanium was exactly what she had suspected. It was a way to move souls in and out of bodies. Except there wasn't enough soul for Ashley to return.

Pi stared at the bottles for a few minutes, even while the fire crackled. "I'm sorry," she said to the vials. "I think this is the only way."

Unlike Camille's mixture, the spell Pi was casting used what was left of the soul, rather than a sampling. She picked what was left of Ashley first.

Pi didn't hesitate drinking it when the spell called for it. She was running out of time. The sudden wash of Ashley's memories through her left her gasping. She felt her parents' love bubble through her like warm cocoa.

She wanted to savor the experience, but time was running out. She performed the second soul absorption, a girl from Senders, which was the Hall that taught mind reading and thought sending. As each soul fragment was absorbed, Pi was overwhelmed with emotions: fear from their last moments before Liam took them, roller coaster rides in the park with family, Halloween dressed as a lion, all the things that Pi had never gotten to do with her parents. It was almost too much. She stopped at the ninth. Was this right of her to do? To take these souls? Was this what they would have wanted?

Pi had an idea how they might escape. Technically, she didn't need any more souls, but would they want to live with her—in her? She asked the question to the thoughts and fragments swirling around in her head, and she heard a resounding chorus of "YES!"

When she realized the last soul, a boy from Metallum Nocturne, wouldn't fit, she began to cry, until Ashley's voice inside her head suggested an answer. She could make room if she removed one of the connections, the one not hooked to the souls, but to her.

"Yes, Ashley," she said, looking longingly at her sister. "I'll do it. Aurie will understand."

Giving up her connection to Semyon Gray and Arcanium hurt more than she would have expected. It wasn't the physical pain, but the idea that she was no longer in the same Hall with her sister. At first she thought she was in no Hall at all, but somehow the partial connections with twelve other Halls was stronger than the one she'd had with Arcanium.

Using the strength she'd gained through the souls, one by one Pi carried her sister, Violet Cardwell, Semyon Gray, and Bannon Creed to the archway in the basement of the statue. It was trivial to reach inside Bannon's unconscious mind and find the correct pattern to escape the statue.

She carried Aurie out first. Violet and Semyon she carried on both shoulders, enjoying the power coursing through her veins. Finally, after putting out the fires inside, she set Bannon Creed on the stairs so he'd have an awful backache when he woke.

Not sure how to get out without alerting the Protectors stationed outside, Pi paced around the room.

When she noticed that Violet was awake, there was a brief staring contest, until Violet said, "Thank you, Pythia."

"I'm sorry," said Pi, remembering the fate of Violet's mother.

"Is she?"

Pi nodded. "She's gone."

Violet surprised her with the next questions. "What about the wards?"

"Weakened, but intact," said Pi. "Aurie kept them together in the explosion."

"What now?" asked Violet.

Pi was unsure about the girl, but didn't have any better ideas. "We need to get back to Arcanium. I'm not sure anywhere else is safe. From there I'll send a message to some friends in Golden Willow. Maybe they can help them."

"I'll take care of it," said Violet, climbing unsteadily to her feet.

"What are you going to do?" asked Pi cautiously.

"If my mother is truly gone, I can contact some friends, get us out of here without being noticed," she said. "There's a coffee shop near the statue. I can call them from there."

The voices inside Pi's head told her not to trust Violet, but something in her gut told her otherwise.

"Yeah. Go ahead. I'll stay here with them," said Pi.

The wait might have been nerve wracking if she hadn't had so many competing memories inside her head to distract her. The decision to absorb the twelve broken souls seemed like it could be a problem in the future.

An hour later, Violet returned. Another standoff was ended when she handed over three bracelets.

"Put these on. They'll obscure you enough that the Protectors won't know who you are," she said. "I'll tell them you work for the *Herald.* We use them to give journalists anonymity in delicate situations. They won't be able to do anything without risking the wrath of the *Herald.*"

Pi hesitated before putting them on herself, Semyon, and Aurie. Then she carried them out of the statue and into the street. True to Violet's word, the officers didn't bother them, though there was visible suspicion. When the limo pulled up to take them back to Arcanium, Pi finally allowed herself to relax.

THIRTY THREE

Aurie woke in her room disoriented and surrounded by her friends. They looked at her expectantly.

"Hello," she said, almost as a question. Her voice was as raw as sandpaper. All the faez she'd channeled had put her body through the wringer.

"Alright," said Pi, "she's awake and it looks like she'll be okay. I told you all that when she got here. It takes a lot more than that to kill a Silverthorne."

The smiles were weak and carried a hint of darkness. Aurie opened her mouth to ask what was wrong, when she saw the headshake from her sister.

Deshawn sat on the corner of the bed. "Are you sure I can't stay?"

"Actually," said Pi, hooking him back into the room by grabbing his arm, "why was Violet wearing your jacket earlier?"

Deshawn blushed, looking like he'd made a mistake. "You're right. I should be going."

As he turned to leave, Pi grabbed him by the arm. "Out with it. Are you and Violet...?"

Pi made a vague hand motion that was loosely translated as crazy-and-sex.

"No! I mean, I think she *would* under the right circumstances," he said, flipping up an imaginary collar. "But no, I'm just trying to be her friend. Sorry, I know she hasn't been nice to either of you, but you have no idea what she's been through."

"Actually, we do," said Aurie.

"You know about the Alton Lockwood thing?" he asked, surprised.

"No," said Pi, "but I can guess. I encountered him at Coterie. I thought you were talking about her mom."

"Well, that too. It all runs together for Violet," said Deshawn.

"That's why you were both in the library," said Aurie suddenly. "The day the soul thief almost got me."

"Yeah," said Deshawn. "We were in the back, talking for hours. I thought for sure you'd figured it out."

"Enough Violet talk. I need to speak with my sister," said Pi.

"Are you...?"

"Out!" said Pi, patting Deshawn on the shoulder.

"Okay, okay, Nurse Ratched. I'm leaving," said Deshawn with a grin, acting like he was being pushed out of the room with great force.

Once the bedroom was clear, Aurie took a good look at her sister. Pi was fidgeting more than normal, and her eye color seemed to shift every few seconds. Her skin had an almost invisible glow.

"What's with the abundant energy? You look like you're pregnant or something," said Aurie.

"That might be one way to put it," said Pi.

"Fess up, little sister," said Aurie. "What's going on?"

"It's hard to explain," said Pi, picking at her fingers like a drug addict.

Living in the thirteenth ward had taught Aurie what a tweaker looked like. Pi had the twitch-energy down, but lacked the scabs and hollow eyes associated with meth. When she probed deeper, Aurie sensed a distance between them, not emotionally, but through her magic. Since her sister had been in Arcanium, she'd felt closer, the connection with Semyon providing the conduit. That feeling was no longer present.

"You're not in Arcanium," gasped Aurie. "I don't understand. Did Camille do that to you? Or Liam?"

"I did it to myself," said Pi, who in a never-ending run-on sentence, proceeded to explain about taking the twelve partial souls, including Ashley, into her body.

It took a few quiet moments for Aurie to process. When she finally spoke, it came out weak. "How does that even work?"

Pi paced around the room, rubbing the shaved side of her hair. "It's...a work in progress."

"Is this like...um...like Liam?" asked Aurie.

"No," said Pi emphatically. "What Liam did was to use the souls as an energy source, like another version of faez. A really powerful version of faez. Really powerful. In this case, the souls are a part of me, like your soul is in you, but they're in me. It's hard to explain."

"Speaking of Liam, what if he comes back? Can we make him take them out of you?"

Another mixed expression passed across her sister's face. Not mixed, fractured maybe. Like a kaleidoscope of emotions filtered through a spotlight.

"He won't be coming back. Inari made sure of that," said Pi.

"Is she back?"

"No. She came close enough to tell me." Pi tapped on her skull. "Through here. She didn't want anyone to see her. As she told me, *Liam swims with the silent speakers, forever.* I wasn't sure what she meant until she sent a picture of a metal ball with antennas on it."

"Satellite? Jesus, she teleported him into outer space," said Aurie.

"Anywhere else and he could have come back. He was a near god with all that soul magic running through him. I think he took a little from each one so he had power enough to break through the wards in all the schools. Probably why he wanted to use Inari, so he didn't have to waste his magic."

"I'm so sorry, Pi."

Her sister sat on the chair, crossed her legs, and got back up again. "It's probably karma I ended up this way. I wanted desperately to have a history about my family. Now, I have so many histories, experiences, whatevers, competing for my attention, that I'm overwhelmed."

"I'm sure we can find a solution," offered Aurie.

"No," said Pi right away, followed by a desperate glance that revealed Pi didn't want to give them up. "I mean, they wouldn't have anywhere else to go. Someone like Creed would just snort them again."

"What about the other souls you rescued?" asked Aurie.

A secret smile formed on her sister's lips. She practically glowed with pride. "I got them back. Seven souls for seven bodies. Thankfully none of their parents had them cremated or anything. A couple had to be dug up. Professor Mali made it happen."

"So all the souls are accounted for," said Aurie, noting a twitch from her sister. "I'm sorry about Ashley. I know you wanted her to be alive."

"She is. I can't explain it, but she's still here."

"Does she want to be inside you? Or the rest of them? Or do you even know that?"

Pi's brow furrowed. "Of course they do. Better than being dead."

A gulf of silence opened between them. Aurie hated it.

"Sorry, sis. *Dooset daram.* I'm just trying to process it."

Pi chuckled. "Tell me about it. I feel like someone has a hundred TV sets on in my head."

Desperate to change the subject, Aurie asked, "What was with the doom and gloom with the others? They seemed happy I was awake, but not really."

"It's Semyon," said Pi. "Whatever Liam did to him has messed with everyone's connection to faez. Can't you feel it?"

She concentrated. It was like standing too close to a two-hundred-foot cliff. The vast emptiness threatened to pull her into the void.

"That's awful," she muttered.

"It's worse than that. Most of the first years and a couple second years have left Arcanium, poached away by other Halls. That fifth year, Beckett, the one that wore that awful Davy Crockett fur hat all the time. He was in the middle of his final dissertation spell when Semyon's soul got rattled. He lit himself on fire in front of the Glitterdome. They put him out and healed him, but they don't think he'll ever be right in the head. A few others are missing."

"I don't even know what to say."

"Neither does anyone else. Professor Mali has been making the rounds, trying to keep everyone together. She's warned everyone not to use their magic until Semyon has recovered."

"And what if we do?" asked Aurie.

"The obvious answer is that you risk faez madness, but you knew that. The second answer, the one that's on everyone's mind is that if someone uses too much, Semyon could die, and *that* would drive everyone connected to him insane, mostly anyway."

"Merlin-on-a-stick. What do I do?" asked Aurie.

Pi scratched at her short hair. "That's the problem. You're linked with him. The older alumni have broken ties as they're strong enough for it not to hurt them, or risk madness. Some of the younger ones too, but with mixed results. Third years up through recent grads are stuck. You can't leave, and you can't use magic."

"And there's no way to fix him?" asked Aurie.

"Trust me, if there was a way, it would have been done already. Dr. Fairlight stopped by with the Rod and even that didn't work. It's some problem with how the soul is connected to the body. It'll take time. That's what she said."

"What about you? You're not in a Hall any longer," said Aurie.

Pi glanced askew. "Technically, I'm part of twelve Halls. Not completely, but the partials form a strong bond like threads in a rope."

"Oh, god. What about my trial? They can't actually ask me to go through with it, can they?"

Pi gave a you-won't-like-this shrug. "The bad news is that the trial is still on. The good news is Professor Mali said using your true name doesn't rely on the protection that a patron gives. That's part of why it's so difficult, because it relies on self-knowledge, rather than access to faez. Or at least that's what the professor said when I asked her."

"That's not totally true. I've been using faez when I spoke my true name," said Aurie.

"Maybe you weren't really doing it," said Pi.

"I swear I was."

"There's a flight to Paris that leaves tomorrow morning. I can book us if you give me the word," said Pi.

"But if I leave, there's no way that Semyon will recover in time. And you know the rest of the Cabal will use this opportunity to get rid of him. Leaving will be the same thing as going to the trial."

"I did some research while you were out. You've got a strong link to faez, so you'll probably be okay if Semyon dies. You might not ever be able to use magic, but you'll be free. If they take it from you, then you'll die, especially after everything you've been through."

The decision was a great monolith looming before her. She wanted to push it away, keep it from crushing her, but there was no avoiding it. Sometimes life left you with no answers.

The hopeful look on her sister's face for Paris would be painful to disappoint. Was it better to be alive than to risk certain death at the trial?

"I can't do it, Pi. I can't run," she said. "If I do, the others don't stand a chance against the Cabal. They don't know what we know. I have to stay and fight, even if it kills me."

"I thought you'd say that," said Pi, rushing out of the room with tears in her eyes.

Aurie was left in a tomb of thought. The world pressed in around her. In two days she'd face the trial by magic. If she couldn't succeed at the task, they'd take her magic, and her life along with it.

A true name was about knowing oneself, completely, and acting on that knowledge to shape her magic. Aurie pulled the covers to her chin. *Who am I? Who am I really? I have two days to find out.*

THIRTY FOUR

The buzzing lights inside the Emergency entrance at the Golden Willow set Pi's teeth on edge. Hood up and hands stuffed into the front of her hoodie, she strolled inside.

Images of the hospital reflected in her mind. She sensed the souls' concern.

"Shhh..." whispered Pi as she approached the front desk.

Herman the guard looked up from his clipboard. The third button on his brown security shirt had popped off, and a glob of tuna salad hung on the front pocket.

"Hey, I know you..."

She waved her hand. His head slumped to the clipboard. Pi reached out and cushioned his forehead. She didn't want him to get injured.

A quick check confirmed that nobody had noticed her entrance. Herman might get in trouble for falling asleep, but nothing more than a reprimand. His only real task was to take names, and Pi had no intention of leaving hers.

The Children's Floor for the Irrevocably Cursed, Magically Ailing, and

Supernatural Virology was lightly staffed. Pi had avoided the few nurses that worked the night shift.

Though the souls did not have voices, their tendencies and habits pulled on her thoughts. One of them had a bit of OCD—she found the slight mistake in the pattern of the tiles to be quite annoying. Another found the lights too bright. It felt like she was carrying around a car full of rowdy adolescents. They weren't changing who she was, but causing chaos in her mind.

It felt strange to come to Golden Willow without her sister. This had been Aurie's place. She'd always thought Aurie should have been in Aura Healers like their father, rather than Arcanium, but maybe working in the hospital had been too small for her.

She envied her sister's sense of purpose. Aurie had always known what she was going to do, and why it was important. Pi wasn't sure she would have tried to hold the city's wards together in the face of Camille's misguided attempt to enter Invictus' realm.

The wards were much weaker after the battle. Professor Mali suggested that another event could shatter their protection, leaving the city vulnerable. Pi couldn't help but wonder if that had been the original intent, except who would benefit?

Her sneakers stopped short, sending up an awful squeak. No one came running, which was good because she was locked in what felt like a waking dream: *shadows approached the city from all sides, faceless men and women stood around intricate summoning circles, colored glass balls sat on velvet pillows.*

When the vision had passed, Pi had to wipe tears from her eyes. She didn't remember crying, but something in the vision had triggered it. The fact that she'd had a vision at all was less surprising, but she gathered it had come from the Oculus student—Laird Thockhollow.

"Hello, Laird," she whispered.

He'd been rather quiet so far, hiding in the background.

"Is that something I need to worry about now?" she asked.

A sense of distance passed through her. She saw a calendar flipping in her head.

"Next year, then," she said.

Each of the souls communicated with her differently, though mostly it was in pictures and feelings.

She took a deep breath and entered Annabelle's room. The whiskers on the girl's face lay limp against her cheeks. An IV bag fed clear liquid into the girl's arm, while a machine pulsed steady beeps. The image before her was a life on pause, an innocent caught up in the struggles for power. That Camille Cardwell had received the ultimate comeuppance didn't soothe the ache in Pi's heart.

"Maybe I should have been paying attention before," said Pi, thinking of the times she came to visit Aurie or go on rounds with her father. But she'd hated being in the hospital, since it was full of almost dead people. She knew that wasn't totally true, that most people left healthy and better off than they came in, but it'd always felt that way to her. Maybe it was because their injuries were proof that the world was not kind. She didn't recall ever seeing anyone with power or money in Golden Willow.

She ran a finger across Annabelle's cheek. The burns had been healed by the doctors, but nothing they'd done had brought her out of her stasis.

Her little mouth formed a tiny bow. Her lips were pallid, crusted dry.

From an inside pocket, Pi produced the leftover vial of soul material. It was the one that had come from Creed's house, the one they'd rescued from the city police headquarters. It didn't feel right to let it go to waste, but she knew Aurie would never agree to use it.

The only problem was that Pi didn't know how. The spell she'd ripped from that book only explained how to put a soul back into a body. What she wanted to do was entirely different.

One of the twelve souls inside of her had come from Aura Healers, but it had been the smallest portion. She hadn't even been sure that it would take given the size, but she'd felt an obligation to try. Pi had hoped that entering the hospital would have awoken that soul fragment and given her the knowledge to fix Annabelle with the leftovers, but no insight came, and she was left staring at the slow rising and falling of the girl's chest.

"What do I do?" she asked the vial cupped in her hand.

As expected, it gave no answer, and neither did any of the souls. Entering the room had quieted their normal chatter. Sensing the importance of the visit, they were watching from the back.

Pi wondered if she'd made a mistake. There wasn't even a tickle of thought coming from the Aura Healer soul. She knew his name had been Justin White, but that was it. Unlike the others, she didn't even know what he looked like. Though mostly she saw them as they had seen themselves. Ashley's nose and backside were way bigger in her thoughts than they had been in real life.

Pi took a step out the door, stopped, breathed a heavy sigh, and returned to the room.

She unstoppered the vial and put it up to her lips. She caught a whiff of body odor, not the bad kind, but a sweet smell, almost like a newborn, but with more character. She sensed a smile that went deeper than the eyes in the essence of that soul, and wanted to drink it for that reason alone.

"No," she said, pushing it away from her lips as if someone had been forcing her to drink it. "Not like Liam."

He'd claimed it made him feel like a god. She feared what that might do to her, even this one small bit.

Before she could have second thoughts, Pi dumped the vial into Annabelle's little bow mouth. A single streamer of smoke slipped from her lips, but otherwise the girl appeared unaffected by the ingestion of the soul.

Maybe that wasn't how it was supposed to work.

Reluctantly, Pi turned around, only to find a furious Nezumi standing directly in the doorway. His black eyes glowered. He clenched his hands in preparation to fight.

"Get away from my little girl," he said, his normally timid speech washed away by anger.

"I wasn't doing anything," she said.

"Your sister put her here," he said, baring a jagged row of teeth.

When the machine gave an extra beep, Nezumi looked past her. His eyes narrowed. "You did something to her, didn't you? Stupid mage. You come to take. Always take."

He pushed Pi out of the way and ran his stubby fingers across his daughter, checking for signs of damage. Pi watched without comment, feeling the weight of many eyes watching with her.

Before she could leave, Nezumi sprung upon her, grabbing her leather coat. Fat tears the size of marbles ran from his black eyes.

"Why mages always take? Why? Annabelle never hurt anyone."

Despite the emotions raging through her, she kept a mask of calm, mostly as a defense against her thoughts. She warred with guilt. Not guilt because she felt bad for Nezumi and his daughter, but guilt that she pitied them more than anything. Pitied them for being vulnerable, for having little power in the world.

Lost in the moment, Pi said, "I have power."

He growled in response. "Nezumi don't care."

Pi opened her mouth to explain. She hadn't meant it that way. When the words came out of her mouth, she was thinking about how she could help, not by fixing Annabelle, or changing the system like Aurie wanted, but by stopping the people who caused the problems. Power only listened to power.

She tried to pull away, but Nezumi held on tight. She could see in his quivering snout that he was working himself up to attack her. He knew he had little chance.

"I'm just trying to leave," she said, gently pushing on his arms.

Removing him with magic would be trivial, but he'd been hurt enough; she didn't want to add to his misery.

"Mages take," he said. "They take and take and take, and Nezumi don't want you to take anymore."

An awful moment rose between them like a restless wave rising up, the crest turning to wind-torn foam, threatening to crash upon an unsuspecting swimmer, hurling them into the bone-crushing coral beneath. At that peak, when the wave could no longer defy gravity and the waters were as black as sin, a lone cry broke through.

It was somewhere between a tiny cough and a cry for her father, but Annabelle was awake. Thoughts of vengeance fled from Nezumi's eyes, which were still beaded with tears as he returned to his daughter and buried his head into her chest.

"Annabelle!"

Over his shuddering back, Annabelle's red-rimmed eyes stared at Pi. The girl's gaze was older than her meager years, either from the long recovery or the vial of soul she'd consumed.

Pi left Nezumi and Annabelle to their reunion and strolled slowly from the hospital, no longer caring if anyone found her.

She couldn't help but consider the difficulties ahead. With Semyon Gray in critical condition, there was no one to take the fight to the Cabal. Before, Pi had only wanted to escape Invictus and flee to Paris with her sister, but the encounter with Camille and then Nezumi and Annabelle changed that. Pi was aware that the chorus of souls inside her might also be affecting her decision.

With a light touch to the back of the head, Pi woke Herman the guard as she strolled out of Golden Willow. Thoughts and decisions about the future weighed on her like chains. It was more than likely that Aurie would not survive her trial by magic in two days, and without her sister, she would have no one to temper her ambitions.

Pi also knew that—

Left!

A shape flew at her from the darkness: the glint of a knife aiming for her abdomen.

She threw herself to the side, the blade catching her thigh. A searing bright line etched itself into her leg. She came down hard on her elbow.

Her attacker came again, his tattooed arm glowing with power as he brought his blade overhead in a two-handed slam. From her back, Pi executed a force shield—a spell particular to the Daring Maids—throwing Liam thirty feet backwards into the brick wall. The impact triggered the automatic doors to open and then reluctantly close.

The cut burned like a wildfire, a numbness spreading up her thigh into her hip. Poison!

Liam pulled himself up, limped towards her. The buzzing lights from the Emergency Room fell upon him. He was a wreck: hair burnt, skin with open pus-filled wounds, lower lip split to his chin. The half-step hitch in his step made him into the monster that she knew he was.

Based on his state of disrepair, he'd used up nearly all his soul magic making it back from space.

Pi tried to get up, but the poison was interfering with her nervous system. Her legs gave out before she could half-rise.

"I've always believed in using the right tools for the job. You'd be surprised at how many mages don't know simple antidote spells." His grin was something out of a nightmare. Two teeth had been pushed into his gums. "Don't worry. It's not going to kill you. I need you alive."

The poison was shutting down her movement. She melted to the concrete, muscles failing on her one by one until she could do nothing but watch him approach with her eyes tilted to the side.

He wanted the souls, hers included.

A spark of thought reached her—the instructions for an antidote spell. The soul fragment of Justin White had woken.

Her fingers had enough dexterity to perform the motions. Liam might have seen, but an approaching ambulance with its lights on distracted him. Pi had to cast the spell twice to get it to work. The first, poor attempt gave her enough movement that her fingers could perform the second with precision.

The spell acted like a giant squeegee. She felt like a bag of icing grabbed at one end and squeezed out. Warm poison ran out of the cut in her leg.

As he leaned down and opened his mouth, she sensed something worse inside him, a rot so foul she recoiled. He wasn't just a fae lord cursed by his ambitions, but a being of hate and hunger.

Sensing her defiance, he whistled, casting a soothing spell. But Pi and the chorus of souls were having none of it. They rose up.

She snatched the blade from his hand. His head snapped up. He realized his danger too late. She was free, and angry.

Pi jammed the blade upward, right beneath his jaw. The being she'd known as Liam had been around a long time. His magic had protected him for millennia, even when he was a weaker version of himself, a god among the dying trees who took sacrifices bound in wicker.

The force of the blade alone would not have injured him. It would have left a nasty wound in his neck that he would have healed easily once he'd taken her soul. But when the chorus of souls—furious from having their lives ripped away—added a twist of magic to the strike that individually would have had no effect, the combined power demolished his ancient protections.

Pi drove the blade into his brain.

The ancient fae lord, the Pied Piper, god of autumn light and blood-soaked wicker, the thief of souls—ruined and rotten to the core—died.

She collapsed back onto the concrete as the ambulance pulled beneath the canopy, the red and blue lights reflecting across her face and the slowly sinking body that turned to dust. She watched as the EMTs hurried to the back of their vehicle and carried a gurney into the building as the shouts of doctors and nurses filled the air.

After carefully wiping the poison off her leg with a rag she found in her jacket, Pi made for Arcanium to spend time with her sister before the trial by magic.

THIRTY FIVE

A pipe in the wall of the waiting room ticked as the air conditioning kicked on. The Court of Three was in the basement of the Spire, the old part of the complex built before the modern age. There were various connected rooms for the members of the trial. Aurie was waiting in a side room for the judges to arrive.

Aurie fidgeted with her smartphone while she waited for the trial by magic, reading the latest articles in the *Herald*. A follow-up piece by a staff writer detailed how the soul thief had been killed in a battle with police and the souls had not been recovered. The unnamed Protector quoted in the article, Protector Cox by his heavy use of the word "y'all," explained the remainder had been sold on the black market.

It was a total fabrication, and Aurie agreed with Violet's reasoning in having them write the article that way. The police were given credit so they could close the case without losing face, and the lost souls was for the students who had been recovered so they weren't hounded their whole lives over the experience of having their souls removed and then restored. Doing it that way left out their role in the whole situation, and gave the police a reason to clear their names, which was also chronicled in that edition of the *Herald*.

If anyone actually investigated the events of the last year, the story would fall apart, but everyone who was involved just wanted to get on with things. Of course, there were already conspiracy theories popping up about what really happened. Pi had sent her links to a half-dozen websites. It was weird to open up a site and see one's face on the front page, but that was always the risk when signing up to be a mage.

A soft knock on the door brought Aurie out of her thoughts.

"Come in," said Aurie.

Professor Mali rolled into the room. The normally dour older woman had a propped up smile on her face.

"How're you holding up?" she asked.

"Well enough," said Aurie, "under the circumstances."

"This really should be Semyon here with you," said Mali.

A second look revealed the dark circles around the professor's eyes. The last week had been rough on everyone at Arcanium, especially the professors, who were trying to hold things together during Semyon's convalescence.

"You're doing your best, Professor Mali," said Aurie.

She looked away, tightening her lips. "We've lost so many students. I'm afraid there'll be nothing left *if* he returns."

"When," said Aurie.

Professor Mali patted Aurie's leg. "You're wise beyond your years, and so calm."

"I'm a mess inside," said Aurie, her heart doing a little pitter-patter dance to prove it. "I'm worried too."

The professor seemed to sense her vulnerability, and straightened up. "My apologies, Aurelia. I'm here for your support, not you for mine. How...how is your progress with your true name?"

"I'm not sure," said Aurie. "I was able to use it a few times during the you-know, but I'm not sure if I wasn't cheating with faez."

"Well, that's good, I guess," said the professor, who took on an introspective cast. "You know, I've been thinking about true names since we talked last. I'm sorry I haven't been much help, but it's not something I thought much about since I learned it myself, and I believe that my breakthroughs had already come when I accepted the injuries to my legs. So using my true name was easier than for most. But I thought back to what had helped me overcome my struggles, and this is what I recalled helping me learn my true name.

"In our darkest hours, when the world is against us and the parts of ourselves we show others gets stripped away, that's who we are. Before my legs were taken, I loved to run and climb, and had dreamed of joining the Explorers Hall. It wasn't until later that I realized I hated the outdoors, the bugs, the poison ivy, the sleeping in tents. What I liked was reading about the outdoors from the comfort of my bedroom. I pushed myself to do those other things because they were what my parents and the other kids in my rural town had expected from me. Don't get me wrong, I miss running, but I love going on a long wheel through the city, and I get to take my books and water bottle with me, and take a break under a canopy in the park to read when I'm tired. That's who I am.

"So consider your darkest moments, and what was most important to you then. Maybe that will give you the clue to who you really are."

Aurie wasn't sure why, but she had a couple of tears in her eyes. Embarrassed, she wiped them away. "Thank you, Professor. That helped."

She looked equally embarrassed. Their collective awkwardness was dispelled when a heavy knock intruded.

"Time to go," said the professor. "Good luck."

Aurie marched into the court, finding the patrons already seated. The blurry shielded form of Malden Anterist took up the center chair, while

Celesse D'Agastine was in the left. The right one sat empty.

On the other side of the room sat a block of marble large enough to carve a museum-sized statue. She recalled the demonstration from Professor Mali of splitting a chunk of stone in half. This stone was fifty times larger.

"Imposing, isn't it?" said Malden.

Aurie let her gaze rest on the empty chair of Bannon Creed. "Not really."

The impact of her retort was unknown because of Malden's shield, but Aurie detected a twitch of amusement from Celesse's lips.

"Do you know anything about what might have happened with Mr. Creed?" said Malden.

"I'm just a student, and not a member of Protectors, so I wouldn't know," she said.

Even through his shield, she could sense Malden's frown. "Come now, Ms. Aurelia. Let's not insult each other. You were at Invictus' statue that night. Tell us what happened."

The initial reason Aurie had thought Bannon had not attended the trial was due to injuries. Based on the line of questioning, she realized his plot had been entirely self-generated. Malden wanted to know because he'd been left in the dark.

Celesse held her emotions in check, as unreadable as a professional poker player. Did she know about Camille's support of Bannon Creed? Or had that been a defection as well?

"You're here to take my magic and you want me to give you information freely? I may be young, but I'm not naive," said Aurie.

"Do not think this information is anything more than a curiosity," said Malden. "At best it might earn you leniency in your failure, in that we might give you a sedative when the deed is done."

"Shall I begin?" said Aurie, turning to face the marble block.

"Let's not be so hasty," said Malden, the blurry form of his hand waving in her direction. "Need I remind you that your Hall is in serious trouble without a patron? It would be unfortunate if anything else happened, tipping chaos into collapse."

"Why would I care?" asked Aurie. "If I lose my magic, then the politics of the Halls will be the least of my concerns."

"Maybe I can offer a little more than that."

Celesse raised the slightest of eyebrows at her peer.

"What are you offering?" asked Aurie.

"A chance at redemption," he said. "It is my understanding that you had a hand in thwarting this attempted perversion of the Halls. We would be monsters not to want you to succeed. After all, there've been so many cruel blows to Arcanium. One more would demoralize your fellow students unnecessarily."

Aurie knew he didn't care a lick about Arcanium, nor did he really care about her. He was pleased she'd stopped Bannon, because otherwise, that would have placed Creed as his superior. What he clearly wanted to know was if Creed had accomplices amongst the other patrons.

"The events of that night are rather hazy to me," she said. "It's hard to remember with this task hanging over my head."

"If you name a coconspirator, you might find your task lightened," he said.

Aurie shot a glance at Celesse. One lie and she could pit these two Halls against each other. It would cost her nothing, and give her a better shot at the trial.

Except that as far as Aurie knew, Celesse had had no hand in it. And the conversation between Semyon and Celesse earlier in the year showed Aurie that the Cabal was held together by fear. If she lied about Celesse's involvement, it might backfire if Malden didn't believe her.

In the end, she wanted to honor the ideals of Invictus, that the Hundred Halls, despite its flaws and cracks, was an important institution that kept the world from descending into chaos.

"I'm sorry, I can't remember," she said, catching a flicker of relief on Celesse's brow.

The privacy shield shimmered. "Very well. Your task awaits. Break that stone in half and you can walk out a free woman."

Aurie approached the marble block. She thought about what Professor Mali had said in the waiting room about times of darkest hours. There'd been many of them in her life, from her parents' deaths to the night in the statue.

"We're waiting, Ms. Aurelia," said Malden.

When she considered those events, the common factor stuck out like spilled paint in a white glove factory; she wasn't sure why she hadn't seen it before. A rustling warmth filled her chest, like a drink of hot cocoa on a cold night.

The only question was which form of her name to use. Should it be Aurie, or Aurelia, or maybe just Silverthorne? None of these resonated with her. They weren't complete. Upon further consideration, she knew what it had to be.

Aurie took the marble stone in her sights. A calmness overtook her like cresting a mountaintop and seeing the horizon stretch out in all directions.

She took a cleansing breath. The shout came from her lips like a hurricane condensed to a knife.

"Aurelia Maximus Silverthorne!"

The room rattled with the force of her true name. The stone block shattered like a piece of glass, shards of dust flowing out in a cloud, settling across the floor.

Aurie returned to her previous spot. She gave a brief bow.

"May I leave now?"

If there was any time she wished she could have seen Malden's face, it would have been in this instant, but she did relish the way he stumbled over his words when he spoke to her.

"This...this trial is concluded," he said incredulously.

"The contract?"

He waved his hand and the contract appeared. A tugging on her chest like a knot being unraveled coincided with the names of the two patrons appearing on the bottom. And with that, she was free.

When she marched from the room, she caught Celesse's appraising stare. Aurie kept her chin held high until she made it out of the Court of Three. Pi was waiting outside with open arms, and Aurie collapsed within the embrace, exhausted.

THIRTY SIX

Pi found her sister on the roof of Arcanium staring at the head of the statue of Invictus that rose above a cluster of office buildings. The statue was the next ward over.

"He looks like he's standing guard over the city," said Aurie, glancing over her shoulder.

"I always thought he looked constipated," said Pi. "Or annoyed by the stupidity of the city's mages."

"You would think that."

Pi hooked her arm around Aurie's, pulled their sides together. "I've been looking all over for you."

"I *was* doing an excellent job of avoiding people until now."

"You'd avoid little ol' me? Your innocent baby sister?" asked Pi, catching a snort of derision from the gallery inside her, Ashley especially. It was hard to hide things from the people living inside her head. They had a habit of poking into memories that even she'd forgotten, like the time she'd put an enchantment on that asshole concrete worker's boots from her third foster home. She'd made it so every time he took a step at work, his boots made random farm animal noises. She'd even tailored the enchantment to slide over to his backup boots if he tried to switch before work.

"I seriously wonder if you've *ever* been innocent. I'm beginning to realize you hide your ways better than when we were younger," said Aurie.

"Or I didn't care about hiding them after Mom and Dad were gone," said Pi, leaning her head on Aurie's shoulder. "What are you really doing up here?"

"Thinking about Invictus. Wondering what he'd think about what's happened to his school."

"Do I need to make you a bumper sticker that says WWID?" asked Pi.

Aurie wrinkled her nose. "What's that?"

"What Would Invictus Do."

"He wasn't Jesus," said Aurie.

"Might as well have been," said Pi. "I'm pretty sure he could turn water into wine, and cure leprosy."

"Does that mean that Jesus was a mage?" asked Aurie, tilting her head playfully.

"Sacrilege! Magic, miracle, it's all the same, right?" said Pi. "Though lately I'm not sure what to think."

"About what?"

Pi sighed. "Everything. Without a Hall, I'm not sure what to do. Professor Mali has said I can live in Arcanium until I decide, though I think she only said that to keep another mage around that can actually use their magic."

There was a hesitancy in Aurie's gaze. They locked eyes for a moment, and her sister looked away. Her cheeks warmed. Pi reached up and fixed a strand of hair that had escaped Aurie's ponytail.

"Did you really use your full name to break the marble block?" asked Pi.

The blush deepened. "What? Is that weird or something?"

"You could have called out Alton Lockwood's name for all I care as long as it broke that hunk of marble," said Pi. "But isn't that a little unwieldy for times of trouble?"

"Mom and Dad gave me that unwieldy name. It's one of the last things I have from them," said Aurie. "What do you think your true name is? Before the others, and after."

"I wouldn't know where to start. I'm starting to forget where they end and I begin," said Pi.

A car backfired in the street below, startling both of them. Once they realized what had caused the noise, they chuckled.

"Dammmmn, we're jumpy," said Pi.

"What are we going to do next year? About the Halls?" asked Aurie. "I can use my true name, but not much else without hurting Semyon. Professor Mali says we can spend the time practicing the spells without adding faez, but what's the use in that? And what if the Cabal attacks again?"

"You mean when the Cabal attacks again. You heard them. They have plots within plots," said Pi.

They fell into silence. Out of the corner of her eye, Pi spied a gondola floating through the air on invisible wires towards the Spire. She nudged Aurie in the ribs.

"Next year we get to ride in those."

"That's about the only thing to look forward to in our fourth year," said Aurie.

"Don't worry, sis. It can't get any worse than the last three years. We've got to be hitting a stretch of good luck going forward," Pi deadpanned.

Aurie eyed her sister with suspicion, so Pi stuck her tongue out to confirm it.

"That's what I thought."

"Part of me was actually being serious," said Pi.

"Which part?"

"I think my pinky toe."

Aurie rolled her eyes. "Ha ha."

Pi had been feeling a little despondent, but finding her sister had been the cure. She squeezed Aurie again, making exaggerated noises as if she was crushing her in the embrace.

"What was all that about?" asked Aurie.

"I was just thinking about how this whole year I've been an idiot wanting to learn about our family, when I've been missing the most important part," said Pi.

"Which part is that? And if you say your pinky toe, I'm throwing you off the building," said Aurie.

"My big toe?" Pi made a gotcha face. "But really, it's you, Aurie. I was so desperate to know some silly facts about our collective past, or learn if we were descendants of sorcerer-kings, or mythical creatures, that I missed what was right in front of me.

"Those things don't matter. What matters is you. My big sis, who gets me up in the morning when I sleep through my alarm clock, who saved me from that douche-nugget Creed, who did like a million cool things for me when we were getting shuttled around all those foster homes, and who was there for me even when I fell for Liam's con."

"*Dooset daram*, Aurie. It may just be the two of us, but we're all the family we need right now."

Her sister not-so-discreetly wiped a tear from her eye. "*Dooset daram.*"

They supported each other as the city moved around them. Pi wasn't sure what the next year would bring, but she knew she didn't want to face it with anyone else but Aurie.

§ § §

A Short History of the Hundred Halls

The magical university that eventually became known as the Hundred Halls started off as a small school called Invictus School of Magic in 1836. The building was an old tavern and inn called the Brownwater, named after the town it was located. Invictus purchased it because the property was attached to a large parcel of land where they could safely practice sorcery without exciting the local populous. As well, the inn had rooms for the first cadre of students, and a place they could all eat together and develop comradery.

In an interview given in the early 1980s, Invictus recounted those early years of the school. He'd recruited students from all over the country, promising them a chance to develop their powers without the threat of madness which plagued early practitioners. Even so, of the fifteen students only nine remained after the first year. Invictus has said little about the loss of his student body, insinuating they left for other professions, but rumors persisted that those students perished due to magical accidents or taking their own lives due to the faez madness they'd already developed before they'd arrived at the school. At this time, Invictus accepted all ages of students and the patron system hadn't been perfected. These early failures are said to be the reason that the cut off age for the Hundred Halls remains at twenty years old.

The town of Brownwater, which existed on the northwestern side of Pennsylvania, became a hot bed of rumors and claims of witchcraft. But Invictus had cultivated the local politicians, either through gifts of sorcery, or outright bribery, keeping the threats coming from outside the boundaries of Brownwater. During the years 1840 to 1858, there were three recorded major attacks on the school. The first claimed the life of Robert Madison when he was caught riding his horse in the countryside, charming birds to land on his hand. A musket shot took him in the head when the ambush surprised him. Four more students perished in the first attack, but all the men that invaded the school were never seen again. Requests to return their bodies were denied by Headmaster Invictus. By the time the second and third attacks occurred, the school had established safety procedures and no more lives of the students were lost. The same cannot be said of the attackers.

When the Civil War broke out in 1861, there were requests from both sides to join the fight. At first, Invictus resisted the requests, not wanting to spotlight the fledgling school and get noticed by the greater powers of the country, but his hand was forced as the war's toll created a rift in the student body which had come from all over the nation. A group of Southern students, led by Conroy Rutherford, left the school and joined the Confederacy. Invictus kicked them out of the school, then allowed those that wished to join the fight on the Union side to leave without concern for their position within the academy. Notable of this time was Evelyn Grace, a blue-eyed beauty that single handedly turned the Battle of Hoke's Run by defeating Conroy Rutherford in a duel of sorcery before routing the southern troops.

By the time the war was over, the Invictus School of Magic had few students and its reputation either tarnished or venerated based on which side it was being viewed from. During the year of 1866, little happened at the Brownwater Inn, and the students that stayed were said to have rarely seen Invictus.

On October 22nd, 1867, the charter for a new school called the Hundred Halls, which incorporated the new and improved Patron structure, was signed. The original signers included Invictus, Semyon Gray, Bannon Creed, Celesse D'Agastine, Priyanka Sai, and Malden Anterist. The history of some of these mages can be traced through the history of the country, while others arrived in the New World seemingly out of the blue. The first five Halls of the original charter were Arcanium, Protectors, Alchemists, Assassins, and Coterie of Mages.

With Invictus removed from direct interaction with the students, the new academy flourished. The Head Patron was able to focus on recruiting new students and growing the school, while the new Patrons taught their specific specialties. Additionally, double Patron system seemed to reduce the problems with faez madness that had plagued the early years.

The first Hall to open after the original charter was the Holistic Institute, also known as Aura Healers, in 1875, followed by the Royal Society of Illustrious Artificers in 1891. Three other Halls started in the years before the turn of the century—Tenebris Hall, The Equus Society, and The Gunpowder Club—but disappeared before the first world war. This became a common occurrence during the century and three-quarters existence of the university, either because of the changing needs of society, the death of the patron, or other Halls incorporating their teachings and making them obsolete.

The two world wars brought the existence of magic into focus for the entire world. Invictus threw the weight of the school behind the Allies, which helped tipped the final result to victory. While the Central Powers, and then Axis, both had mages in their regiments, they were prone to faez madness and there were numerous examples of destructive sorceries impacting their own troops unexpectedly.

It was the success of magic in the World Wars that led to the passing of laws that codified the Hundred Halls supremacy and forbid the opening of rival schools in other parts of the world. To facilitate these laws, Invictus promised to open up the school to the entire world and the American government, keen to keep the school on their territory, agreed. This paved the way for the Sorcerous Education Act of 1951 which allowed the school to make major land grabs in the region north of Philadelphia and west of New York, creating the structure that would become the city of Invictus.

In the years after the second World War, the Hundred Halls flourished. Before then, there'd only been about thirty different halls at the university, but they swelled to a number over eighty (no one knows for sure). Researchers have suggested that the number has been oscillating between sixty and seventy-five since, though others have argued that the true number is north of a hundred because Invictus does not publish the list of Halls and some form without ever taking a student. These "Ghost Halls" are sometimes created by ambitious mages that wish to use the association with the school for research, or other purposes.

Wards in the City of Sorcery

First – The ward is considered to be the financial home of sorcery related businesses worldwide and many of the wealthiest mages live in its boundaries.

The Order of Honorable Alchemists [Hall] – This school is the premiere place in the world to learn the arts of alchemy. Celesse D'Agastine, its patron, uses it as a place to recruit its future products.

Second – Known as the other entertainment capital of the world, this ward receives the majority of tourists.

The Academy of the Subtle Arts [Hall] – No one knows exactly where the hall is located, but in official literature of the school, its home is noted as the second.

Glitterdome – A massive stadium dedicated to music, big events, and the occasional sporting match.

Ashnod's Theater – The premiere theater for students of the Dramatics Hall.

Herald of the Halls – The newspaper wholly devoted to reporting on the Hundred Halls, the city of Invictus, and related subjects.

Third – Adjacent to the second, this ward receives its fair share of visitors intent on leaving the city of sorcery with a bit of magic to make their personal lives a little bit better—or more interesting.

Protectors [Hall] – A functional looking building where mages are taught to become future law enforcement members, or the military. The most advanced members have often been recruited to other realms as mercenaries.

Left Tower Books – A mainstay of the literary circuit. Authors of books about magic must always make a stop at this wonderful depository of literature.

Fourth – This ward has no singular identity but given its location in the inner ring of the city, it has similar functions to the first three wards.

Coterie of Mages [Hall] – Along with the Statue of Invictus, the Spire, and the Stone Flower of Stone Singers, the Obelisk is one of the most recognizable architectural wonders of the city. A towering structure of pure obsidian, the school provides its home to the most elite of mages.

Statue of Invictus – An enormous statue of the founder of the city. It was gifted by an unknown benefactor. Invictus is said to hate the replication.

City Library – The massive library is a place of scholarship for mundane and sorcerous topics.

Fifth – Many businesses make their home on the eastern half of the ward while the western section that borders the thirteenth is mostly residential.

Arcanium [Hall] – The academy focused on the study of truth and knowledge, this medieval castle supposedly contains more books than all the libraries and bookstores of the city combined.

Acoustic Architectural Institute of Design [Hall] – Commonly known as Stone Singers, the giant stone flower that makes up the building opens and closes daily with the shining of the sun.

Sixth – Has the highest concentration of banks in the city, but also maintains a large residential area.

Holistic Institute [Hall] – This school contains a teaching hospital that is frequently used by the poor and non-humans of the city.

Museum of Magical Artifacts – A world famous museum dedicated to the display of historically significant artifacts.

Seventh – A mix of residential, restaurants, and bars make this a great place for the recently graduated to enjoy their time.

Canal District – A series of canals, modeled after Venice, snake through this area filled with restaurants and bars.

Eighth – A mix of residential and businesses.

Society for the Understanding of Animals [Hall] – This hall has the largest campus in the city and is tightly interwoven with the zoo, which it helps maintain.

Oestomancium [Hall] – Known as the Weird Circus to most, this halls dedication to exploring the possibilities of transhumanity makes it unique at the school. Their yearly Carnival held each Halloween is a delight and horror to those that attend.

Invictus Menagerie and Cryptozoo – The second largest cryptozoo in the country holds a wide variety of supernatural creatures, but unlike the larger zoo in Portland, this one specializes in the less dangerous kinds.

Ninth – A mix of residential and businesses.

Freeport Games – A quaint gaming shop that has existed in the city since the 1970s.

Tenth – A mix of residential and businesses.

Metallum Nocturne [Hall] – Steam and the stench of burning metal rises frequently from this hall as they are the arcane metallurgists of the wizard world.

Wizard's Wax Museum – A wax museum dedicated to showcasing the history of wizards and mages. True historians find this place rather sketchy on details.

Eleventh – A mostly residential area that has seen better days.

Enochian District – One of the earliest settlements of the city, this district has been forgotten in recent times. It's one of the few places that non-humans dare to live in the light.

Twelfth – This area has the few industries left in the city, though most have left due to the laws passed restricting their operation. Tends towards cracked concrete and rusted out buildings.

Thirteenth – This ward has been partially reclaimed by nature. Few visit this part of the city, despite its border with the prosperous fifth.

The Spire – The tallest building and/or structure in the world. Serves as the administrative home of the Hundred Halls. The top section is the home of Invictus. The enormous tower serves many functions including the Merlin Trials, and the Second Year Games.

Undercity – The region beneath the city stretches as wide as the confines of the outer wards, but moving around is fraught with supernatural danger. A vast majority of this area is unmapped due to the heavy influence of faez, the paranoia of its residence, and the dangers posed to explorers. There are a few known settlements within the Undercity that tend to be the home of non-humans that are unwelcome on the surface.

Big Dave's Town – The largest and most well-known settlement in the Undercity, this kidney-shaped cavern has a population in the thousands. The Devil's Lipstick or the open air market are the most frequently visited. Undercity gangs keep the peace.

Voodoo Land – A village deep in the Undercity populated by a people infected by a sentient fungus.

Wells of Power – Known or seen by few, the four wells are places that faez leaks through the barrier between realms. Each one is protected by a guardian that was placed there by the Patrons.

Other Realms

The Hundred Halls is not just a magical school. The magic of portals creates a network of realms where mages with access can move about freely. Realms do not exist at fixed positions to each other, but move in relation to each other for unknown reasons, creating unusual and sometimes unexpected connections. The Academy of the Subtle Arts is the Hall most connected to the multi-realms, but others such as Coterie of Mages for the Infernal realm are known experts.

The Eternal City – The home of the maetrie, sometimes called city elves, is a place of high magic and high danger that doesn't follow all the rules of more stable realms. In the Eternal City, locations don't always remain in the same place, and even those are ruled by the various courts: Jade, Diamond, and Ruby. Only the most brave (or foolish) mages visit this realm, and of those that do, most never return.

Ruby Court

Queen: Lady Amethyte

Diamond Court

Queen: Lady Zaire

Jade Court

Queen: Lady Kikala

The Infernal Realm – An early precursor realm that was one of the first to stabilize out of the fledgling universe. The understanding of this brutal place is limited and most scholars think, probably wrong. It is awash in demonic creatures that defy human knowledge.

The Veil – This realm exists at the barrier between life and death. Ghosts, apparitions, and otherworldly creatures sometimes pass through into other realms, causing problems and sometimes opportunities. It is rumored that the mages of the Academy of the Subtle Arts can briefly step into this realm to pass out of sight.

Harmony – A stable realm of harsh beauty, Harmony is known to few. The fearsome and explosively fast mystdrakons come from this place and its jungles hide other dangerous creatures that frighten even the most hardened explorers.

Fae – The realm most commonly portrayed in folktales and legends is the place of the seelie and unseelie. Access to this realm has become more difficult in the last century, making its influence less known than the past.

Ice Hold – A cold and inhospitable place that has become a vacation spot for the ultra-wealthy mages that wish to experience winter sports in an entirely different realm than their own. Most only visit the lodges in the mountains, though some adventurous explorers travel further than the known regions.

Montanhas – A mountainous region that was settled by Portuguese colonists a half-century ago and then again by the company Lifestone. The enormous Montas live in this realm alongside the settlers. Surprisingly little is known about the native race.

Caer Corsydd – A backwater fae realm of swamps and bogs. Its dangers are only matched by its beauty. As the home of the Gwyllion, the outcasts of Fae, it is a mix of fairy and unsettled country. The rules that apply to most fae realms do not here, because it was not their homeland.

Danir – The home to a pastural race that is quite civilized. Their extensive farmlands are surrounded by jungle. Early explorers learned about the existence of *mágrithral* which is commonly called magesteel, a material that can easily hold enchantments. The value of magesteel is astronomical, though the Danir no longer produce it, citing environmental issues as the cause.

Black Council – The existence of this realm has not been confirmed. Researchers claim that it's a den of malicious thievery. Serious researchers avoid this realm as a topic of scholarship due to the string of unfortunate accidents that befell their compatriots that sought to unearth the truth.

Brodaria – Home to the Brodarians, a battle-hungry people that spent their days in constant conquest. Mercenaries and fortune-hunters have been known to visit this realm to ply their dangerous trade.

Major Figures of the Hundred Halls

Invictus – The most famous mage in the world, considered to be the oldest living being. Speculation has him to be at least five hundred years old, though many consider him to be much older.

Malden Anterist – The head of Coterie of Mages keeps himself hidden from scrying and other methods of sight through the use of obfuscation enchantments. The reason for this unusual setup is the subject of much speculation.

Celesse D'Agastine – The third most famous person (after Invictus and Frank Orpheum), the head of D'Agastine Industries runs one of the largest multinational corporations in the world. Celesse is known as a fierce business woman who has destroyed those that have attempted to stand in her way.

Semyon Gray – The least vocal of the Original Five, Semyon is known for working quietly behind the scenes to guide the politics of the Hundred Halls in a more humane direction.

Priyanka Sai – The head of the Assassin's Hall is infamous across the realms.

Bannon Creed – As head of the Protectors, as well as the Blackstone Security, Bannon's mages are involved with law enforcement, and the military across the realms. It is rumored that he often plays both sides of conflicts to maximize his financial interests and accusations about drugs or other unsavory acts have often been met with unusual deaths. Journalists steer clear of any topics related to the mage, which only burgeons his untouchable reputation.

Frank Orpheum – A legendary entertainer and head of the Dramatics Hall, after Invictus, he's considered the most famous in the world. His magic tricks have defied explanation, even by those who understand his methods.

Radoslav – The reclusive owner of the Glass Cabaret is an ex-pat maetrie with ties to organized crime across the city. His jazz bar attracts tourists curious about the city fae, and those who wish a favor from him—but at a price. He is the son of the Ruby and Jade Queens, and is known as the Black Butcher for his role in the destruction of the Ebony Court.

Hemistad – The owner of Freeport Games is a curious figure that not much is known about. Mages that have visited his gaming store suggest that he is not who he appears to be, but the extent of his powers are unknown. He makes frequent trips into the Undercity for his own purposes.

The Societies

The societies were originally created to help the city protect itself from the dangers posed by the infernal realm. Their members are pulled from the top halls with the intention of providing a cross-section of skills. Each has its own location in the Undercity where it meets and initiates new members, but the four societies gather together on a yearly basis for meetings, and then again, every four years for a ceremony called the Convergence, which is meant to help gauge the threat of the infernal realm. All four societies have a role in the Convergence.

There are many other smaller societies that were created for other purposes, but these original four are what most think of when "secret societies" are brought up in the city.

Well and Stone – Dedicated to the understanding of faez and the role of the wells of power.

Snake and Tome – Dedicated to developing charisma and the cunning to change the world.

Chroma and Key – Besides Coterie of Mages, this society is a repository of demonology.

Silence – This society focused on predicting the future through the use of augury.

Timeline of Season One

2003: Invictus disappears / Nadia's Triumph

2013: The Reluctant Assassin

2014: The Sorcerous Spy / Wild Magic

2015: The Veiled Diplomat / Bane of the Hunter / The Warped Forest / Song of Siren and Blood

2016: Agent Unraveled / Mark of the Phoenix / Gladiators of Warsong / House of Snake and Tome / Trials of Magic

2017: The Webs That Bind / Arcane Mutations / Citadel of Broken Dreams / Storm of Dragon and Stone / Web of Lies

2018: Enter the Daemonpits / Untamed Destiny / Sonata of Shadow and Thorn / Alchemy of Souls

2019: Plane of Twilight / Well of Demon and Bone / Gathering of Shadows

2020: City of Sorcery

2022: The Order of Merlin / Infernal Alliances / Tower of Horn and Blood

Hundred Halls – Professors / Instructors

Arcanium – Semyon Gray (Patron)

Joanne Mali

Sebastian Longakers

Gill

Moonie

Alain Chopra

Coterie of Mages – Malden Anterist (Patron)

Augustus Trebleton

Phillip Sinclair

Isla Kingsley

Protectors – Bannon Creed (Patron)

Avani Blue

Alchemists – Celesse D'Agastine (Patron)

Alysson Cho

Assassins – Priyanka Sai (Patron)

Carron Allgood

Marilyn Pennywhistle

Maggie O'Keefe

Alliette Noyade

Percival

Matt Konig

Dionysus Minoan

Stone Singers – Ester Starwood (Patron)

Marin Zeng

Asa Lacuerda

Sven Larsen

Art Williams

Robin Leech

Animalians – Adele Montgomery (Patron)

Didi Applebrook

Kako

Cassius King

Vladmir Constantine

Ansel Park

Ernest Valentine

Dramatics – Frank Orpheum (Patron)

Lilly Hathhammer

Glossary Terms

Merlin Trials - The entrance exams to the Hundred Halls that can only be taken during the ages seventeen through nineteen. There are three stages to the trials.

Faez - The raw stuff of magic. Faez is the energy that when shaped by spell or other means creates magical effects. Faez is dangerous to humans, but a tolerance can be built up over time if somehow protected. The patronage system of the Hundred Halls is the most common method.

Patron - The founder of a hall within the Hundred Halls. The patron extends their magical protection to students, keeping them safe from faez madness, and teaching them a specific skill set within the magical world.

Faez Madness - Prolonged use of faez without protection results in irreversible damage to the user's ability to understand and interact with reality.

Second Year Contest - These games require cross-Hall teams to compete against each other for a grand prize utilizing special facilities that keep the participants from physical harm.

Maetrie – Commonly called city elves, though they have no relation to the Fae. Their home is the Eternal City, a realm closer to Invictus than any other.

Major Halls

Arcanium

Nickname: Arcanium

Patron: Semyon Gray

Est: 1867

Motto: Knowledge is Power

Description: Arcanium believes in the value of gaining knowledge, not only about the world around us, but of ourselves. Before we can master magic, we must hone the tool the magic originates from, because a poorly trained mage will not only be a danger to themselves, but society at large. Once a student is capable, they may learn the art of changing spells on the fly using lexology, or how ancient runic languages are the key to solving the world's most difficult problems. Join Arcanium and be a part of the solution.

Coterie of Mages

Nickname: Coterie

Patron: Malden Anterist

Est: 1867

Motto: Limitless

Description: Anything is possible. Here in the Coterie of Mages, we don't believe in limits. If you can imagine it, you can do it. We push the boundaries of what magic is capable of. If this frightens you, then Coterie is not the Hall for you, but if this elicits a sense of excitement and wonder, then apply to the Coterie of Mages. We are the elite.

Academy of the Subtle Arts

Nickname: Assassins

Patron: Priyanka Sai

Est: 1867

Motto: Anyone can be persuaded

Description: Human connections make the world go round. We at the Academy of the Subtle Arts strive to bring people, companies, and countries together. Our mages are the world's most effective diplomats and heads of state. If you seek to join the interconnected world of politics, then the Academy is the right Hall for you.

The Order of Honorable Alchemists

Nickname: Alchemists

Patron: Celesse D'Agastine

Est: 1867

Motto: Perfection is Achievable

Description: The human vessel is a sacred thing. We believe in maximizing our potential through better alchemy. Our potentials cannot be met if we rely on the ordinariness of humanity.

Protectors

Nickname: Protectors

Patron: Bannon Creed

Est: 1867

Motto: To Protect and Control

Description: Order requires commitment. Protectors are committed to the value of human life. To being the shield against those that would tear down society, and create chaos. The Protector Hall teaches the ultimate defense, not only for yourself, but for the world at large. If being on the front lines of the world's conflicts appeals to you, then Protectors is your Hall

Acoustic Architectural Institute of Design

Nickname: Stone Singers

Patron: Ester Starwood

Est: 1891

Motto: Building through song

Description: A song is made up of many notes, just like a bridge is made of many stones. Society cannot function without the infrastructure to hold it together. The Acoustic Architectural institute of Design teaches how to shape the world with only a song.

Society for the Understanding of Animals

Nickname: Animalians

Patron: Adele Montgomery

Est: 1945

Motto: We Are Not Alone

Description: All life is sacred. From the industrious dung beetle to the majestic horned dragon. We at the Society believe that Earth must be shared with all her children and when we do we will truly unlock her endless possibilities.

Holistic Institute

Nickname: Aura Healers

Patron: Sir William Jenner III

Est: 1875

Motto: Health Starts in the Soul

Description: When someone gets hurt, are you the first to run to their side to tend their wounds? If so, then the Holistic Institute is for you. We'll teach you how to mend even the most grievous wounds.

Minor Halls

Gamemakers

Nickname: Gamemakers

Patron: Aldophus Dimple

Est: 1961

Motto: Life is a Game

Description: Life is a game to be perfected. We at the Gamemaker's Hall know the importance of games as the training grounds for life.

Metallum Nocturne

Nickname: Night Metal

Patron: Edward Canterbury

Est: 1908

Motto: Strike. Spark. Surpass.

Description: When the hammer hits the forge, great energies are released. Metallum Nocturn is that hammer against the forge of your soul. Join us, and find out what possibilities we can make.

The Daring Maids

Nickname: Palimaidens

Patron: Alice Hayword

Est: 1908

Motto: Stand

Description: The world is filled with unspeakable cruelty. We seek justice for those who cannot protect themselves, no matter the place. Join us in our fight against oppression.

Hundred Halls – Season One Series

Season One

THE HUNDRED HALLS

Trials of Magic

Web of Lies

Alchemy of Souls

Gathering of Shadows

City of Sorcery

THE RELUCTANT ASSASSIN

The Reluctant Assassin

The Sorcerous Spy

The Veiled Diplomat

Agent Unraveled

The Webs That Bind

GAMEMAKERS ONLINE

The Warped Forest

Gladiators of Warsong

Citadel of Broken Dreams

Enter the Daemon Pits

Plane of Twilight

ANIMALIANS HALL

Wild Magic

Bane of the Hunter

Mark of the Phoenix

Arcane Mutations

Untamed Destiny

STONE SINGERS HALL

Song of Siren and Blood

House of Snake and Tome

Storm of Dragon and Stone

Sonata of Shadow and Thorn

Well of Demon and Bone

THE ORDER OF MERLIN

The Order of Merlin

Infernal Alliances

Tower of Horn and Blood

HUNDRED HALLS SHORTS

Nadia's Triumph

The Ghostly Light of Hallow's Eve

The Ascendant Cup

The Whistling Man

Summer Spies

Fear is Forever

Balancing the Ledgers

A Slip of the Tongue

Shades of the Past

Continue the action with book four of
The Hundred Halls

GATHERING
OF
SHADOWS

The Hundred Halls Universe

SEASON ONE

THE HUNDRED HALLS
Trials of Magic
Web of Lies
Alchemy of Souls
Gathering of Shadows
City of Sorcery

THE RELUCTANT ASSASSIN
The Reluctant Assassin
The Sorcerous Spy
The Veiled Diplomat
Agent Unraveled
The Webs That Bind

GAMEMAKERS ONLINE
The Warped Forest
Gladiators of Warsong
Citadel of Broken Dreams
Enter the Daemonpits
Plane of Twilight

ANIMALIANS HALL
Wild Magic
Bane of the Hunter
Mark of the Phoenix
Arcane Mutations
Untamed Destiny

STONE SINGERS HALL
Song of Siren and Blood
House of Snake and Tome
Storm of Dragon and Stone
Sonata of Shadow and Thorn
Well of Demon and Bone

THE ORDER OF MERLIN
The Order of Merlin
Infernal Alliances
Tower of Horn and Blood

ABOUT THE AUTHOR

Thomas K. Carpenter resides in Colorado with his wife Rachel. When he's not busy writing his next book, he's hiking, skiing, and getting beat by his wife at cards. He keeps a regular blog at www.thomaskcarpenter.com and you can follow him on twitter @thomaskcarpente. If you want to learn when his next novel will be hitting the shelves and get free stories and occasional other goodies, please sign up for his mailing list by going to: http://tinyurl.com/thomaskcarpenter. Your email address will never be shared and you can unsubscribe at any time.

Lightning Source UK Ltd.
Milton Keynes UK
UKHW042057011122
411486UK00009B/140/J